MAKE US TRAITORS

Gilda O'Neill was born and brought up in the East End, where her grandmother ran a pie and mash shop, her grandfather was a tug skipper and her great-uncle worked as a minder for a Chinese gambling-den owner. She left school at fifteen but returned to education as a mature student. She is now a full-time writer, and *Make Us Traitors* is her eleventh novel.

Gilda O'Neill has also had four non-fiction books published including the highly acclaimed *Sunday Times* bestseller, *My East End: A History of Cockney London* and *Our Street: East End Life in the Second World War*. She lives in East London with her husband and family.

Praise for Gilda O'Neill

'Her vivid, flint-edged picture of London's East End in the sixties leaps off the page with its sardonic dialogue and sharply realised characters . . . you'll find it very difficult indeed to put this one down' Barry Forshaw, *Crime Time*

'This novel has everything . . . a cracking read' Martina Cole

'A thumping good read' Lesley Pearse

'A sharp eye, a warm heart and a gift for story telling' Elizabeth Buchan

'Every page is a delight' *Daily Mail*

'Peopled with an irresistibly vivid cast of characters and told with warm-hearted sympathy . . . a great read' *Oxford Mail*

'The characters . . . . he dialogue is spot on . . . . or the time and t . . . . .

A BOND OF FATE TRILOGY

Part Two
Make Us Traitors

GILDA O'NEILL

arrow books

Published by Arrow Books in 2004

1 3 5 7 9 10 8 6 4 2

Copyright © Gilda O'Neill, 2004

Gilda O'Neill has asserted her right under the Copyright, Designs and
Patents Act, 1988 to be identified as the author of this work

First published in the United Kingdom in 2004 by William Heinemann

Arrow Books
The Random House Group Limited
20 Vauxhall Bridge Road, London, SW1V 2SA

Random House Australia (Pty) Limited
20 Alfred Street, Milsons Point, Sydney,
New South Wales 2061, Australia

Random House New Zealand Limited
18 Poland Road, Glenfield
Auckland 10, New Zealand

Random House South Africa (Pty) Limited
Endulini, 5a Jubilee Road, Parktown 2193, South Africa

Random House UK Group Limited Reg. No. 954009

www.randomhouse.co.uk

A CIP catalogue record for this book
is available from the British Library

Papers used by Random House
are natural, recyclable products made from wood grown in
sustainable forests. The manufacturing processes conform to
the environmental regulations of the country of origin

ISBN 0 09 942746 X

Typeset by SX Composing DTP
Printed and bound in Great Britain by
Bookmarque Limited, Croydon, Surrey

For Andy McKillop

May 1963

In a dramatic climax to the trial that has been gripping the nation, Eileen O'Donnell, 44, was today sentenced to life imprisonment for the murder of her husband, Gabriel, a crime to which she freely confessed in September last year.

Gabriel O'Donnell, long suspected of being the driving force behind one of the two powerful criminal mobs that have been terrorising the streets of the East End, was never indicted on any of the many charges brought against him and his family. O'Donnell, like his sons, Brendan and Luke, and his son-in-law Peter MacRiordan, had always claimed to be a legitimate businessman.

Sources, who had to be promised anonymity, so great is the fear stalking east London, spoke to this paper about the sham of their so-called businesses, claiming that they are nothing more than a cover for the O'Donnells' nefarious dealings.

In the run-up to the trial, continual attempts were made to persuade Eileen O'Donnell to admit to the involvement of not only her own family, but also of their associates, the Kesslers, in the crime wave that has been sweeping London, but she was only prepared to speak about her own culpability in murdering her husband.

The police are understood to be very disappointed by Eileen O'Donnell's refusal to cooperate, as they are believed to view the halting of the activities of these two families as the only way forward in making the streets safe again for decent people. A campaign that this paper not only supports, but which it promises to pursue.

See page 5 for your chance to add your name to our petition demanding government action.

November 1973

Eileen O'Donnell, 55, who, 11 years ago, sensationally confessed to the murder of her husband, Gabriel, the notorious East End gang leader, was released from prison early this morning.

Wearing a cream-coloured suit, and looking arrogantly ahead of her, O'Donnell was met by her wealthy businessmen sons, Brendan, 35, and Luke, 34.

Luke O'Donnell, bachelor, drove his mother away in a luxury Daimler saloon. Surprisingly, they were accompanied by Sophie Kessler, 53, the wife of millionaire Harold Kessler.

After the trial, a source close to the O'Donnells and the Kesslers linked the murder of Gabriel O'Donnell to a feud between the two families. But whatever its cause, his death was the final horror in a series of terrifying and brutal events, which shook the East End and appalled the country as a whole.

At the time of Eileen O'Donnell's conviction, unsubstantiated rumours about the families were buzzing through every London pub. The most often heard was that the troubles between them began when Gabriel O'Donnell found out that his youngest daughter, Catherine, was in a secret relationship with Samuel, Harold Kessler's youngest son. There was further speculation in the underworld, when the body of Catherine O'Donnell, aged just 18, was pulled from a blazing car, that her death was a result of something far more sinister than a road-traffic accident. Everything from sawn-off shotguns to the involvement of one of her own family was suggested. One of the most sickening events was the sudden death and hurried burial of Stephen Shea, one of Gabriel O'Donnell's closest associates. There was much fevered speculation at the time, confirmed by those in the know, that Shea had been assassinated as part of the appalling gangland grudge match between the families, and that, in a shocking gesture of power, his body parts had been fed to Gabriel O'Donnell's Alsatian guard dogs.

Bad feeling escalated between the families, finally reaching crisis point, when Rachel, 21, Daniel Kessler's heavily pregnant wife, was killed in an explosion, which was never satisfactorily explained, although whispers were heard, and fingers were pointed in the direction of the O'Donnells.

It was O'Donnell's death that saw this newspaper launch its ground-breaking campaign to bring safety back to our streets. Since then, matters have been mostly quiet between the families, with word among the criminal fraternity that the O'Donnells agreed to 'tolerate' the presence of the Kesslers on 'their' patch, providing no 'rules' were breached.

Many are now wondering if the release of Eileen O'Donnell will open old wounds, and if terror will return to our streets.

Additional comment and pictures pages 3, 4 and 5.

Chapter 1

In the early-morning gloom, the tall, darkly hand-some man opened the boot of his car, and took out a plain, blue nylon shopping bag. It would probably have looked more at home on the arm of a bargain-seeking housewife than in the hands of the driver of a sleek, black Mercedes.

Brendan O'Donnell shut the boot with a heavily expensive clunk, and set off through the car park of the motorway service station. Head angled down-wards, he pulled the collar of his sheepskin coat up about his face – apparently avoiding the rain – and moved fast and confidently towards the café, with its dim, improvised lamp lighting. The unions were on strike again, playing havoc with the electricity supply, and although, as a rule, Brendan had no time for the bastards, right now he could have kissed the shop stewards bloody personally. These blackouts made the conditions for what he had planned just about perfect.

Halfway along the pedestrian path, Brendan stopped. He secured the bag between his feet and, snatching a glimpse over his shoulder, bent low as if to tie his lace. Satisfied he wasn't being followed, he picked up the bag before heading towards the tall, conifer windbreak that shielded the area where the lorries and rigs, and their slumbering drivers, were parked up from the night before.

'Half four and packing already? We'll be sorry to see you go, hen. Made a nice change, having a lady down here among us lowlifes.' The brass-yellow blonde squinted through the darkness, baring her tobacco-stained teeth in an unpleasant smile. 'Even if you are a no-good, murdering whore.'

Eileen O'Donnell didn't flinch. In her eleven years inside she'd learned her lesson well on how to react to such remarks – or rather how not to react. The resulting isolation had at least saved her from further beatings after the initial attacks that had been her payment for daring to act in a way that the other prisoners had decided was snooty and stand-offish. Paradoxically, it was the reputation of the man she had killed – her husband – that would, in the past, have been her protection. But Gabriel O'Donnell had done too many things, to too many people, and Eileen had paid many times over for his crimes as well as her own.

The blonde heaved herself up to a fleshy crouch, folded her beefy arms across her cerise nylon nightdress, and watched as Eileen collected together the last of the few possessions she had allowed herself to put on show. The trinkets and photographs, she knew, had only added to her vulnerability with the likes of the Glaswegian witch with whom she had been forced to share so much of her meagre living space for the past twenty months.

In some ways, the last few of those twenty months had been the most difficult to endure of the whole time that Eileen had been in prison, because she knew what, and who, waited for her on the outside.

Brendan O'Donnell stopped halfway along the hedge, took a gold cigarette lighter from his coat pocket, held it at eye level and sparked it three times. On the third flame, two men appeared at his side.

Brendan was immediately on the alert. 'Where's Barry?'

Kevin Marsh stared down at his feet and let out a long, slow breath. 'Sorry, Brendan. Barry never showed. Them guts of his must be playing him up again. Probably didn't wanna risk it.'

'Fair enough.' Brendan's face betrayed nothing. 'So, it's down to me and you then.'

'What? I'm not here, I suppose?' It was Peter MacRiordan, Brendan O'Donnell's red-headed lump of a brother-in-law.

Kevin nodded as if the exchange between Brendan and Pete Mac hadn't happened. 'Yeah. And I brought Pete Mac along just in case.'

Brendan looked at his brother-in-law, sighed with resignation, and then opened the nylon bag. From it he took three pairs of department-store driving gloves, the sort that would soon be being gift-wrapped, ready to be placed under family Christmas trees all over the country to surprise dads and grandpas.

'Here you are, lads, these'll keep your hands nice and warm.' Brendan took the empty cellophane packaging from them and then pulled on his own pair before dipping back into the bag.

This time he took out a length of lead piping bound in cloth. 'And this'll open the truck door quicker than any set of twirls.'

'But ain't the driver expecting us?'

'Not this time he ain't, Kev. No.' Brendan jerked his head towards the line of lorries. 'Because this is not a usual pickup. This time we're gonna help ourselves to the load in that nice big green truck down there. The one with *Kessler* written on the side in pretty red letters. See, I've had a whisper that it might be worth our while.' He shrugged down into his sheepskin. 'In more ways than one.'

Kevin's response was a tight frown, but Pete Mac, working as ever from a different agenda, came out with one of his usual, annoying comments. 'Fucking Barry Ellis. Bad guts? D'you reckon? There's me out here in the pissing down of rain, freezing me goolies off, while he's tucked up indoors, nice and warm with his Sandy. And Kevin's still making excuses for him. Everyone knows the bloke's off his nut, so why do we all keep on pretending?'

13

Kevin grabbed the lapels of Pete Mac's trench coat. 'Just shut it for once, will you, Pete? He's been a good and loyal friend to me, and to the rest of us.'

'Brendan?' Pete Mac was clearly offended. 'You gonna let him treat me like this?'

Brendan looked at him coolly. 'We're meant to be working here, Pete, not rowing like bloody schoolgirls.'

'I still don't think it's right. Barry gets away with murder just because he can't face the fact that he found Stephen Shea's body – well, the bits that was left of it.' He snorted, a derisive mix of laughter and contempt. 'Big fucking deal. That was over ten bloody years ago. More, when you work it out. So why don't he just get over it?'

'Pity it wasn't you what got chewed up by fucking dogs.' Kevin was now very close to punching him.

'Have you two finished?'

Pete Mac looked at his brother-in-law for as long as he dared, then shrugged non-committally. What was the point in arguing? He never listened to him anyway.

'Good. Now let's get going.'

Brendan led the way over to the Kesslers' truck, and then climbed up the steps to the cab and rapped on the steamed-up window.

Jimmy Harris looked at his watch and groaned. Half four in the bloody morning. What now? It was bad enough the trouble he'd be in when he got back

14

home as it was. Nancy was bound to say it was his fault that he'd been told at the last minute to make an extra pickup in Spain. And his fault that the wait had sent him over his driving hours. Course it was his fault – even though the contact had never shown and so he might as well have kept on the road as originally planned. Everything was *always* his fault. That was to say, everything Nancy didn't like was his fault. Anything that went the way she wanted, well, that was an entirely different matter. Mind you, the stopover had been worth it. He'd had a right laugh with that bunch of Paddies he'd got talking to while he was hanging around. He still had the hangover to prove it. But Nancy'd never believe him even if he told her the truth. And as for trying to explain that it wasn't possible for him to push on because of the hours – good as useless. But he couldn't drive legally for another three hours, and that was that, because, as always, Daniel Kessler had warned him: don't do *anything* to draw attention to yourself or the rig, just do as you're told and you get the extra wedge. It was funny how she never complained about that.

And now some bugger was knocking on his window, disturbing his sleep. He couldn't move until at least half seven, and here was this arsehole about to tell him he had to get out of the lorry park. Well, he was just about ready for him.

Jimmy wound down the window. 'What?'

It took him no more than a split second to register

the face, but it still didn't make sense. 'O'Donnell?'

'Got it in one, moosh. Now we're gonna move this rig somewhere nice and private.'

'I don't think so.'

'Sorry?'

'Daniel and Sammy'd kill me stone dead. And if their nutty cousin Maurice found out, I'd be better off dead.'

'And you really think you should be more afraid of the Kesslers than of me?'

'Look here, O'Donnell –'

Even in the quiet of the early morning, the cloth wrapping on the lead pipe did its job, the contact with the man's skull making little more than a dull thwack.

Jimmy slumped sideways across the bench seat, a thin trickle of blood running from his nostril.

Brendan tossed the lead pipe into the cab and turned to Kevin. 'I'll go and get the Merc. Then I'll drive by here nice and slow and lead the way. You follow me in the truck, but not too close, all right? And, Pete, you bring up behind in the other motor.'

The black Mercedes, followed by the Kesslers' green truck, and then Kevin's maroon Cortina, were soon heading along a rural byroad that had become little used since the building of the nearby motorway. It was now almost enclosed, tunnel-like, by the overhanging branches of the trees that shielded it from the fields on either side.

Brendan flashed his lights twice then killed them as he pulled into a cinder-surfaced lay-by.

The others drove in behind him.

'Let's have the keys.' Brendan took the driver's keyring from Kevin and started working through them, searching for the one that matched the locks on the back of the truck.

Kevin stood beside him, watching silently.

Pete Mac leaned against the cab and lit a cigarette, kicking the back of his heel against the wheel rim. Why couldn't he have driven the truck? Brendan was treating him like a spare part again, and Pete Mac was getting really pissed off with it. Thirty-eight years old and still being treated like the fucking van boy.

It was then that he spotted the car. It was swerving all over the lane as if the driver had lost control.

Now here was a chance to show Brendan he deserved a bit of respect, and that he was just as capable as the others. He threw his unsmoked cigarette to the ground, searched hurriedly through the cab for the lead pipe, and then scrunched his way round to the back of the truck.

'Ssshh!' he warned the others. 'There's a motor coming.'

The three of them stepped back into the shadows just as the car skidded into the lay-by, scraping across the cinders as it came to a juddering halt. The driver either wasn't in the best of moods or was drunk. Maybe both.

'Shit,' spat Brendan. 'What does he want?'

Then the passenger door was flung open and a young woman in her late teens, wearing hot pants that barely covered her buttocks, got out and wobbled towards the lorry on thigh-high platform boots. She was followed by the car's driver, who was dressed rather more soberly in a heavy, floor-length army-surplus greatcoat.

'I gave you so many chances, Neil,' the girl gasped through her tears. 'I told you, if you so much as looked at one more girl, I never wanted to see you again. And what do you do? You go and snog my best friend.'

'How many more times? No, I didn't.'

'And how many more times have I got to tell *you*, you horrible pig? She told me, Neil. She told me what you did.' Her words started to catch as her sobbing grew louder. 'And I know it's true, because she said you had really wet lips.'

'But, Sookie . . .'

Sookie? Pete Mac stifled a laugh.

'You know it didn't mean anything. We'd all been drinking and smoking and messing about. It was nothing. Look, how about we get back in the car?'

He reached out to her, but she wouldn't let him touch her. He was getting seriously annoyed with this. They'd been driving around all night as he tried to explain that nothing had happened at the party, while she grabbed at the steering wheel and demanded to be let out. Well, she'd got her wish now – they were standing in a lay-by in the middle of bloody nowhere, in the pouring rain.

Why couldn't that stupid Marsha have kept her mouth shut? It wasn't as if he'd screwed the silly cow. Mind you, if she'd have been up for it, he wouldn't have said no.

The girl threw back her head and wailed theatrically. 'I loved you, Neil Barrett.'

He dredged up his last bit of patience from somewhere very deep inside him. 'This has gone beyond being silly. Look at you, you're soaked through. And you must be freezing in that outfit. Come here, Sook. Come on.' His voice was now soft and cajoling. 'Let me give you a cuddle. Warm you up.'

'A cuddle? You must be joking, you animal. I've got no intention of ever getting back in that car with you ever again.' She pointed accusingly at the vehicle as if it were somehow as guilty as its driver.

'I know,' she went on, her chest rising and falling with temper. 'Why don't you go back to college and *cuddle* Marsha? I'm sure she'll be only too happy to oblige. Everyone knows she's the bloody common-room bike.'

Neil snorted dismissively. 'So how are you going to get home?'

'I'll hitch.'

'Fine, if you really want to be on the front page of

the papers tomorrow. *Student murdered by maniac.* Just because she was too bloody stubborn to admit she was wrong.'

'If you cared about me, you wouldn't have kissed her in the first place.'

'Tell you what, I agree with you. So let's just forget it, shall we?'

They heard the car door slam, and the window being wound down, and then his sharp, angry voice: 'It's your bloody funeral.'

The car revved away into the early-morning darkness.

Pete Mac was about to say something, but Brendan slapped a hand over his mouth.

'Pig,' they heard her snivel, as she came round the side of the truck and walked slam into them.

It was bad luck for Sookie that Kevin had decided to bring Pete Mac with him, and also that Pete had had just about enough of being told what to do.

This was the moment when he would prove, once and for all, that he was more than capable of handling difficult situations.

He tore Brendan's hand away from his mouth, barrelled forward and smacked the girl across the back of the neck with the lead pipe.

Her knees gave way, and she folded up on herself, all neat and tidy like a pop-up book being closed after a child's bedtime story.

Brendan dragged Pete Mac back into the hedge.

'Are you completely off your fucking nut?'

Pete Mac could barely speak with the injustice of it all. 'But you just whacked the driver.' He spat belligerently at Brendan's feet. 'What was I supposed to bastard do?'

They'd just finished hauling the girl up into the cab, shoving her in from the passenger's side, and wedging her fast against Jimmy's body, when a horsebox reversed smoothly up to the front of the Kesslers' truck.

'What the fuck's going on now?' Kevin was beginning to sound as agitated as he felt. This wasn't going well. And he couldn't help wishing that he'd left Pete Mac back in Stepney, or, better still, that he himself had stayed at home like Barry.

'It's okay,' said Brendan. 'Calm down. I'm expecting her.'

'*Her*?' Pete Mac wasn't agitated, he was furious. Left in the dark as usual. Why hadn't Brendan told him about any of this?

A young woman in her early twenties, wearing jeans and a waxed jacket, and with her long dark hair caught up high in a ponytail, jumped down from the driver's side of the horsebox and made straight for Brendan. She kissed him on the cheek and asked in a whisper: 'Where's the lorry driver?' Her accent was Irish, cultured.

'Don't worry about him.' Brendan winked, his

own gruff cockney sounding harsh in comparison. 'Dab of chloroform. Sleeping like a baby in the cab.'

She nodded to Kevin and Pete Mac and then turned back to Brendan. 'And where's Luke? Didn't fancy putting his hand to a bit of manual labour, I suppose? Or maybe this is too exciting for him.'

Her smile broadened into a grin, folding her cheeks into the dimples that made her look the image of Brendan's kid sister Catherine. And that had his stomach flipping over as his head filled with images of Catherine dying on the filthy couch in his father's scrapyard.

'Well?' she demanded.

'All right, Ellie, keep it down. We just didn't need him – okay?'

Pete Mac let out a grunt-like laugh. 'Why lie to her, Brendan? You know Luke's picking up Eileen later this morning.'

'She's coming out of prison?' asked Ellie, her eyes fixed on Brendan. 'Today?'

'Yeah.' Brendan returned his attention to the driver's keyring. 'Now, are we going to get this lot unloaded or what?'

Ellie reached up and touched his cheek. 'Are you going to meet her?'

Brendan bowed his head. 'I'm not sure.'

'She'll be expecting you.'

Brendan shrugged. 'Maybe.'

Pete Mac muttered something under his breath.

Brendan rounded on him. 'What did you say?'

'I said: it's not right having birds involved. They're too fucking soft for this sort of work.'

'If you must know, Pete, *Ellie* is driving some merchandise back over to Ireland for me.'

Ellie stared at Pete Mac, her eyes suddenly hard, as she pointed at the horsebox. 'There's a beautiful, sorrel bay filly in there. A truly gorgeous creature. And I'm responsible for that vehicle's safe delivery.'

'I don't get it.' Pete Mac screwed up his nose as if someone had just farted. 'If she's just moving horses about, then what's she doing here?'

'Because I've got a little surprise.' Brendan slapped the flat of his hand against the truck. 'Not only all the tobacco and hash that I hear the Kesslers have packed in nice and tight among these loads from Spain, but a little something extra that I had slipped in, while the driver was being entertained by friends of mine down in Fuengirola.' He chucked Ellie under the chin. 'And you're going to give it a lift over the water for me in the horsebox, ain't you, sweetheart?'

Brendan was pleased with Ellie, he knew she was bright, but she was also willing. She'd immediately done as she was told, keeping watch on the roadside, while he, Kevin and Pete Mac unpacked the avocado-green lavatories and washbasins from the back of the truck.

23

Ellie glanced over her shoulder every now and then, to check on their progress, noting the look of increasing puzzlement and then pleasure on Brendan's face as they searched carefully through the straw packing in the wooden crates. As he pulled out yet another of the plastic-wrapped parcels, each the size of a flattened bag of sugar, to add to the growing pile at his feet, he weighed it in his hand, and prodded it experimentally with his fingertip.

'Looks like my information was out of date, chaps. Seems like the Kesslers have been branching out.'

'There aren't just chaps here, you know, Brendan.'

Brendan grinned at Ellie's cheek. He hadn't seen much of his dad's 'little mistake' when she was growing up – though, God knows, just her very existence had irritated the hell out of his mother – but once Eileen had gone inside, Ellie had been able to get closer to her half-brothers. She seemed to fancy herself as a chip off the old O'Donnell block, and had become increasingly desperate to get away from the stud farm in Ireland, where she'd been kept hidden away all those years with his dad's sister Mary.

A life in London and a chance to work with Brendan, that's all Ellie wanted these days. And maybe if she carried on being as useful as this, perhaps Brendan would have no objection.

Satisfied that they had finally cleared out the whole lot, the three men stowed the packages in the boot of Kevin's car. Then Brendan rubbed his hands together to warm his fingers, and took a small, pencil-slim torch out of his pocket.

'And now for the little surprise I *was* expecting. The one I had planted. Ellie, you keep a lookout, girl.'

Holding the torch between his teeth, Brendan knelt on the ground, apparently oblivious of the damage the soaking wet cinders were doing to his trousers, and felt under the chassis, seeking out the clips he knew he would find there.

'Gotcha!' he said round the torch, as he released the smooth, cold metal.

What looked like the fuel tank suddenly came loose and dropped down on two sturdy brackets.

But it wasn't a fuel tank.

He opened the hidden lid of the metal container and stepped back, letting the other two men see inside.

'They're fucking guns,' gasped Pete Mac.

'Nothing gets by you, does it, Pete?' Brendan shone the torch so they could get a better look. 'And better to risk the necks of them bastard Kesslers bringing them over from Spain than risking our own, eh, lads?'

Brendan and Ellie worked together clipping the truck's dummy fuel tank to the underneath of the horsebox, Ellie occasionally breaking the silence with soothing noises to calm the filly whenever it spooked.

25

'Good girl,' said Brendan when they'd finished, in unconscious imitation of Ellie speaking to the horse. 'That was a nice job. Now drive carefully and smile at any nice man from customs who wants to have a talk with you, all right?'

'Sure, and don't I smile at all the fellers?'

'And you've got the address for the drop in Wicklow?'

'*Yes.*'

'Go on then. They'll be expecting you.'

The three men watched as Ellie drove off.

Pete Mac, not best pleased to have been left out of so many of the plans, edged closer to Brendan. 'Fancy getting your own sister involved in gun-running,' he needled. 'All them bad boys with all them bombs and that going off over there. It don't seem right to me.'

'Far as I can see, Pete, there's no more bombs over there than there are over here at the minute. And anyway, Ellie's my half-sister, not exactly the same, now is it?'

'Jesus, I've gotta hand it to you, Brendan. People reckon I'm a nasty bastard, but you've got no sentiment in you whatsoever.'

'Interested as I always am in your opinion, Pete, why the fuck don't you shut up and let me think? I've had it up to here with you and your fucking screw-ups.'

'*My what*?'

'Well, it ain't my frigging fault that we've got a dead girl on our hands, now is it? But it is up to me, of course, to come up with a way of dealing with it.' Brendan checked his watch again.

'It's gonna start getting light soon. So I want that truck torched before anyone starts nosing around. And make sure you rip the tart's clothes up first, and rub one of his spanners, or the wheel brace or something, in the blood. Make it look like he's tried it on with her and they've had a fight.'

He took out his car keys, tossed them in the air, and snatched them into his fist. 'Anthony's waiting for you over at the flat in Bow Common, so get over there and unload the gear with him, have yourselves some breakfast, and see me back at the cab office at, say, half ten, eleven.'

With that he walked over to his car and drove off as casually as if he'd just finished another ordinary day's work.

Chapter 2

Eileen O'Donnell stepped through the prison gate, threw back her head, and let the cold, fresh rain fall on her face. She crossed herself as she breathed the same prayer she'd uttered every day since she had finally got rid of Gabriel. She wasn't asking for forgiveness for what she had done – no, she had no regrets about that – but she desperately wanted guidance for her family. Because Eileen had plenty of regrets about them.

But now at least she was free. Or as free as a woman could be who had murdered her husband, and who had refused to let her children see her while she had done her time in prison.

Despite her greying hair and her much slimmer, almost skinny frame, Brendan spotted his mother straight away. If Ellie hadn't have said anything, he didn't know if he would actually have come, whether he'd have decided to wait until later, but he was here now . . .

He got out of the car and took a single step towards her. But then he stopped. There was a cluster of what could only be journalists making towards her.

Then someone else, a woman, calling his mother's name – *Eileen!* She was running towards her with an umbrella held out ready to protect her from the rain.

He could hardly take in what he was seeing. But it was her, he was sure of it now. It was Sophie Kessler, Harold Kessler's old woman. And Luke was running right along beside her.

Like they were together.

Brendan started running too, and, as he drew closer, he heard Sophie Kessler talking to his mother.

'Eileen,' she was saying, her face full of pity – *damn the interfering old cow*. 'I know all about my Sammy and Catherine. He told me everything. And I wanted you to know that I understand what you did.'

Brendan barged past her and grabbed Eileen's arm. 'My mother don't need your fucking understanding. Come on, Mum, come with me. I've got the motor over there.'

A burst of flashbulbs exploded in the grey morning air, followed by a barrage of questions.

'Mrs O'Donnell! Over here! Do you have any comment about your time inside?'

'Did you have special privileges because of who you are?'

'How did the other prisoners treat you, knowing you murdered Gabriel O'Donnell?'

'Eileen! Here! Are you worried about your sons following in their father's footsteps?'

Eileen didn't seem to notice them, nor did she look

at Brendan, she just stared down at his hand resting on her arm. 'Let go of me.'

She turned to Sophie Kessler. 'I'm very grateful for your words.'

Then she turned to Luke. 'You'll give Sophie a lift home, will you?'

Luke nodded, then jerked his thumb at the reporters. 'Brendan, get rid of them lot.'

Brendan stalked over to the huddle of raincoated men without a word, or at least without one that Luke could hear.

Sophie Kessler smiled pleasantly at Eileen. 'Don't worry about me, my love. I just wanted to be here today. You know, to see you out safely. You'll be wanting to be with your family just now. I'll go and find myself a cab.'

'We wouldn't hear of it, would we, Luke?' said Eileen.

Luke held open the back door of the car, gulping back the tears that were threatening to spill down his face, as he listened to the soft Irish voice of his mother. The voice still barely tinged with the cockney tones of her children. The voice he hadn't heard for eleven long years.

'You won't get a cab in this weather, Mrs Kessler,' he said, pulling himself together. 'Please, get in out of the rain. It'll be my pleasure to give you a lift.'

Luke made sure that Eileen and Sophie Kessler were settled in the back seat of the Daimler, before closing the door and turning to check on his brother.

Luke was surprised to find Brendan standing right behind him. He was holding a smashed camera, and the journalists were slouching away, muttering threats.

Before Luke could speak, Brendan was jabbing a finger in his brother's chest. *'It'll be my pleasure*?' His face contorted in disgust. *'Mrs Kessler*? Luke, what the fuck d'you think you're doing even talking to that woman?'

'Forget all that for now, Brendan. There's more important things to worry about. It's Barry Ellis. He got a tug. Early hours of this morning. His Sandy phoned me. She heard someone banging on the front door – guessed it had to be the law at that time – but she couldn't wake Barry up.' Luke rubbed his chin nervously. 'He'd had too much to drink, see. So she shot out the back and over the fence. I picked her up from a phone box and took her to one of my places over in Stratford.'

Brendan was *not* about to show any gratitude. 'You're being helpful for a change.'

'Don't have a go at me cos you've got the hump about Mum. I just thought you should know, that's all.' Luke took another step away from the car, moving closer to his brother. 'Cos let's face it, Brendan, it'd be a shame if anything happened to bring the law to the house today, and to upset Mum, wouldn't it? And anyway, even if Barry didn't work

31

for us, we've been mates with Sandy since we were kids. We owe her that much.'

Brendan took out his cigarettes and lit one, unable to say thank you, or well done, or even to argue. 'Was there any gear in the house?'

'Sandy reckons no, but I'm not so sure. Not now.' Luke paused. 'I made a few enquiries. They reckon, when they eventually woke him up, Barry lost it and gave one of the coppers a right whacking.'

'You're kidding?'

'No.'

'Why'd the silly fucker have to go and do that?' Brendan raked his fingers through his thick, black, collar-length hair, realising for the first time since he'd left the others in the lay-by that he was wet through. 'So even if there was nothing dodgy in the house then, there's sure to be plenty in there now?'

Luke shrugged. 'Reckon that's about the size of it.'

'I'll get into the office and make some calls.' Brendan tapped on the car window. 'See you later, Mum.'

Eileen looked straight ahead.

Luke got in behind the wheel. 'Right then, we'll take you home first, shall we, Mrs Kessler?'

'Thank you, dear, but just drop me in Oxford Street, if you don't mind. There's a few bits I need to pick up from Selfridges. Harold thinks I'm up here on

32

a shopping trip. Though why he thought I came out so early!' It was typical Sophie, chatty and friendly as ever. She took off her chocolate-brown leather gloves and put them in her matching handbag, then unfastened the buttons of her camel cashmere coat and eased it away from her neck. 'You know, I've never seen it rain so hard.'

Eileen said nothing, nor did she do anything to try to make her damp, old-fashioned two-piece any more comfortable as it clung limply to her body. She just stared out of the window, watching the world flash by, a world that had somehow become so busy, fast and crowded. She felt stunned by the clatter, and colour, and rush of it all, the details coming at her like a kaleidoscope.

'You wait till you get home, Eileen,' Sophie was saying. 'You won't know the place. The East End's changed so much. The world's changed. There's this ridiculous new decimal nonsense – I still convert back to the proper, old money, or they have you over in the shops if you don't watch them. And then there are all these young girls, they think nothing of living off the welfare nowadays. No man involved, a lot of the time. Just girls by themselves with babies. Shocking.'

As she carried on her commentary on the changing world, Sophie didn't seem to notice that Eileen continued to gaze out of the rain-streaked window, sitting there as if she were alone, cocooned in her own place, where no one could reach her.

'And everyone goes abroad for their holidays now. Did you know that? Everybody. Never used to hear of that in our day, did you? Not unless you had a good business and were well off. And they've all got phones and cars – all of them – and central heating. They expect it, even on the estates. You should see the tower blocks that have shot up all over the place. And the kids running wild while their mothers sit about smoking and drinking coffee all day. Not like we used to live, eh, Eileen?'

Even Sophie was beginning to realise that she was prattling on, but what else could she do – sit there in silence?

'Me and Harold, we got fed up with the way things were going, so we moved out. We're in Essex now – Abridge. Nice place. Classy. My Harold thinks he's lord of the manor, the silly old sod. You should see him in his wellington boots when he takes the dogs out. Green they are, like the ones he's seen the neighbours wearing. An East End Jew in green wellies! I daren't laugh at him though, he's so touchy about things like that. He's still in charge of the businesses, of course, but the boys do most of the day-to-day stuff. Tell you what, you'll have to come over and see us sometime. Have a bit of dinner with us. Catch up on old times. And who knows, once you see the fields and trees, you might even want to buy a little bungalow for yourself out there. I'd like that, you being nearby. What d'you think, Luke, d'you think your mum'd like the countryside out our way?'

'Dunno, Mrs Kessler,' he said, smiling politely into the rear-view mirror. 'Not really thought about it.'

Sophie returned his smile with a weak effort of her own, relieved that at least one member of the O'Donnell family was acknowledging her. 'Hark at me, chatting on. I'm so excited to see your mum, I'm forgetting myself. So tell me, Eileen, tell me how you are.'

Eileen considered for a moment, and then at last the words came spilling out.

'I told the Review Committee that I'm a Catholic and I'm very sorry that someone died. It's not right that a man should have lost his life. But what I didn't say was that it might have been a sin, and a crime, but I'm glad I did it. Being in there was terrible, but I'd go through it all over again if I could have my Catherine back for just one day.'

Sophie could think of nothing to say so she patted Eileen's hand.

Eileen pulled away as if she'd been attacked. 'I'm sorry,' she said, her voice so small that Sophie and Luke could barely make out what she was saying. 'It's a long time since anyone's touched me without meaning me harm.'

In the O'Donnells' minicab office on the Bethnal Green Road, Pete Mac sat on the corner of the desk tapping the end of a pencil up and down like a drumstick.

Paula, the cab controller, pressed her headset closer to her ears. 'Sorry, love,' she said into the little hands-free speaker, 'you'll have to repeat that.' She flashed a look at Pete Mac. 'Only it's a bit noisy in here.'

Kevin Marsh screwed up his eyes as if in pain and grabbed the pencil from Pete's hand. 'Who are you? Keith Moon's ugly uncle?'

The door opened and Kevin swung round, knocking cold, sugary tea all over the bookings log. Paula said nothing, she just pulled a box of tissues from the desk drawer and began mopping up.

'Out the back,' said a grim-faced Brendan, walking straight past them.

'Brendan,' Kevin called after him as he followed him through into the private office. 'About Barry –'

'Yeah, I know, Kev. He didn't turn up this morning cos he got collared.'

'On my life, Brendan, I only just found out. Sandy called my Gina and she called me here. I swear I didn't know.'

Pete Mac pulled a face to show he doubted that very much indeed.

Brendan dropped down into a tan leather armchair that stood beside the big black ash desk in the back office. 'What I've heard is that they pulled a fucking drugs raid on him – the bastards. As if I don't pay them enough to leave us alone, they have to go and fit up poor old Barry for dealing.'

Kevin felt as if his breakfast was about to make a reappearance. 'I think it's a bit worse than that, Brendan. He went off his head and gave one of the coppers a good hiding.'

Brendan forced the heels of his thumbs into his eyes. 'So I heard.'

Pete Mac puffed out his already chubby cheeks. 'I bet they got the right needle with him over that.'

'No?'

For once, Brendan's sarcasm silenced Pete immediately, but it didn't stop Kevin. He wanted to make it very clear that he hadn't known what had happened to Barry. 'Yeah. And they've fitted him up for some other nonsense as well, over Haggerston way. A post-office job. They're saying he smashed the clerk's head in with a pickaxe handle in front of a queue of punters waiting for their fucking pensions or something. But everyone knows he ain't got the bottle for nothing like that since he found Stevie Shea.'

Pete Mac rolled his eyes – here we go again, more excuses for that bloody moron.

Kevin glared at him. 'And my Gina wanted to go over and see if Sandy was all right, Brendan, but she said she had to keep her head down for a few days. Keep out of the limelight.'

'Yeah, don't worry yourself about Sandy. Luke's got her sorted out.' Brendan dragged the nails of both hands through the dark shadow of stubble on his chin. 'But all I can do for Barry right now is to get a brief over to see him. And anyway, we've got other things to worry about.' He stood up. 'I've got to get home for a bit, get changed and shaved, and I want you two to get yourselves back over to Bow Common and move Kessler's gear into one of the new lock-ups. And tell Anthony to give the place a good clean-up. We've got no idea who might be nosing around later. Or what might have been said.'

Despite it being against his habit or inclination to ever question Brendan, Kevin felt compelled to speak up for his old friend. 'Barry would never grass anyone up, Brendan.' But then he paused and added quietly, 'Not if he's in his right mind, he wouldn't.'

'In his right mind?' Pete Mac threw up his hands. 'You said it, Kev. The bloke's a bloody nut job.'

Chapter 3

Brendan took the stairs two at a time down into the big basement kitchen of the house on the Mile End Road where he had lived for all of his thirty-five years.

He was a fit man, apparently at ease with himself, and in control of everything that surrounded him. But those few who knew him well would have noticed the bottom lip drawn back between his teeth and the slightly narrowed eyes, and would have realised that, in reality, he was desperately trying to control his temper as he figured out why things weren't going the way he wanted them to.

He checked out the room. Eileen was sitting stiffly upright in an easy chair next to the now redundant kitchener that had become little more than a shelf for displaying an arrangement of dried flowers and wheat ears. Then there was Luke sitting at the perfect pine table that Brendan had bought to replace the one that had been in the kitchen since Eileen and Gabriel had first moved into the house all those years ago. Caty, his twelve-year-old niece, was sitting across from her Uncle Luke staring morosely through drooping curtains of glossy, chestnut-brown hair, while her mother, Patricia, was busying herself filling the kettle at the shiny stainless-steel sink. High above her, the narrow window, set up in the wall at street level, let in little of the grey mid-morning light, streaked as it was with the rain that was still coming down in sheets.

'D'you like the way I had the place done up for you, Mum?' Brendan asked, tossing his keys down on the table. 'The old place don't look too bad, does it, eh?'

Eileen didn't reply.

Patricia looked over her shoulder at the elder of her two brothers. 'Tea, Brendan?'

'Thanks.' He straddled a chair, facing his mother, and tried again. 'I suppose you've heard about these petrol shortages and all this electricity blackout shit – sorry, Mum, I forgot myself – all this blackout business that's going on. Well, none of it's going to worry you. I'll see to that. You won't want for anything. And what do you think of your new cooker? It's got what they call a griddle and everything. You'll be able to cook a turkey in that thing as big as our Luke's head come Christmas.'

Still no response.

Caty stared down at the table, her eyes as blue as Brendan's had been at her age – before he'd taken to the drink almost as enthusiastically as his father had done before him. She was absorbing every awkward moment.

Brendan wouldn't let it go. 'Why didn't you let us come and see you, Mum?'

'In that place?'

He sat up straight. At least she'd answered him. 'We were all so worried about you. You should have let us visit. It wasn't right keeping us away.'

Patricia set down the tea things next to Brendan, deliberately making them clatter against the tray. 'Luke's doing well for himself, aren't you, Luke? Tell Mum about your business, go on.'

Brendan was about to light a cigarette, but instead he pulled it from his mouth, flicked off his lighter and cut off his brother before he could say a single, boastful word. 'Yeah, Luke's doing really well, Mum. But you know him, he's far too modest to say so himself. He's got properties all over the place. Even some right over in Stratford, Plaistow and Forest Gate. He's bought up all these houses and turned them into flats. Just like old man Kessler used to over in Notting Hill. Mind you, Luke's the first one to get in round that way, so there's no real competition, no threat from any nasty Rachman types for him to worry about. Not like Harold Kessler had. And now he's the regular king of the slum landlords round there, aren't you, mate? Gets them old tenants out no trouble. And now – this is a bit of a new venture – a few of his places have some very attractive young ladies living in them and all.'

Luke jumped to his feet. 'What's got into you, Brendan? Today of all days.'

'What, my business is always *dirty*, is it, but anything you set up is somehow clean? Don't get it myself, Luke. Maybe Mum understands.'

Eileen, recognising how close she was to weeping, dropped her chin until it almost touched her chest, and put her fingertips to her mouth – so much bad feeling between her children. Bad blood some would say. And maybe they were right.

Caty held the glass of milk that Patricia had given her, eyeing Brendan, the uncle she rarely saw, and Eileen, the grandmother she didn't know at all, over the rim. She was fed up being treated like a child. Everyone kept everything from her. But these people were her family, and, creepy as they were, she was entitled to know what was going on with them. It was bad enough being sent to the rotten church school in Wanstead now she was in the seniors. The girls there all thought she was dead common, living in Stepney, and all the girls in Stepney thought she was a snob because of the disgusting uniform she had to wear. It was as if she didn't fit in anywhere, even in her own family. It was all so unfair.

Patricia slapped her hands on the table. 'Right, Caty,' she said, trying, but failing to sound cheerful. 'We'd better be going, love.'

'Mum!' She dragged the word out to three whining syllables. 'I've not finished my milk yet.'

'And I thought you were always saying you hated the stuff. Now come on.'

'Sit down, Pat.' Brendan kneaded his temples with his thumbs. 'Let's just forget it, all right?' He sighed loudly and then turned on a smile. 'You can have a bath later on, Mum. I've had the boxroom converted into a bathroom, and a top-of-the-range suite put in for you. Dark claret it is. With gold taps shaped like dolphins. It's got a shower cubicle and everything. Looks like a posh hotel up there. And wait till you see the cream shag pile I've had put through the house.'

Eileen raised her head and looked at her daughter. 'I think I'll be going up for a rest.'

Brendan felt panic rising from his stomach to his chest. He had to take control. 'I gave Pat the money to get you a load of nice clobber and all, Mum. It's up in your new wardrobes. I had them fitted by this firm from down the Roman. White they are, with brass handles. Really smart. One of them's got a mirror that covers the whole door.'

Patricia picked up her handbag. 'Brendan, just leave it for now, eh? Mum needs a bit of time. She's tired. Come on, Caty, don't let me tell you again, Nanny wants a bit of peace.'

'I'll get one of the lads to drive you.'

'It's okay, Brendan, I've got the car.'

'What – I can't do anything for anyone no more? So what's wrong with my help all of a sudden?'

'Pat's right, Brendan,' said Luke, ruffling Caty's

43

hair. 'We should let Mum rest. Come and get your coat, Caty, and I'll see you out.'

As Caty reluctantly followed her uncle over to the stairs that led up to the ground-floor hallway, Eileen rose to her feet.

'Wait.' She reached out to her daughter and hugged her, holding her close. Then she walked hesitantly over to her grandchild.

Doing her best to smile, Eileen brushed her lips against the top of Caty's head, breathing in the scent of her hair. 'You're a beautiful, beautiful girl, Caty. And I'm so proud of you. You're just how I've imagined you all these years.' She stepped back to look at her, holding her at arm's length. 'And that gorgeous auburn hair. It made a great mix, your mum being a brunette and your dad being a redhead. You probably won't believe this, but you're the girl of my dreams. I used to fall asleep at night and see you. And you're exactly like I hoped you'd be. All I could ever wish for. Your mum's done a grand job with you.'

Eileen closed her eyes, her chest rising and falling as she felt the air filling her lungs – air that hadn't been breathed in and out by all those other women. Then she turned and took her daughter's hand. 'So, Patricia, how is he then?' Another hesitation. 'Pete Mac.'

'You know him, Mum, same as ever. We're all fine.'

Eileen nodded as if she were no longer listening.

'I'll be off now.' With that, she climbed unsteadily up the stairs and left them standing in the kitchen staring after her.

Patricia blew her nose. 'She looks so old.'

Brendan was stunned. After all he'd done for her – not a word for him. Not a single, bloody word. Having a kid, was that really all it took to get her to be proud of you? How fucking hard could that be? He'd settle down with Carol and have a bloody houseful of kids if that's what she wanted. And it'd be something her precious Luke wasn't ever likely to beat him at, not unless some sort of miracle happened that changed him overnight into a real man.

Luke took Patricia and Caty out to their car and then came back down to the kitchen. He was concentrating on buttoning up his long, black leather coat, anything to avoid looking his brother in the eye. The last thing he wanted was another row, but he couldn't leave without saying something.

'Nice one, Brendan. You managed to upset everyone in one single pop. That takes some doing that does, even by your standards.'

'Not staying, Luke?' Brendan opened one of the new oak kitchen units and took out a bottle of brandy. 'Better things to do up Soho, have you? Got some nice feller waiting for you?'

'If I had, do you really think I'd tell you? Wait for you to laugh at me? Call me filthy names?'

'You bring it on yourself.'

'Look, Brendan, this ain't to do with me. It's Mum I'm thinking of.'

'Blessed St Luke of fucking Stepney.'

'Just listen to yourself, will you? This is all too much too soon for Mum. Go easy on her at least till she settles back in.'

Luke started back up the stairs, but then turned and looked at his brother. 'Before I go, I just want to say one more thing. While you were mouthing off about me and my properties, Brendan, I didn't hear you complaining about that gaff of mine over Bow Common I lent you to stow your hookey gear. Or about the place I came up with for Sandy to stay in.'

'Just piss off, will you, Luke? And leave me alone.'

Brendan sat by himself at the table with the still-full bottle in one hand and an unused glass in the other. He had been there for almost an hour, fighting his craving to drink the stuff until he was insensible, so he could just wipe away all his resentment at Luke, the resentment at him being their mother's favourite that had come flooding back – just as if she'd never been away. But, as always, he was also battling with his terror of turning into his father.

He couldn't stand it any longer. He got up and emptied the alcohol down the sink.

He threw the bottle in the bin and filled the kettle

instead. Perhaps he really should think about settling down. Why not marry Carol and have kids? He'd have to do it one day. Why not sooner rather than later? And why not with her? He was sick of being treated like he didn't matter in his own poxy home. Let his mother try and ignore him when he had a whole tribe of little chavvies running around the place.

He spooned coffee into a mug and glanced up at the wall clock. Ellie should be well on the way to the ferry by now.

Christ, his mother was going to be shocked – no, not shocked, she'd have fucking kittens – once she realised just how far her husband's bastard had ingratiated herself with the family, especially with Eileen's beloved Luke. And all while she'd been rotting away in prison . . .

But she still wasn't going to be half as shocked as Brendan had been that morning, when that Kessler woman had turned up and had got into Luke's car just like she had every right.

That whole fucking family made him sick to his stomach. They had more front than bastard Brighton.

Chapter 4

He might have been standing in a drab, cement-floor lock-up, behind a row of grubby terraced houses in Leyton, with the only light coming from a single, bare swinging bulb, but Brendan was no longer the sour-faced man who had left his mother to her rest just a few hours earlier. In fact, his mood had improved no end, and he was looking very pleased indeed.

'Bloody hell, we've had a right touch here. Look at this little lot.' He ran his hand over the stacks of plastic-wrapped packets that half filled the runs of wooden shelving standing against the far wall. 'I knew there was a lot, but when you see it in the light, all set out like this . . .'

'I don't know about you, Brendan,' said Anthony, who usually looked after the O'Donnells' working girls, but who, because of his enormous size, was also brought in on other jobs when a bit of extra muscle might be called for, jobs such as collecting money owed, frightening people who stepped out of line – or minding valuable merchandise – 'but I reckon that's speed.'

'Well, it definitely ain't the packets of Golden

Virginia we was expecting.' This wasn't just one of his sometimes terrifying mood swings, Brendan was genuinely happy. Okay, his mum wasn't acting as if she was exactly pleased to see him, but he was going to work on that, and anyway, he knew he had to cut her some slack. It was understandable her being a bit confused after what she'd been through. But why shouldn't he be happy? He had all that lovely dough to look forward to from the arms run. And now, to cap it all, here was this very nice, and unexpected, little bonus.

As far as Brendan knew, speed hadn't been a part of the Kesslers' trade – not until now. His information was that they had decided a few years ago to stick to importing what they knew – hash, rolling tobacco and porn films. It was where they had the contacts, and they'd made good, regular money. Life had been easy, and they had been content. But they'd obviously changed their markets, realised that it was speed that was getting to be the real earner.

It made Brendan laugh. If you read the papers or listened to people talking, you'd think there was no money about, that the whole bloody country was in trouble. But he'd heard the dealers who supplied the clubs and pubs saying how they couldn't get enough of the stuff. It was what all the kids wanted now. And not only the kids. The older lot didn't mind a bit of it, if it came in pill form.

He was looking at a very tidy little sum on those shelves.

But best of all, what made Brendan the happiest, what made his grin so wide, was that it had once *all belonged to the Kesslers*. Every last grain of it.

Sweet.

Kevin puffed out his cheeks. 'They must be well in with customs if this is the kind of load they're bringing in.'

'Too true, Kev.' Brendan did another mental count of the packages; it was like bloody Christmas come early. 'Anthony, what's that kid's name?' he asked over his shoulder. 'You know, the one who hangs around in Arty Burns's snooker hall. Always goes in there alone. Obviously doing a bit of trade.'

'The freaky-looking one with the big-soled boots and all that blond curly hair?'

'That's him.' Brendan's hand went unconsciously to his immaculately tied silk tie – stylishly wide but nothing lairy, that wasn't his way. 'Dresses like a clown.'

'That's Milo,' said Anthony. 'Timmy Flanagan's youngest.'

'Yeah, old Timmy's boy – God rest his soul. Go and get him and bring him round the cab office. I might have a job for the young chap.'

Brendan took a final look at the shelves, and then walked over to the narrow access door that had been set into the up-and-over shutter. He stepped outside, checking that no one was hanging around in the alley.

'By the way,' he said, poking his head back inside the lock-up. 'Either of you got any idea where that prick Pete Mac's got to?'

Kevin's and Anthony's embarrassed shrugs told Brendan everything he needed to know. His brother-in-law was hanging around with some tart somewhere.

Christ, he really was a waste of space. If he hadn't have been married to Patricia, he'd have been long gone, Brendan would have seen to that. Still, at least when he was screwing around he wasn't causing anyone any trouble.

Pete Mac smiled contentedly. He had met the two Liverpudlian sisters in a club a couple of weeks ago. They'd had a few laughs about the three of them being redheads. The girls had given them his number and he hadn't thought much more of it. That's what birds did when you bought them drinks. But then, and he still couldn't believe his luck, he'd been going through his jacket pockets, checking for handker-chiefs with lipstick on them, odd earrings, that kind of thing – otherwise there'd be more nagging when Patricia took his suit to the dry-cleaner's – when he'd come across the cigarette packet with their number scribbled on it.

Why not? he'd thought.

Now, not only was he lying here in a big double

bed in a hotel – well, a B & B – in Paddington, having had a big smile brought to his face by the two very cute red-haired sisters – three redheads in a bed, there must be a word for it, yeah: bliss! – but the girls reckoned that back home everyone knew they were two of the best hoisters in the business. And now they were talking about settling in London for a while, and – this was the tasty bit – lifting to order for him. Fur coats, jewellery, and all that fancy gear that posh birds, and tarts with old men who had a few quid, couldn't get enough of. And all he had to do was get them a flat.

Would he be interested?

Now, let's think about it. He was thirty-eight years of age. His wife took no notice of him. His kid had more time for Luke, her fruit of an uncle, than she did for him. Brendan treated him like he had shit for brains and had no right to do anything – even though he'd been part of the bloody family since he was a teenager – and he still paid him wages like he was a fucking employee.

So, would he be interested . . .

Not many, Benny!

Pete Mac might as well have died and gone to heaven.

As Anthony walked through the door, a few people looked up. But most of the men, and they were all men, carried on smoking, chalking cues, and taking apparently languid, but actually totally focused shots at the coloured balls on the dozen tables that filled the twilight world of Arty Burns's personal fiefdom – a snooker club over a row of shops on the Barking Road in Plaistow.

The only person really to take notice of his entrance was Arty himself, who, compared to Anthony's mountain-like build, was more like a small molehill.

'Anthony! Surprised to see you here today. How are you? Let me get you a beer. Something stronger? You do remember you picked up Mr O'Donnell's share two days ago, don't you? We've not got anything like full cash boxes again, not yet. You can look for yourself. Would you prefer a cuppa tea? Cheese roll or something? Nice and fresh they are. The old girl in the baker's made them up for me this morning.'

As Anthony put one of his huge hands on the man's shoulder, he felt the little man's skinny frame become rigid with fear. 'You're all right, Arty. I'm here looking for someone.' He stretched out his arm and beckoned with a saveloy finger to a relaxed-looking man in his twenties, who was leaning against the door jamb of the lavatory, hands in his pockets and a self-contented smile on his face. 'And he's standing right over there.'

The young man raised his eyebrows, pointed to himself and mouthed, 'Me?'

Despite his misgivings, Anthony nodded. He was

sure that Brendan knew what he was doing – he couldn't have run all his businesses so successfully if he didn't – but this bloke made Anthony feel very uncomfortable. Anthony himself had made one or two concessions to changing fashion: his shirt had a longish collar, his jacket had a bit of a waist and his lapels were wide. He even had a droopy moustache – although that wasn't really from choice, he thought it looked daft with his shaven head, but his wife had insisted he grow it, so that had been that.

But this bloke was something else.

Big, blond, permed afro hair; flared, dark red, velvet trousers, pink shirt – pink, for Christ's sake! – a paisley kipper tie, rainbow-striped tank top, and blue platform-soled boots.

Brendan was definitely right about one thing: he could have stepped straight out of the circus.

Deep breath. 'You're Milo Flanagan.'

Milo nodded cheerfully. 'That's me.' His accent was pure East End. At least there was something normal about him.

'Brendan O'Donnell wants to see you.'

'I'll get me coat.'

Anthony might have known to expect the fur-trimmed, floor-length embroidered afghan.

Milo winked at Paula as Anthony hurriedly steered him through the minicab office and into the doorway of the private room at the back.

54

Brendan was waiting for them.

He was about to invite them in, but he didn't have the chance. Before Anthony could stop him, Milo was across the room with his hand extended in enthusiastic greeting, like a hyperactive candidate canvassing votes before a general election.

'Hello, Mr O'Donnell.'

'You've heard of me.'

'Course I have. Everyone's heard of the O'Donnells. My old feller was always saying how he knew the family.' He turned to Anthony to reinforce his point with a friendly grin, and then back to Brendan. 'Your dad made you lot famous.'

'Yeah, the old man was a legend.' Brendan pointed Milo towards one of the leather chairs. 'But me, I'm different. Gabriel wanted to know everyone – and wanted everyone to know him. He loved it, being seen with all the faces in the pubs and clubs, and hanging around with all the celebrities and stars. But me, I like keeping what they call a low profile. I value my private life, see, because I'm a businessman, and being private's a sensible thing to be. That's why I employ people for their skills. They do their job, and, other than that, I don't wanna know. So long as they keep their noses clean, and don't draw attention, they lead their own lives.'

'Cool with me, Mr O'Donnell.' Milo made himself comfortable, folding his arms and resting a booted ankle on his knee. 'Now, I'm guessing that if you wanna talk to me it'll be about drugs.'

'You're a straightforward bastard, I'll give you that.'

Milo shrugged, his afghan moving up from his narrow shoulders like a living creature. 'No point in beating about the bush, you being a businessman and everything. And I know that you know my business is drugs. Just another commodity to be bought and sold. And I'm good at that – buying and selling.'

Milo was clearly warming to his topic. 'You see, it's simple, Mr O'Donnell. At the bottom of the heap, there's the pushers. They're the ones who get the kids interested. Hang around the school gates and that. They let 'em have the gear for a good price – good quality and all – get 'em hooked and reel 'em in. Now the pushers, they buy their bits and pieces from local dealers, and they in turn buy from the bigger dealers, the ones who supply on a more serious level. And them dealers – they buy from the importers. And the importers do their business with the producers.' He rubbed his hands together. 'Importing. Very nice game. I'm gonna have some of that one day.'

Anthony winced. He was talking to Brendan as if he was an amateur. He might have heard of the family, but did this little herbert really have the first idea who he was talking to?

'But until then, what can I do for you, Mr O'Donnell?'

Brendan looked at Anthony and exploded with laughter. 'Cheeky little fucker, i'n he?'

Harold Kessler was sitting in what his wife called his den, a large room overlooking the grounds at the back of their Essex mansion. Hidden behind high walls and electronic gates, the recently built house looked as if it might belong to a pop star or a footballer. But Harold was neither of those, he was the head of the Kessler family, and the one with ultimate responsibility for the family businesses – businesses which might be described as being slightly less conventional than either sport or music. Although it could, in all honesty, be said that he was also in the entertainment industry. Then there was the haulage company, a very useful sideline and cover for their other activities, and, very importantly, a convenient explanation for the family's wealth.

Harold Kessler's sons Daniel and Sammy sat on the large, deep-buttoned plum velvet sofa that ran along one expensively – if flashily – flock-papered wall, while his nephew, Maurice, lolled in a wing-backed chair, his leg slung over one of the arms. A not unusual scene in the Kessler household, because although the 'boys' were now in their thirties and had places – and a succession of casual relationships – of their own, when they weren't working or playing, the three of them spent most of their time at Harold and Sophie's place in Abridge. And it had to be said that

Daniel's supposed live-in girlfriend Babs didn't object to the arrangements. She and their three children – David, Michelle and Paul – lived in a nice detached house in Gidea Park, handy for her mum and dad's place on the estate at Harold Hill, and near the market, park and schools. Everything that Babs had ever wanted, in fact.

What was unusual on this dull, November afternoon was the presence of two police officers, each balancing Sophie Kessler's second-best china on their knees as if they were having tea with the vicar – or perhaps the rabbi.

'So, the way we see it, at the moment, the best bets are, from the look of it,' one of the officers continued, tiptoeing carefully through the minefield of suggestions, 'is that your driver had been having it away with the bird, and her husband's found out and he's had them. And burnt out the truck in temper.' Pause. 'Unless she was just a hitchhiker who came unstuck with her choice of lift. But that wouldn't explain the fire, of course.' Another, longer, more awkward pause. 'But you know what vandals are like nowadays.' He took a mouthful of the now cold tea, then added a bit feebly: 'They'll put a match to anything.'

Luck was with the officer. Harold Kessler had no interest in making him squirm. Not today.

'Thank you, gentlemen,' Kessler said, with an apparently obsequious dip of his shiny bald head. 'You've been a real help over this terrible business.

Two deaths, such a waste.' He tutted sadly. 'I'll contact my insurance company. Tell them what you said. Doesn't seem as though anything need be too difficult about the claim. Now . . .' He opened the desk drawer and took out a thick padded envelope. 'My son, Danny, will see you out.' He handed the packet to the officer who had done all the talking. 'A little thank-you for your kindness, gentlemen. For the widows' and orphans' fund, of course.'

'Of course, thank you, Mr Kessler. Very generous.'

Daniel, solemn as an undertaker, showed the men out to their car. When he returned, his expression was rather different. He dropped down on the sofa next to his brother.

'Top-quality fucking speed that was, Dad. Good enough to cut to at least double the quantity. Maybe more. And it had to be this time we lost it. The time I risked bringing in enough of the fucking stuff to spot for all the gaffs I had lined up for the massage parlours. Twelve properties, and all at just the right sodding price, and in the perfect bloody area. Good as in my hands they were. I was gonna start having all the East End trade right out of that queen Luke O'Donnell's hands. And what happens? This. So what am I gonna do now? Ask the Baxters if I can have the places on fucking HP? I'm gonna look a right bleed'n mug.'

Sammy reached over and patted his brother's leg.

'Sorry, Dan. I know how long you've been planning this.'

Daniel held his head in his hands, flattening the springy blond, Pre-Raphaelite curls that had, at last, come into fashion. But style was the last thing on Daniel's mind.

'I'd bet my last fiver it was them O'Donnells who did this. It's got their fucking name written all over it. That dirty-eyed bastard of a driver must have found out what he was carrying and gone and told them.' He gripped his hands into tight, angry fists. 'The fucker's just lucky he burnt to death before I got hold of him. Cos I tell you what, the O'Donnells are gonna be sorry they ever did this to me.'

Harold raised his shoulders and spread his arms in an extravagant shrug. 'So it's happened the once, son, and it's very upsetting. But do we really want to start all that business again with the O'Donnells? We're not doing too badly, are we, boys? The Soho shops are making us a nice living with the films and magazines. And the betting always shows a good profit.' He took a cigar from the humidor on the inlaid rosewood desk. 'And, thank God, at least they left no evidence in the truck.'

'It gets to me, Dad, that's all. That lot come out on top every bloody time, while we scratch around, having to be grateful for whatever business the bastards *allow* us to get on with.'

Maurice put down his cup and saucer on the onyx

and brass side table, swung himself around off his chair and strolled across the room to the window behind Harold's desk. He looked out at the mist gathering over the river that ran along the bottom of the garden.

'Do you know,' he said, his Manchester accent still as broad as on the day he had first been sent by his parents to stay 'for a bit' with his Uncle Harold's family in London, 'I love the life I've got down here, and, like Danny, I hate the thought of them Irish bastards messing with it. So, if you're interested, like, I know how to get hold of a bit of scratch in a hurry. In fact,' he turned to face them, his face cracking into a nasty grin, 'I've got the perfect plan.'

Perfect plan?

They should have realised there and then that there was going to be a problem.

'The way we get the stake for your property, Danny, is with a bank job. A big one. I've been working on it for a while now. And you and Sammy are more than welcome to be part of it, cos it's gonna take a team. Not a big one, just the three of us.' He smiled politely at his uncle. 'No offence, Harold, but this is a young man's game.'

Harold didn't look offended, he looked sceptical. As did his two sons. Very sceptical.

Maurice sat himself down and waited for their reaction.

Daniel was the first to speak. 'Look, Maury, I know you're family – so I'm really sorry to have to say this – but, first thing that comes to my mind is, why didn't you tell us about it before – if you really have been planning it for so long?'

Maurice was about to interrupt, but Daniel ploughed on. 'And second, we all know how you get. Let's face it, you're not a calm bloke, are you? And I really don't know if I wanna take the risk of you getting all twitchy, and doing something that I might think's a bit daft. Like you getting bored and pissing off and leaving us there roasting on the pavement.'

Maurice grinned happily, more than pleased with himself. 'That's what you don't understand, feller. We won't be going across the pavement. We are going to pay Mr Bank Manager a private visit at his lovely home in Surrey.'

Sammy looked imploringly at his father. 'Dad, you tell him.'

Harold Kessler shrugged. 'Maybe you should think about it boys. Sounds less risky than going in team-handed into the local high-street branch and putting the wind up the tellers. All these bloody have-a-go heroes crawling out of the woodwork, wanting their pictures in the papers, they're making it dangerous out there.'

'All right then, Maury, sell it to us. Prove you've thought it through.' Daniel Kessler sounded about as convinced as his brother looked, but he wanted those properties and, to do the deal, he needed a proper stake.

When Maurice had finished outlining the bare bones of his plan, he sat back in his chair, speech over, ready for questions.

And Daniel had plenty of those. He and his family had seen and done some pretty unpleasant things in their time – it was part of the tough and violent world in which they had chosen to live – but his cousin Maurice was a one-off and could shock even him. So he wanted to be very clear about what exactly this job would involve.

'You absolutely, stone-bonking guarantee we're not taking any guns, and that there's no strangers involved? Just you, me and Sammy. We're all the team that's needed?'

'Positive, feller. Two of us hold the wife in the house – big, scary, bad men, like – while the manager takes the other one of us to the bank. Then he opens the vault, gives us the cash, and before you know it we're back home. You've got the money you need for your properties, we've got a nice cut for ourselves – and a divvy for Uncle Harold, of course – and the fleet's lit up, feller. Simple as that.'

'We're gonna have to think about this.'

'Think all you like, Dan, but I'm gonna go in there in two weeks' time with two blokes willing to help me. I'll leave it up to you whether you're one of them or not.'

Harold broke the ensuing silence. 'I know you've all got a lot on your minds, boys, but come on, this won't buy the baby a new bonnet.' He pulled back his sleeve, exposing a sparkling, diamond-encrusted watch. 'Time you three shifted your arses up to Soho to check they've all got plenty of stock in, and while you're at it, you can pay a visit round the betting shops to make sure no one's having a weed. Expensive time, Christmas, and I don't want any of them bastards thinking he can treat his old woman to a mink stole on the strength of my earnings.'

When Sophie poked her head round the door of the den, Harold was lounging back in his chair, luxuriating in the ritual of lighting a cigar.

'They all gone?' she asked, collecting the dirty teacups and saucers on to a tray. 'The boys and the law?'

'All gone,' puffed Harold through a veil of lavender-blue smoke, and then added absently, 'So how was Eileen?'

Sophie perched on the edge of the sofa, facing her husband's desk and set the tray down on the floor. 'It's so sad, Harold. I think she's going to have a right time of it, adjusting to life outside again. I tried my best to get through to her, but I don't think she heard a word I said. It was like talking to a brick wall.'

She shook her head sadly. 'I just hope her daughter, or her boy, can help her.'

Harold frowned. 'Her boy? What, Brendan?'

'No, I mean Luke.'

'Him?'

'I know he's as bent as a nine-bob note, Harold. God help him. But he's a kind boy. Thoughtful. He gave me a lift, you know. Wanted to bring me all the way home. But I said that wasn't a good idea, that I'd told you I'd gone shopping.'

'Yeah?' said Harold, looking down his nose to study the red-hot tip of his Cohiba as he puffed away, drawing in the smoke.

'I didn't want Luke telling that brother of his that you knew I'd gone to meet Eileen. You know, Harold, that Brendan really is a nasty bit of work. There was his poor mother, bewildered by everything, upset, standing there in the pouring rain. And him? He wanted a row.'

She stood up. 'And there were all these newspaper people there, shouting questions and taking pictures of her.' She bent down to pick up the tray. 'I don't suppose they had a clue who I was, do you?'

Chapter 5

Brendan was whistling cheerily to himself as he turned the key to the street door of Carol Mercer's house. It was a three-bedroom end-of-terrace on a new estate in Hackney that Brendan had 'arranged' for her to move into through a friend of his – a friend who was something to do with the council. It wasn't a place he'd have chosen – Stepney and Spain did for Brendan – but she loved it, treating it more like a doll's house than a home, forever rearranging the furniture, getting new curtains and cushions, polishing and cleaning . . . And that was all just fine by Brendan. In his experience, if you kept a bird happy, then you saved yourself a lot of grief. And Brendan was going to make her a very happy bird indeed – he was going to marry her. And Christ knows, she'd been nagging him about settling down for long enough. And it would certainly get his mother approving of him for once.

'Carol, you ready, girl?' he called down the hall, staying outside on the step so he could keep an eye on the Morris Marina he'd borrowed from a driver at the cab office. If she was going to keep him hanging around, he'd have to treat one of the little chavvies playing football in the street to mind the car. It was hardly like leaving his Merc out there, but he'd appreciated the loan, and didn't want the bloke's motor getting damaged.

'Course I am, lover.' Carol came out of the back bedroom and wiggled her way along the passage towards him. She was wearing brown, knee-length suede boots, a mid-calf orange dress that was slashed almost to the crotch, and which dipped into a low V at the neck. The outfit seemed to be held together by nothing more than the metal-studded, brown suede belt she had slung low on her hips. She put her hands behind her head, puffing up her already big blonde hair. Standing as she was against the geometrically patterned silver wallpaper that dazzled visitors as they entered the place, she made quite a sight.

'So, what do you think?'

Brendan eyed her admiringly. 'Beautiful as ever, darling. And if we weren't going out . . .'

She lowered her chin and peered up at him through heavily mascaraed lashes. 'Seeing as you're in such a good mood, we could always go out later.'

'Tempted as I am, babe, I've gotta shoot round to see Sandy Ellis first. Make sure she's all right, and that there's no . . .' He hesitated, weighing up how much he could trust a bird like Carol. 'Problems.'

Carol's hands dropped from her hair. 'Aw, Brendan,' she whined. 'When you phoned you said you were taking me out. You never said nothing about going round to see Barry Ellis's old woman.' She flapped about a bit, not knowing how to vent her anger, then, deciding to sulk, she hopped on to one leg and struggled to undo the zip of her boot. 'So I got all dressed up for nothing, did I? Thank you very much.'

'No you didn't, Cal. Now get that boot done up again. You've gotta come with me.'

'What, to see Sandy Ellis? You having a laugh?'

Brendan's jaw clenched. Marry this cheeky bitch? Not in this fucking lifetime. He stabbed his finger at her face. 'Don't you *dare* question me, or I really will have a laugh – after I give you a good slapping. Now get out to that car.'

As he shoved her towards the doorway, Carol caught her shoulder on the jamb, making her flinch with pain, but she knew better than to cry out.

Brendan drove through the rush-hour traffic along Cambridge Heath Road, and Carol sat silently, still sulking, beside him. She was fed up and her shoulder stung from where the bastard had pushed her. As usual, the rotten sod had just had to get his own way.

When Brendan whistled it wasn't just dogs that he expected to come running. It made her so angry.

The trouble was, she liked being his girlfriend. He was generous – very – with his money, and he was really good-looking – a big plus considering some of the animals she'd been with – and Carol liked it when other girls couldn't keep their eyes off him. That and the fact that he was one of the most powerful men – if not *the* most powerful man – in the East End.

And she *loved* it when people were scared of him. That really turned Carol on.

But she liked it a whole lot less when she was the one he was scaring.

She glanced at him sideways, taking in the strong profile, the dark brown, almost black hair that curled into soft gypsy curls as it skimmed his collar. Then there were his eyes.

So blue.

All right, she'd give him one more chance.

But this time she really meant it.

Brendan steered the car off the Romford Road and pulled into a side turning, slowing down and ducking his head to check the door numbers of the neat little Victorian terrace.

Carol sat up straight. 'Why are we stopping in Stratford, Brendan? What are we doing here?'

'Sandy needs to keep her head down till this trouble with Barry's been sorted out.' A worrying thought popped into his mind. 'And this has to be a secret, right, Carol? No one's to know that she's staying here. Or that we've been over here to see her.'

Carol wrinkled her nose. He was taking the piss, wasn't he? Who on earth would she want to tell that she'd been visiting someone round here? These houses were awful – really old. And this one they'd stopped outside was worse than the rest. The little front yard was piled high with rubbish, and the curtains looked like they'd been hanging there since the place had been bloody built. It was disgusting.

'Don't worry, Brendan, I won't be telling anyone. I can promise you that.'

'Good.' He turned off the ignition. 'Now you ready?'

Carol didn't answer; she just stared at the house. At least it explained why he'd come out in such a dodgy-looking motor. He wanted it all kept quiet that he'd been here, and driving this crappy car'd do that all right. Who the hell would expect to see Brendan O'Donnell in this piece of shit?

'I said: you ready?'

'Look, Brendan, I don't wanna be difficult or nothing, but d'you mind if I wait for you out here?' She saw the look on his face. 'I'm not feeling that good.' And she'd feel even worse if she had to go in there with him, she could just imagine the stink.

Brendan threw open the driver's door, furious he'd even thought that the stupid little mare would know how to behave when you went to visit a bird while her old man was banged up. 'Please yourself.'

Brendan had to knock twice before he heard Sandy's wary voice asking who was there.

When she opened the door, he was shocked. Sandy

was almost as old as he was, and a good fifteen years or so older than Carol, but she'd always taken good care of herself and had never really looked her age. But, today, she showed every one of her thirty-four years. Her eyes were hollow; her usually glossy, shaggy lion-cut hair was unbrushed; and as for what she was wearing – it looked like one of Barry's old shirts, and as if she'd slept in it.

He acknowledged her with a nod and stepped inside, straight through the street door and into the sitting room of the little two-up two-down.

When he turned to look at her, Sandy's lips were pressed together in apology. 'The old girl only moved out recently, and Luke's not had a chance to clear out the furniture or anything. But you don't notice the smell after a while.'

She looked exhausted, defeated. 'Sorry.' She pulled the shirt collar up to her throat. 'I had to get out on the quick. And this was the nearest thing I could lay my hands on before I legged it.'

'You don't have to apologise to me, San.' He looked about him, deciding which of the threadbare chairs would do least damage to his suit. He settled for the manky-looking sofa by the side of the gas fire.

Sandy waited for him to sit down, visibly squirming as he put the flat, stained scatter cushion down on to the floor. 'Can I make you some tea? No, sorry . . .' She thought for a moment, gnawing at her thumbnail. 'Sorry, Brendan, I wasn't thinking. I'm

71

not sure if there is any. The cupboards're not exactly full, and what there is, well, it looks a bit iffy. You know, old . . .'

'But you've been here since first thing yesterday morning. How've you been managing?'

'It's all right, the water's still on. And so's the gas, thank goodness, or I'd have frozen to death in this weather. And at least no one knows I'm here.'

Despite the strange circumstances, as Sandy dropped down on to the armchair facing him, Brendan couldn't help but notice her legs. They were long, and sort of polished-looking. Very nice.

He caught himself staring at her and immediately pulled himself together with a straightening of his shoulders and an unconvincing cough. 'Carol Mercer's outside. You know her?'

'Let me guess, young blonde girl?'

Sandy's attempt to lighten what was obviously not an easy situation for either of them passed Brendan by. 'That's the one,' he said. 'Like I said, she's waiting for me outside, so there's nothing funny about me being round here with you.'

'Course not. I never thought there was.'

'Don't think she fancied coming in.'

Sandy shrugged. 'She's only a kid.'

Brendan winced, and then – at last – treated her to a grin. 'Don't rub it in, San. I know I'm a few years older than her, but I'm not drawing me pension just yet, girl.'

'You can't fool me, mate. I know exactly how old you are. You were the year above me – remember? Well, you were when you did the teachers a favour by coming in for the odd day now and again.' She tried another smile. 'I fancied you something rotten back then. All the girls did.'

Brendan frowned. 'I never knew that.'

'Liar. You knew all the girls were after you.' Her smile faded as she reached out for one of the packs of cigarettes piled on the old-fashioned tiled mantelpiece. 'And Luke knows me, eh, Brendan? Knew I'd be climbing up the wall if I didn't have plenty of fags.'

'At least he got something right.' Brendan shook his head in wonder. 'I can't believe he brought you here.'

'Don't be like that. The poor sod didn't have much choice, did he? It was bloody four o'clock in the morning when I called him. Pitch dark and pissing down with rain. I must have sounded hysterical, not knowing what was going on, standing in a phone box, freezing cold and wearing nothing but Barry's shirt. Not even a pair of slippers on me feet. What else could he do?'

'Maybe.'

She offered Brendan a cigarette and they smoked in silence for a while. 'Luke said Eileen's back home. How's she doing?'

'Your old man's being held in police custody, you

don't look like you've had any sleep – which don't surprise me, the state of this dump – and you're asking me about Mum?' For want of something better to do, Brendan loosened his tie. 'I appreciate you asking, Sandy. She's fine.'

He spent a bit more time on his tie, tightening it again and then smoothing it down. 'So, how are you, if it's not a stupid question? Which it definitely is.'

What was up with him? He sounded like a sodding teenager.

'Brendan.' She leaned forward, resting her elbows on her knees, her hands clasped in front of her. 'I'm gonna tell you something. It's about Barry. I think you've got a right to know, seeing as how good you've been to him – and me – over the years. It might explain a few things.' She tapped her thumb nervously against her teeth. 'But you've got to promise me you won't hold it against him.'

'Go on.'

'He's got into drugs.'

'Don't be daft, San.' Brendan sounded relieved. 'We all like a bit of a smoke. If anything, he's got more sense than me. I worry I'm getting too much into the booze. Like the old man did.' *Why was he telling her this? It was like he was in the sodding confessional or something*. 'A bit of puff's the least of his worries.'

'No, Brendan, you don't understand. It's more than that. A lot more.' She took a long, deep drag on her cigarette. 'It started after he got ill. You know, after finding Stephen Shea. At first it was tranqs, on prescription. But then that wasn't enough. And lately, well, let's just say it's got worse. A lot worse. He's been spending so much money. So much more than he's been bringing in. That's why that post-office thing they're blaming on him . . .' She looked away, unable to meet his gaze. 'I think he probably did it.'

'Bloody hell, Sandy. You are kidding me, right?'

'I only wish I was. I've been working in a launderette on the Commercial Road just to pay the rent. But Barry don't know that, Brendan. And promise me you won't tell him.' She laughed mirthlessly. 'It was the only bloody place I could think of that he wouldn't go in. But I even had to leave there, when one of the customers told me he'd been in dealing of a night.'

Brendan smacked the side of his fist on the arm of the sofa, and Sandy's head snapped up. She'd said too much.

'Brendan, I –'

'It's all right, San. It ain't your fault, girl.'

'It was heartbreaking seeing how he got. Everything he earned went up his nose, or in his arm, or down his throat.'

'If it was that serious, why didn't you say something?'

'You'll never know the number of times I nearly phoned you. But I could only think about how you'd

75

all react if you knew he'd been using like that. I suppose I was surprised you never noticed.'

Brendan ground out the stub of his cigarette. 'We all just put everything down to his nerves. You know, after what happened. And that he'd sort of –'

'Gone off his head?'

'Yeah.'

'He might as well have done. In the end I didn't know which way to turn. I'm sure he must have been borrowing money, cos he'd sold everything indoors that wasn't bolted down months ago. Then I got a letter last week, threatening to cut off the electric, so I borrowed a few quid off Gina, you know, Kev's wife. Pretended I was buying Barry a surprise for Christmas.'

'Jesus, Sandy. I had no idea, girl. Look, you mustn't worry. When all this is straightened out – and it will be – I'll find you something to do. A nice little number in the minicab office during the day shift.'

'But you've got Paula in there already. And she's got kids to keep.'

'I don't believe you, San. Always looking out for other people.' He took a roll of notes from his inside pocket, took a small wad for himself, and held the rest out to her. 'You take this for now. No one knows you round here. You can go out safe enough.'

'Thanks, but I don't need it. I mean, I'm not exactly dressed for shooting round the supermarket, now am I?'

'Take it anyway. Go on. Just in case. And in the meantime I'll send someone round with a bit of shopping for you. Just let me know if you need anything special.'

'I wouldn't mind some clothes.' She looked around the grimy little room. Another smile. 'And a few bits of cleaning stuff wouldn't go amiss either.'

Brendan stood up. 'I've, you know, enjoyed this.'

She looked puzzled. 'Eh?'

'Talking. To you.'

'Good. I'm glad.'

He surprised them both by kissing her gently on the forehead. 'I'll be in touch, all right?'

For some reason, that simple gesture was too much for Sandy; she dropped her chin as her eyes began to well up, the tears spilling down on to her cheeks.

'Sandy, look at me.'

She peered up at him through a watery blur.

'You mustn't worry yourself, okay? We'll get him straightened out. Get him off everything. The lot. Christ, I can get his supplies cut off –' he snapped his fingers '– as easy as that.'

Brendan got back in the car and slammed the door angrily.

Carol ignored him; she was too busy checking her make-up in the rear-view mirror that she had twisted round to bother herself with him and his moods.

He steered the car away from the kerb, but before

they'd even reached the end of the street, he stamped on the brake, shooting her forward, and leaving her with a smear of Damson Shine lipstick streaked across her jaw. He snapped off the courtesy light, leaving them in the dark save for the rain-diluted orange glow of the street lamps.

'Brendan! What is wrong with you? How am I meant to see what I'm doing?'

'*What?*'

'Well, you drag me over here and then you –'

The force of the back of Brendan's hand smacking her across her face had Carol reeling back in her seat.

He reached inside his jacket, pulled out what was left of the roll of notes and, using just one hand, guided the car back into the kerb, ignoring the angry driver of the car behind him, who was hooting and gesturing as he was forced to swerve to avoid him.

He peeled off a few fivers for himself and threw the rest in her lap. 'Here, get a cab. I've got things to do.'

'But it's pissing down out there.'

He reached across and opened the passenger door. 'Out.'

He jerked the mirror back into position, and drove on into the early-evening traffic, heading west, back towards Stepney.

He didn't even look at her as he sped away, didn't even bother to check in the mirror to see if she was all right. He had other things on his mind. Important things.

Like why the hell was the thought of Sandy being stuck alone in that shithole getting to him so much?

And what the fuck was he going to do about Barry Ellis?

Chapter 6

By the time Brendan pulled up outside the phone box opposite the Little Driver pub in Bow Road, he had calmed down and his mind had cleared.

First he made a couple of calls to reliable contacts, men who could ensure that regular deliveries would get through to Brixton with no questions asked except how much they would be getting paid. Then he searched in his wallet for the direct, personal line of DI Hammond, a police officer who'd recently transferred down to London from Birmingham. A man Brendan had been introduced to at a charity boxing evening in Bethnal Green. A man who had put a very interesting proposition to him.

Brendan shot his cuffs, straightened and tightened his tie, smoothed back his hair – a man in control – and dialled the number.

'Mr Hammond?'

'Speaking.' The Brummy accent identified him immediately.

'It's Brendan O'Donnell here. Remember? We had that little chat at the boxing do the other night.'

'Of course, I remember. It was a most enjoyable evening.'

'And d'you remember how you said you might be able to get me into that place you was talking about?'

'Certainly, I do.'

'Well, I'm at a bit of a loose end tonight, and I was wondering if now would be a convenient time.'

'I don't see why not.'

'Good, cos there'll be a drink in it for you, Mr Hammond. A right nice one.'

'I shall look forward to that.'

As Brendan drove into the red-brick garden square that sat on the vague borders of the City and the West End, where residential and corporate properties became almost indistinguishable from one another, he could just make out DI Hammond, through the swishing swoop of the windscreen wipers, waiting for him on the far corner.

Save for the concession of a cheap, chain-store raincoat, the police officer was apparently oblivious to the rain. He was a mild-looking man, in his late forties, and a bit old-fashioned. If you were being honest, dull would probably be how you'd describe him – undeniably more civil servant than dashing crime fighter.

And that suited Brendan just fine.

He let the car cruise to an easy halt and pushed the passenger door open wide.

'Mr Hammond, good to see you. Please, get in.'

*

'So I really won't need you with me?' Brendan was studying the very ordinary piece of card that was, apparently, his pass down into the Aladdin's cave that lay hidden beneath the police station close to Holborn. 'I must admit, it seems a bit unlikely, Mr Hammond. Say they recognise me? Like I told you, I was a bit of a rascal in me youth.'

'You'll be fine, Mr O'Donnell. Any friend of mine is as good as family down there.'

Brendan nodded, taking it all in. 'So, how's the real family then, Mr Hammond? Well are they?'

'Actually, since you're asking, Mr O'Donnell, I have to say: no. Mrs Hammond hasn't been too well at all. It's a shame, but she's taking a bit longer to settle herself down here in London than either of us had expected. But then the leafy suburbs of Birmingham are a very different kettle of fish to this place. She's seen the doctor, of course, but all he could suggest was that she could do with a break, a rest away from it all. But you know what policemen's wages are like, Mr O'Donnell. Public scandal in my humble opinion. Still, that's the price of being a public servant in today's world. Shame, it would have been nice to give her a little treat.'

Brendan clapped his hand on the steering wheel. 'Don't say another word, it's as good as done, Mr Hammond. You can take her down to my . . . to my *friend's* gaff in Estepona. Lovely part of Spain, that is. And let's face it, if every bleeder on the old jam roll's having two weeks away every year, then I'm sure a hard-working man like yourself and his wife deserve getting a fortnight's worth of sun on their backs.'

'That's very generous of . . . of your *friend*, Mr O'Donnell. And I'd really like to do that for my Betty. Be sure to thank him for me, won't you?'

'It'll be my pleasure to do that, Mr Hammond. Go over there for Christmas if you like. Or wait till the weather warms up a bit. Whatever you fancy. Just let me know and I'll make sure you get the keys. There's a local couple keeps it all in order over there – English they are, so no problems with the old lingo or nothing. And, while we're at it, how about calling me Brendan?'

'Thank you, I will – Brendan.'

'You know, Mr Hammond, I like to be sure of the strength of a man before I do business with him, know how he'd react at the death, and from what I can see, I think we're gonna get on just fine together.' He held out his hand to seal the deal. 'There's gonna be money in that hand next week, Mr Hammond. Gonna be a nice little drink for you to treat yourself, while you're down in Spain.'

Mr Hammond's smile could have lit up the gloomiest of November evenings. 'Thank you, Brendan, I'm touched. And please, I'm Bert to my family and friends.'

*

It was ten o'clock. Brendan had left DI Hammond a couple of hours ago and, being eager to try out the apparently magic pass he had been given, he had gone directly to the police store in the basement in Holborn, and – to his surprise – he had actually been let straight in. Just like Hammond had said.

Now Brendan was standing in the entrance to the Bellavista, a club and barely disguised knocking shop, in a cul-de-sac in Shoreditch. Despite the decor being a bit dated, the place was buzzing.

The red velvet and gilt had once been state of the art, when the O'Donnells had taken it over back in the early sixties, and had had it refurbished as the first of their new-look East End clubs. It was still a place that had the power to make Brendan feel tingles of nostalgia for the 'old days'.

He scoped the room and laughed quietly to himself. As always, it was full of punters wanting to drink and meet willing women. The old man had been right, that would never go out of fashion. As he'd got older, Brendan had come to realise that Gabriel, when he wasn't pissed, hadn't been quite the fool that his son had sometimes thought he was. But it was hard respecting your father, when you were a flash, hot-headed kid with more going on in your trousers than in your brain. Shame he'd never had the opportunity to tell his dad that. And a shame his dad couldn't see what a success his eldest son had made of his life.

He spotted Kevin up at the bar.

'All right, Kev?' He settled himself on one of the high stools and accepted the glass of whiskey from the barman without a word.

'Yeah, all right.' He sounded fed up. 'I was just, you know, thinking about Barry. The poor fucker.'

'Yeah.' Brendan scratched at his chin. 'You're right there, mate. He is a poor fucker.'

Brendan had thought a lot about Barry tonight: when he'd been looking into Sandy's eyes, and after he'd chucked Carol out of the motor. And that was why he'd made the decision to phone his contacts, to make sure that Barry had plenty of gear while he was stuck inside on remand. Brixton was a real rathole, a place where it wouldn't take a lot to break someone as unbalanced as Barry Ellis. So, from Brendan's point of view, and despite what he'd told Sandy, keeping the bloke nicely topped up was a very sensible thing to do.

The fact that he was going to keep Barry supplied didn't make Brendan feel guilty. He wasn't going to waste his sympathy on a tosser like him, even if he had known him all his life. All Brendan cared about was that the bloke kept his trap shut. And, thank Christ, Sandy had inadvertently shown him a way to make sure that that's exactly what he would do. No cravings equalled no need to get upset. That was why Barry would have everything his little heart desired.

'You know, Kev, I had a meet with that copper,' Brendan said, in between sipping his drink, and calculating how many of the girls were sitting idle and how many were upstairs with punters. 'He gave me this pass thing.' He leaned in close to Kevin. 'Gets you into this massive basement place, right under this nick up the City. You should see it. Like a fucking cash and carry, it is. Magazines, films, photos, the lot. All the really hard stuff they pull in during the raids. Some stuff even Anthony would close his eyes at. And more than I'd ever bloody hoped for. But they want some serious cash.'

'How much?'

'Let's just say we're gonna have enough from that gear we chored off the Kesslers to make a start, but we're gonna need another bit of bunce every bit as big, to show them we're not fly-by-nights. That we intend to take this business seriously. Then we can have what we like.' He raised his glass. 'There's some very valuable merchandise down there, Kev.' He snorted with laughter, unable to believe it. 'They'll even copy the bastard films for us. You should see all the confiscated equipment they've got.'

He leaned back and folded his arms. 'You know, I think we're gonna need a meet with the Kesslers in the very near future – explain how they'll be taking our supplies for their shops from now on. And at our own very special prices.'

Kevin raised his eyebrows. 'Blimey, meeting up with that lot? Now that does sound serious.'

Brendan was finding it hard to wipe the grin off his face. 'Very serious. And, aw yeah, before I forget. Take a ton out of the till before you leave tonight. I want your Gina to get some things for Sandy Ellis. Clothes, a bit of grub and that. The poor cow's in a right state in that pisshole Luke's stuck her in. And make sure you give Gina a few quid to say thank you to her. From me.'

'Sure, course I will. Gina'll know what to get her. But you don't have to treat her or nothing. She'll be more than happy to do it.'

'No, I'd like to. She's a good girl, your Gina.' Brendan spoke as he moved towards the door.

'Thanks, Brendan, she'll appreciate that.'

'And another thing,' said Brendan, stopping and turning around. 'Tell Gina that Sandy needs some tea bags, will you? She ain't got none, poor cow.'

Kevin didn't laugh. He honestly wasn't sure if Brendan was having a joke or not.

Just a couple of miles up the road, on the other side of the now metaphorical, but still very real boundary of what had once been the solid divide of the old City wall, DI Hammond sat with his colleague, DC Medway, in an ornately tiled pub. It was actually an old gin palace, one of the few remaining examples of the Victorian art of dispensing hard liquor to the masses. And Bert Hammond, with his own interest in control, particularly of the lower orders, found the place very much to his taste. It showed how such things could be done. And that was also why he wasn't drinking alcohol: he didn't like to lose control of himself either. So he was sipping at a glass of soda water with the merest hint of bitters to colour and cloud the liquid.

But it didn't mean he wasn't enjoying himself. He was enjoying himself a great deal.

'Not a bad evening's work, eh, Medway?' Hammond winked – a gesture that didn't look entirely right coming from the very proper DI. 'And next time there's going to be a *nice little drink in it*, as that slimy Irish git might put it.'

He took a small taste from his glass and brushed his finger across his unfashionably clipped tooth-brush moustache. 'Plus we get the O'Donnells and the Kesslers back at each other's throats, of course.'

'Just like in his father's day,' said Medway, remembering it all too well. They were memories he didn't really care for.

'So I understand from studying the files.' Hammond rubbed his hands together. 'Divide and rule, eh, Medway? Divide and rule. A good lesson for us all.'

'Yeah, great, another turf war, just what we want.'

'I do hope that's not an example of your patronising London sarcasm, Medway.'

Medway put down his pint and shook his head. 'Course not, sir. Course not.'

Chapter 7

Carol had to grab hold of the edge of the seat as the taxi driver swerved through the afternoon traffic, but she was too lost in her thoughts to complain. It was a whole week since Brendan had dumped her in the street in Stratford, and just three weeks until Christmas, yet she still hadn't heard a single word from the rotten, conniving git.

She looked at the bags stacked by her feet on the floor of the cab. Christ, she was pissed off. She'd just been shopping in the West End and she'd had to choose – choose, if you don't mind – between two pairs of shoes. She'd caught the superior look on the stuck-up mare of a saleswoman's face. It was humiliating, that's what it was.

And another thing, how exactly was she meant to buy Christmas presents if Brendan wasn't giving her any money? She already knew what she wanted to get him: something really expensive.

How, exactly, was she supposed to do that?

There was the money she had stashed away, of course – having carefully put two-thirds of everything Brendan had ever given her into a special account. But that was emergency money, not bloody shopping-for-rotten-Christmas-presents money.

'Here. Stop here,' she ordered, tapping on the glass partition.

The taxi driver hadn't been surprised when she'd given him the address on the dodgy estate. The floor-length silver fox might have cost a few quid, but it was obvious that a kid like her didn't get that sort of clobber by spending her days in a typing pool.

She counted out the exact fare, and swung the cab door shut with an angry slam, making the driver call after her, but she didn't give a bugger. Carol Mercer had other things on her mind. Like getting Brendan back exactly where she wanted him.

Carol was about to put the key in the front door, when she pulled back, a perplexed frown on her face.

The front-room curtains were closed.

She'd never have left them like that when she went out this morning. It looked horrible, like she had a coffin in there or something.

She put her bags carefully to one side of the step. Took off her fur coat, folded it up and put it on top of the pile, then slipped off her high heels. She hadn't been looking after herself since she was fifteen for nothing.

Making as little noise as possible, she let herself in, ready to scratch the eyes out of anybody who'd been stupid enough to dare to touch any of her lovely things.

She was momentarily fazed to see Anthony standing there, blocking her way into the hall.

But even Anthony – who despite her best efforts to keep quiet had heard Carol coming in the door – was no match for her.

'Take one step towards me, you fat bastard,' she said, her sparkly blue fingernail jabbing him in the chest, 'and I'll tell Brendan you tried to touch me up. Now get out of my way.'

'All right, calm down.' Anthony backed away from her, until his way was blocked by the firmly closed door of the front room.

'You can't come in here, Carol. Sorry, love.'

'Aw can't I?' Carol aimed a swift kick at his shins. It didn't hurt – she wasn't even wearing shoes – but Anthony was so shocked that someone so little had so much front, that it gave her the benefit of surprise. She was under his arm and through the door before his brain had had a chance to crank into gear.

'What's going on?' She was stunned, riveted to the spot.

There was this bright light. It was weird, really intense, throwing shadows that made the room – *her lovely front room* – look totally different. Unfamiliar. And there were men. Strange men. Standing around smoking. *In her house*. She'd never have allowed that.

So what the hell was going on?

She shaded her eyes with her hand as if she were

looking out to sea. This was her room – her own beautiful room – but everything was wrong. It was as if she'd never seen the place before. Well, not like this she hadn't.

It took her a moment to make out what she was seeing. And even then it didn't make any sense.

Brendan was there. And so were what looked like a film crew – four men she'd never seen before, complete with camera and a microphone. And along the far wall on her sofa, under the front window, were two completely naked women – one black and one white – and they were touching each other. *On her brand new, bloody sofa*.

'What the fuck do you think you're doing?' She launched herself across the room at them, but Anthony wasn't about to be caught out again. He grabbed her round the waist as if she were no more than a toddler and hoisted her off her feet.

Up until then, the men in the room – Brendan included – had been too engrossed in the action between the two women to notice Carol's entrance, but now, all eyes were on Anthony and his wriggling, kicking, cursing captive.

'Bloody hell, Carol,' said Brendan, with a little snort of laughter. 'What's up with you, girl? You look like your drawers are on fire.'

The two women started giggling.

'Letting brasses fucking *do it* on my sofa? You bastard, Brendan.'

Being told off by a little trollop? Brendan didn't like that. He didn't like that at all. 'There's no need to get excited. We're only testing out a bit of recording equipment.'

'Look at them. Look at what they're doing. On my bloody new sofa.'

Anthony was finding it increasingly difficult to keep hold of her. 'Can I put her down?'

Brendan wasn't interested in Anthony's problems. 'No need to pull that face, Carol. You wasn't exactly a ballet dancer when I met you, now was you?'

'Stripping's one thing, but that,' She pointed angrily at the two women, her legs still flailing around. 'That's filth.'

Brendan turned to the man who had been operating the camera. 'Hark at her,' he said, with a salacious smirk. 'She was dressed up like a cowboy who'd forgot to put on his shirt and strides, when I met her. Hat, boots and a gun holster, that's what she was wearing. Very classy.'

Everyone in the room except Carol started laughing.

'Don't you dare talk about me like that.'

Brendan didn't bother looking at her. 'Go to bed, Carol.'

Her objections were growing quieter, her thrashing around less wild. 'It's three o'clock in the afternoon.'

This time he did turn to face her. 'Do us all a favour and just piss off out of it.'

They didn't even wait for her to close the door.

'Who's that?' It was one of the men.

'No one, just some little scrubber. Now, you two, get back down to it, or you can piss off an' all.'

Carol leaned against the wall in the passageway, flinching as someone slammed the door shut behind her.

She could hear the men talking and laughing.

This was all that Sandy's fault. Until Brendan had gone to see that horrible slapper, he'd been all over her, couldn't get enough of her. Now she might as well have been something he'd trodden in, something that had spoilt his fancy, handmade shoes.

The men had stopped laughing. Carol moved closer to the door.

'So you definitely reckon the Kesslers don't make their own films.' It was Brendan speaking.

'From what I've heard and seen –' it sounded like the man with the camera '– it's all French and Dutch merchandise they stock. Everything imported. Comes in off the boats, then they distribute it in their lorries.'

Carol leaned closer.

The Kesslers. Brendan was always going on about them. Always saying how much he hated them.

She listened a bit more.

'Well, that's all gonna change.' It was Brendan again. 'Because, I tell you now, they ain't gonna be able to resist taking our stuff for their shops. Not only have I got personal access to the sort of gear that'd make your hair stand on end – if you had any –' more laughter '– but a good friend of mine has offered to make as many top-quality copies as I want him to of our own private productions. And all in a nice safe place where no one can touch us.'

She heard a round of approving chuckles.

'And the artistic efforts we're offering are going to be something a bit special.' This time it was only Brendan laughing. 'I mean, some of these birds coming into the country are so desperate they'll do bleed'n anything. I've already had this pair. Like *Last fucking Tango in Paris* it was. With me playing Marlon sodding Brando. But I had to use marge, didn't I? I mean, couldn't afford best butter, now could I?'

The other men joined in with his laughter, and one of them said: 'You dirty bastard, Brendan.'

'Yeah, good, innit? They're so fucking strung out, they'll do anything for their next fix.'

Carol made the mistake of slapping her hand against the door in temper.

Brendan was out to her before she had even realised what she'd done.

'I told you to get in that bedroom. Now, before I get wild, I suggest you get out of here. Right now.'

'But this is my place.'

'*Your* place? Don't be stupid, Carol, and don't go getting me any more wound up than I already am, or I might just lose me temper with you. In fact, I'll tell you what, you've done me a favour. You've made me realise I've had enough of you. So go on, get out, and don't let me see you hanging around here again. All right?'

Carol narrowed her eyes. She wasn't going to have this. 'What a big man,' she hissed at him. 'Throwing your own unborn baby out on to the street.'

'My what?'

'I'm nearly seven weeks late, Brendan. *Seven weeks*. I was gonna tell you, but I didn't know how you'd –'

'Do you think I'm a complete idiot?'

She stepped back, the wind completely taken out of her sails. 'How d'you mean?'

'You're no more pregnant than I am.'

'Yes, I am.'

'Bollocks, you are.'

'I am!'

'Here you are then.' He grabbed her hand, pulled some money from his pocket and slapped it into her palm. 'There's more than enough there to get rid of it. If you really are carrying. And I'm sure you know plenty of old witches who can help you out. Now get out of my sight, we're trying to work here.'

'But what about all my things?'

'Give me fucking strength.' Brendan rapped his knuckles on his teeth. 'Look, you can come back in the morning. I'll give you till midday to get your stuff together. Then, and I mean this, Carol, I don't wanna see you anywhere near here again. Right?'

It was just before nine the next morning. Luke let himself into the O'Donnell family house on the Mile End Road and crept quietly along the hallway in case his mother was still sleeping.

As he started down the basement stairs to the kitchen, he was taken aback to see Brendan sitting at the table, nursing a mug of tea.

'You're up early.'

'Blimey, you're sharp, got new blades, have you?'

Luke sat down opposite his brother. 'It was you I was hoping to see as it happens, Brendan. Wanted to know about Sandy, if she still needs to stay over there in –'

'What, got tenants queuing up to move into that stinking gaff, have you? Can't let her have it for just a few more days?'

Luke threw up his hands. 'Here we go. Why do you always have to think the worst of everyone? We're not all as bloody awkward as you, you know. I was just wondering if she needed to be moved somewhere else. *Somewhere a bit nicer.* Now we haven't got the law on our heels, and we've got time to think about –'

Brendan jumped to his feet. 'And why do you think I give a fuck about what happens to Sandy?'

Luke held up his hands in surrender. 'Bloody hell,

Brendan, keep you hair on, mate. What the hell's got into you?'

Brendan sat down again and poured himself more tea, then – begrudgingly – held up the pot by way of offering some to his brother.

Luke nodded, and Brendan got up again to fetch him a mug.

'It's that bloody Carol Mercer. She's got me all agitated,' he said, opening the cupboard over the sink. 'I chucked her out yesterday, and what does the rotten cow do? She goes and announces she's bleed'n pregnant.'

'And you still chucked her out?'

'Course I did. I mean, how do I know whose kid it is? She ain't exactly the fucking Virgin Mary, now is she? So I gave her some dough to get rid of it. But for all I care she can keep the money and use a bloody knitting needle and a bottle of gin.'

'*You watch your filthy, blasphemous mouth.*'

Brendan twisted round to see his mother, in her ancient candlewick dressing gown, gripping the back of Luke's chair to steady herself.

The mug slipped from Brendan's hands and smashed into pieces in the stainless-steel sink.

'Mum, you don't understand.'

Eileen turned on her heel and hauled herself back up the stairs, clinging to the banister as if it were a mountaineer's rope. 'Don't you dare speak to me.'

'But even if she is telling the truth, d'you really

want me to be like Dad, and have a bastard hanging round me neck for the rest of me life?'

Eileen stopped at the top of the stairway. 'No matter how much I despised what your father did,' she said, without turning to face her son, 'I'd never have wanted the child's life to be taken before it was even born.'

It was now a few minutes to ten that same morning, less than an hour since Brendan had walked out, leaving Luke to deal with their mother. He had driven from Stepney to Stratford in far less time than it should have taken him, having driven with an anger-fuelled recklessness that made even his usual aggressiveness behind the wheel seem mild in comparison. But as soon as he spotted Sandy in Maxine's All Day Café on the Romford Road he relaxed. A smile came to his face, and he swaggered through the doorway as if he were entering the grand dining room of a distinguished restaurant rather than a greasy spoon in east London.

Sandy was sitting at one of the only three occupied tables, Brendan having guessed rightly that the full-English breakfasters had long since left for work, and the tea-break rush was yet to begin.

'Been waiting long?' he asked, pulling out one of the ill-matched, vinyl-covered chairs.

Sandy shook her head. Her hair, now clean and glossy, fell about her face in soft, fair wisps, and, he couldn't help noticing, the red roll-neck sweater she wore tucked into her plain black maxi-skirt emphasised the womanly curves of her body in just the right way. Sort of feminine, not showy or tarty like Carol would have looked.

'No, not long. And anyway,' she lifted her chin to the window, indicating the second-hand car lot across the street, 'I've been busy guessing which of the passers-by would stop to admire the "car of the week".'

'What, that Capri?' His tone was dismissive.

'You might not like it, but I do. Barry always used to say he'd get me one. You know, one day. A purple Capri, with real leather seats. Aubergine, did you know that's what they call that colour?'

'No, I didn't.'

She offered Brendan one of her cheap cigarettes – she'd long since run out of the stack Luke had left her, and wasn't about to blow the money Brendan had given her on expensive brands.

She lit one for herself. 'Not gonna happen now though, is it? I'll never have my dream car.'

'What I don't get is why you protected him for so long.' This was just as much of a mystery to Brendan as the relationship between his mum and Luke.

'I'm loyal,' Sandy said, with a resigned shrug. 'And he needed me. So . . .'

'D'you love him then?'

That threw her. 'That's my business.' She swirled

the burning end of her cigarette around in the debris in the ashtray, unwilling to meet Brendan's gaze, then said quietly. 'Truthfully, Brendan, he wasn't the Barry I knew any more. Not once that stuff got hold of him. But how could I just leave him to it? We've been together such a long time. So I just did what I had to do – the best I could – to look after him. Still, it's out of my hands now, innit?' She raised her eyes to meet his. 'Do you reckon he'll get sent down for very long?'

'If it's my turn to be truthful, San – yeah, I do.'

Her head slumped forward. 'Shit.'

'I know. But if you're still interested, at least I've got a job for you.' He leaned back in his chair – casual, not bothered. 'The pay's good. Regular.'

Her head jerked up, she was almost smiling. 'Really?'

'Yeah. And it's got a nice little place to live in and all.'

'Brendan, you don't know how much this means to me. I could start as soon as you like.' She leaned forward, excited to be seeing a way out of at least part of the crap she was in. 'Is it all right for me to be back in circulation then? I'm not being ungrateful or nothing, but I can't wait to get out of that place.'

'I've spoken to some people and, so long as Barry keeps schtum about you being in the flat with him at the time of the raid, there's no need for you to be involved in any of this. And from what I've heard, he ain't saying nothing to no one. And . . .' He hesitated, considering his words. 'Look, Sandy, I don't even know if you wanna hear this, but I've had some gear sent in to him. Nothing too serious,' he lied. 'Just something to ease the pain a bit. I didn't like the idea of him suffering in there.'

'Thanks, Brendan.' Sandy's eyes brimmed with tears. 'Mad, innit, I'm grateful that he's got the stuff that got him and me in all this trouble in the first place.'

'It took some doing, San, believe me. He really did give that copper a good hiding.' Brendan reached out and took her hand. She was shaking. 'Now, about this job. I'm setting up one of these new agencies. For escorts. And I want you to run it.'

She pulled her hand away and patted herself hard on the chest as she almost choked on the smoke she had just inhaled. 'Escorts? You're kidding, right?'

'Don't go getting the wrong idea, this ain't gonna be nothing nasty.'

'No? So what is it gonna be then? A dating agency for young ladies?'

'I don't take that sort of lip from no one, Sandy.'

'And I ain't running a bloody knocking shop. I've done some things in my time – plenty I ain't very proud of – but running toms ain't one of them.'

'If you'll just listen to me. I've gone right into it, and I guarantee your part will all be above board. Not a lot of difference from what Paula does in the cab office. You take the bookings, and we charge the punters a basic fourteen quid a night. And we'll have nice girls – clean and that.'

'So there's no "extras" involved then?'

He flinched at her sarcasm, but didn't comment on it. 'That's up to the girls. If they want to charge for anything else, fine. And we trust them to pass on to us whatever percentage we've agreed beforehand. And we'll know they're not cheating on us, because every now and again we'll slip in a ringer to see if they're doing it by the book. And because it'll be run properly, by you – if you fancy it, of course – they'll never know if it's a plant working for us, or a genuine customer they're dealing with.'

'How much will they bring in for you then, each of the escorts, after these percentages have been worked out?'

'Three, three and half a week.'

'*Three hundred and fifty quid?* Bloody hell, Brendan.'

'Exactly. A lot of money. And that's why I need someone I can trust to run the books. You've got a brain, and you're classy, and that's why I'm asking you to do it.'

'What, needs someone classy to run toms, does it?'

'There's no need for that sort of talk, Sandy. Like I said, they don't have to do anything they don't want to.'

'So they'd be happy to work the whole night for a

bit of dinner and a few gin and tonics, would they?'

His handsome face creased into a broad grin. 'You've got me there, girl. I said you had brains. But come on, you've gotta at least give it a try. And I know that if you're sorted out, Barry'd feel a lot better.'

She couldn't argue with that. 'Say I didn't like it?'

He shrugged. 'Fine. No bad feelings, you just walk away.' He took a moment to stub out his cigarette. 'And I'm sure we could come up with some sort of arrangement so's you could stay on in the accommodation. Till you found somewhere else to live, of course.'

Chapter 8

While Brendan tried to convince Sandy that she had a great future working for him, Carol was standing in the front room of what she had stupidly believed was her home, staring down at the two pathetic suitcases full of clothes and make-up – the sum total of her life.

At least the bastard had coughed up the cash for an abortion. The thought brought a thin smile to her lips; not only was the money an unexpected bonus, but she'd actually conned big man O'Donnell into thinking she was pregnant. She'd well and truly treated him like a mug. And that was more than a bonus – that was a real pleasure.

But Carol had little else to smile about. She picked up the cases with a sigh, carried them outside and set them down by the doorstep before locking the door as the note on the coffee table had instructed her. She was about to post the key back through the letter box, but decided against it and slipped it into her pocket. She'd drop it down the first drain hole she came to. Let him sort that one out. Then she snatched up the bags again and tottered unsteadily down the path, balancing on her high, platform shoes, with her silver-fox coat flapping around her legs in the stiff wind that threatened yet more rain. She glared straight ahead, just daring her neighbours to even twitch at their curtains.

She paused at the gate. What now? What exactly was she supposed to do?

As a last resort there was always the tiny flat over the bookie's in King's Cross, the one she used to share with two of the girls from the Cactus Parlour. But they were a thieving pair of bitches, and Carol wouldn't be able to close her eyes once they got back from the club, in case they turned her over.

Or there was always that pillock, Peter MacRiordan . . .

He couldn't keep his eyeballs in their sockets whenever she was around, and she knew there was no love lost between him and Brendan. And if what everyone said was true, Pete Mac wasn't averse to setting up little love nests to keep his bits of stray well out of sight of his Patricia. In fact, she guessed that he'd take great pleasure in thinking he was having one over on his condescending bully of a brother-in-law.

He was so stupid she could probably even get him to tell her all sorts of things. She'd learned from a very young age that having information about people was never a bad thing, and knowing something that might somehow cause Brendan aggravation was very appealing. Because, whatever else happened, she wasn't going to let him get away with treating her like this.

She checked her watch. Quarter past ten. Brendan had given her till dinner time. She had plenty of time to go back inside and call him.

As she unhooked the telephone receiver from its holder on the kitchen wall, Carol Mercer looked around the immaculately clean and tidy room for what she knew would be the very last time. She could have cried with the injustice of it all.

'O'Donnells' Cabs, how can I help you?'

'Paula!' she said, putting a happy smile in her voice. 'Is that you, babes? This is Carol.'

''Lo, Carol. Wanna make a booking, do you?' Paula knew Carol would prefer to roll in wet tar and then walk over broken glass rather than get in one of the O'Donnells' scruffy minicabs, but it amused her to aggravate the toffee-nosed little trollop. 'You'll have to hang on, I'm afraid. Not sure what I've got available at the moment.'

'Er, no, you're all right, thanks, Paula. I'm fine. I just wanted to speak to Peter MacRiordan. Is he there?'

Why would Carol Mercer want to talk to Mr Potato Head? 'Er, Pete Mac, you say?'

Carol noted the pause. 'I've got a message for him. From Brendan.'

Paula nodded to herself – that explained it. 'He's in the back office. I'll let him know.'

'Can't you just give me the number?' Carol's smile was fading fast. 'I'll call him direct.'

'Sorry, sweetheart, Brendan's express orders. I don't give that number to no one.' Paula was more than up to Carol Mercer.

'But this is urgent.'

Oh, yeah? Why was that then? Perhaps this wasn't as straightforward as Carol tart-features Mercer was pretending.

'Tell you what,' said Paula, all helpful suggestions, 'you give me *your* number and I'll get him to call you back.'

When the telephone finally rang – nearly ten minutes later – Carol was just about ready to pick up her bags and go round to that bollocking cab office and stick Paula's mike right up her fat arse. She could imagine the ugly, soapy mare taking her time, finishing her coffee, writing down bookings, and then – how kind – shifting her lazy, rotten carcass from her chair and walking through to the back office to give Pete Mac the message.

Carol was getting pissed off being treated like muck by everyone who had anything to do with the O'Donnells. But there was something she wanted from Pete Mac so, as far as he was concerned, she was going to be sunshine its fucking self.

'Hello, Peter,' she purred.

'Yeah? Who's this?'

Bloody hell, he was dim. 'Peter. It's me, sweetheart, Carol Mercer.'

That bucked him up. 'Hello, darling. What can I do you for?'

Keep smiling. Keep it going. Stick out your tits to get the mood right. 'I'm sorry, but I had to tell you, Peter. It's been driving me mad.' Pause for effect. 'Peter, I can't help myself. It's just that I'm really attracted to you.'

'Fucking hell, girl.'

Now she definitely had his attention.

'Brendan'd go fucking potty if he knew.'

'I know. That's why I've had to keep it hidden from everyone. You know how he gets.'

No answer. What was wrong with the man? She was offering it up on a bloody plate.

'Peter, can we meet up? Today maybe? I know Brendan's busy, and I can jump in a cab. Right now if you like. He'd never find out.'

Like a dinosaur slowly coming to the realisation that it was standing on a sharp stone, Pete Mac's brain gradually and painfully whirred into action.

Shit. He was already on a promise from the redheaded sisters, and he didn't want to upset them. They were all set to go hoisting for him, which would definitely help with all the expenses he was mounting up. But he couldn't turn this down.

110

'I can't tell you how sad it makes me to have to say this, Carol, but I can't. How about tomorrow?'

Sod it, she'd have to go to a hotel. But she was buggered if she'd pay out for more than one night. Or even one night for that matter.

She bit her tongue to stop herself from telling him to go fuck himself, and did a quick run-through of the places she'd be prepared to stay for a few days. Not too expensive – she didn't want to frighten him off before she'd even started working on him to get her something more permanent. And somewhere she wouldn't be familiar to some cow of a receptionist from the old days – when she'd still been charging by the hour.

Got it.

She breathed down the phone at him: 'I can't say I'm not disappointed, Peter, because I am. Very. It's taken a lot of courage to make this phone call. But I can wait. In fact, I'll be ready and waiting for you tomorrow.' She added, pointedly: 'First thing in the morning, okay? At the Winchester Hotel in Bloomsbury. Do you know it?'

Pete Mac was sniggering like a twelve-year-old. 'Don't worry, Carol, I'll find it.'

'You've made me so happy.' She treated him to a tinkly little giggle. 'You won't keep me waiting, will you, Peter? Promise me you'll be there by ten at the very latest, or I'll think you've changed your mind, won't I? And that'll make me ever so sad.'

'I'll be there, darling, you can bank on it.'

Gotcha! He'd be there before checkout time. She wouldn't have to pay the night's bill. 'I can't wait, sweetheart. See you in the morning.'

As he put down the phone, Pete Mac was grinning like a panting hound. The red-headed sisters, and now Carol Mercer . . .

He'd always known his day would come.

The following morning, Carol Mercer, dressed only in a bath towel, opened the door to find Pete Mac standing outside in the hotel corridor, just as she had expected. What she hadn't expected was the bunch of tired-looking carnations that he was pointing at her like some parody of a Victorian suitor coming to call on his young lady.

She just about managed to stop herself from bursting out laughing.

'Peter,' she cooed. 'How sweet.' She took the flowers, puckered her lips and kissed the air about a foot away from his mouth. 'Come in, please.'

As he swaggered into the room, he took in the chintzy, English-country interior, and Carol took in his expensive dark blue suit, his slightly tatty brown suede shoes, his thinning red hair, jowly face and his heavy, wobbly belly.

'Still raining,' he said.

'Oh, Peter, I'm so glad you're here. I've decided that this isn't a temporary thing, I've walked out on

112

Brendan for good.' Carol threw out her arms to him, and the loosely fastened towel fell to the floor.

Pete Mac's jaw dropped open, and, as he ripped his shirt in the zip of his fly in his hurry to pull down his trousers, Carol Mercer knew that not only did she not have to worry about her hotel bill, but, from the look on his face, getting a more permanent roof over her head wasn't going to be too much of a problem either.

To Carol's further relief, Pete Mac's performance was mercifully brief and unadventurous. He went through the motions and was propped up on the pillows, and halfway through a cigarette, all in ten minutes flat.

Carol snuggled into his chest.

'Peter, you do know the reason I walked out on Brendan, don't you? I couldn't get you out of my mind.' She tried an experimental sniffle – would he crumple when she cried, or run a mile?

He fannied about finding an ashtray on the bedside table, then ground out his cigarette and wrapped his arms around her. 'Poor kid. Why didn't you say something before?'

'I wanted to, but I didn't know what you'd say.' Sniff. 'You being married to Patricia and everything. And Brendan being your brother-in-law.'

'Pat don't mean nothing to me, Carol, I just feel sorry for her, that's all. That's why I've stuck by her and the kid for all these years. How could I leave the poor mare, when she thinks the bloody world of me?

And as for Brendan – not got no time for the bloke. No time whatsoever. Never have, never did.'

'He scares me.' She let a tear drip on to his arm. 'What am I going to do, Peter? I've got no money, but I can't go back home. He'd kill me if he knew what I felt about you. So where can I go?'

Pete Mac considered this puzzle. He had a flat, but he'd got the red-headed sisters holed up in there. And he didn't want them upset. They weren't only up for anything, but they'd soon be bringing him in a good few bob with their hoisting. He'd just have to find somewhere else for her.

'Don't worry, darling, I'll give you some money and you can stay here for a few days, while we get you a place sorted out somewhere.'

'You are so sweet.' She ran a finger through his sparse wiry chest hair. 'And I'm really glad you don't like Brendan. That makes me feel a lot less guilty.'

Pete Mac cupped her breast in his hand and leaned over her, licking at her nipple. 'But I hope it don't make you feel a lot less naughty.'

'Course it doesn't,' giggled Carol, ready to gag at the stench of him. 'And we know who else doesn't like Brendan. And we know he *hates* them.'

'Who's that then?'

'The Kessler family. So why's that then, do you think, Peter?'

*

'What's this all about, O'Donnell?' Having refused to sit down, Daniel Kessler was standing in front of Brendan's desk in the private office at the back of the cab firm. He was flanked by his brother Sammy and his cousin Maurice. They were all dressed in long dark overcoats, which they had no intention of taking off.

This definitely wasn't a social visit.

Daniel sunk his hands deep into his pockets. 'We get this call out of the blue demanding a ridiculous amount of money to be paid over. For what exactly?'

'Aw blimey, did I forget to explain?' Brendan slapped a hand against his forehead. 'My memory.' He leaned forward and flicked through some papers, as if too busy to be having this conversation. 'We've got some merchandise for you. For the shops. Films, magazines. Proper hardcore. Expensive stuff. Good earners.'

'Say we don't want it?'

'You ain't got no choice, pal.' Brendan stacked the papers into a neat pile and weighted them down with a heavy stone ashtray. 'Remember, you're only working in the East End because we tolerate you. Or do you want to start rowing again?' He scratched distractedly at his head. 'Me, I'm more than ready to take you on, Kessler. More than ready.'

For want of something to say – and to save himself from landing Brendan fucking O'Donnell a square

115

one right on the chin – Daniel sucked at his teeth. He just knew it was him who'd had the speed out of that lorry.

Brendan leaned back in his chair. 'Good, we understand one another. Now, I think you need to start thinking fast, because now we're in business, I'm gonna give you one week – seven whole days, mind – and you are gonna have that money for me. Or I am going to be very cross with you, Kessler. And, who knows, I might just find myself having to get someone in who can run the shops properly. The way I want them run.'

Brendan stood up and walked over to the door. He pulled it open and said over his shoulder, 'Turn the light off when you leave, lads.'

With that he walked out, leaving them standing there.

'Fuck you!' Daniel Kessler spat out the words as if they were poison. 'The money that bastard's talking about, even if we stripped every betting shop, and then managed to get enough together to fund another consignment from Spain, we'd never do it in time.'

Maurice sat himself down in Brendan's chair, and clasped his hands behind his head. 'Now I know we're all agreed that we ain't ready for a full-scale battle with the bastards.' He lifted up his legs and plonked his feet down on the desk, the heels of his shoes leaving greasy black polish marks in disrespectful tramlines across its shiny glass surface. 'So, my bank-job idea suddenly seem attractive to you then, does it, fellers?'

Chapter 9

Luke finally reached out for the phone that stood on his black acrylic bedside table. It was the fourth time it had rung – or rather trilled its irritating trill – in the last ten minutes. Whoever it was was certainly persistent.

'Yeah?'

'Luke, it's me, Ellie.'

It sounded urgent.

'Ellie? What's wrong?'

'You! You haven't called to let me know the arrangements for coming over to London, and I am so fed up with waiting. It's driving me demented over here. I'm telling you, if I don't get away from Aunt Mary and this bloody farm, they'll be taking me away in handcuffs.'

Luke hoisted himself up to a sitting position. 'That's not funny, Ellie. Now take a deep breath, and calm down. You're sounding just like a whiny kid wanting another sweetie.'

'I don't mean to, Luke. Honestly. But it's Friday night, ten days before bloody Christmas and there is absolutely nothing to do over here. Nothing. Not a single, solitary party.' There was a slight hesitation.

'Well, except for deadly family things. And I'm twenty-two years old, for Christ's sake. Twenty-two. Not fourteen. And I want a bloody life.'

Luke reached out for his cigarettes and lighter. 'D'you think you might be exaggerating a bit, Ellie? Overreacting?' He frowned as he drew in the first lungful of smoke. 'And making a big mistake. Because I'm telling you, things ain't exactly easy over here at the minute either. Brendan and Mum are at each other's throats, and I'm stuck in the middle of the pair of them.' He put his hand over the mouth-piece. 'Ssshh, Nicky. In a minute.'

'Ignore me then.' Nicky rolled over, tugging the bedcovers away from Luke.

'And if she ever finds out that Brendan got you involved in doing that delivery over to Ireland for him, that would just about put the tin lid on it.'

'I don't need you starting on me as well, Luke.'

'I know, I'm sorry, love.' He smiled to himself, imagining her standing there pouting at the phone.

'It's not as though I don't deserve a bit of fun. I work like a slave with those horses. You should see me. I'm practically running the place. Luke, please, let me come and stay in London with you. Please.'

'I told you –'

'Only for a while. I won't get in the way. I promise. I've really thought about it. I was going to ask Brendan, but I already guessed what Eileen would have to say.' Ellie sighed dramatically. 'You

119

probably don't want to hear this, Luke, but you should hear the things Aunt Mary has to say about Eileen. Honestly, she is such a cow. And while I don't understand the half of it, your mam's still her sister-in-law, when all's said and done.'

'Ellie, like you said, you don't know the half of it.'

'But I know what it's like living over here in Kildare. It's like living with a witch. You should see the schedule she's got mapped out for me over Christmas. If I'm not mucking out, I'm expected to be in the house smiling at the bloody priest and the old bags from the village, while they down tumblers of sweet bloody sherry after Mass. Then I'll be expected to help with the mountains of sodding food she'll insist we all swallow. And that's without the washing-up. Oh, Luke, *please*. I'm truly going to lose my mind if you don't let me come over and live in London.'

Luke ground out his cigarette. 'Finished?'

'I suppose so, but you have to –'

'Ellie, I'll see what I can do.'

'Promise?'

'I promise. I'll try and sort something out, and I'll call you back tomorrow or Sunday. Okay?'

'Oh, Luke –'

'Bye, Ellie. Aw, and you might start watching that tongue of yours. I don't like to hear women swearing.'

Luke put the phone down and ran his hand over

Nicky's strong, muscular back, just the touch making him smile with pleasure and longing. 'If you want to go to that club, we'd better think about getting up.'

Nicky turned over and smiled back up at him. 'I'd much rather stay here in bed with you,' he said, pulling Luke down on top of him.

He touched his lips gently against Luke's. 'You know, I like it, the way you're nice to your little sister. You really care about her, don't you?'

'Nearly as much as I care about you.' Luke looked down into Nicky's eyes and wondered at how his life could have changed so much in just six months. How being with Nicky had made him happier than he could ever have imagined.

Carol Mercer paid the cab driver. She'd have liked to have told him to wait for her, but she couldn't afford to waste any more money. This was the third club she'd been to in search of Sammy Kessler, and the few pounds she'd allowed herself for the evening were running out fast. She'd now got plenty of information about him and the other Kesslers from Pete Mac, and even more about the O'Donnells. And it was about time she started making use of it. She could hardly credit some of the things Pete Mac had told her. It was bordering on the ridiculous – he was such a big mouth, and worse, he was dumb with it. A very dangerous combination that had made her realise pretty quickly that she'd have to be careful about every single word she said to him.

Unfortunately, there was one thing the lard ball hadn't been able to blab about – well, not with any certainty, anyhow – and that was where Sammy Kessler spent his Friday nights. So Carol had had no choice, she'd had to jump in and out of cabs, visiting all the places Pete Mac had so much as mentioned.

She'd had to go by cab as she could hardly walk through the streets or jump on a bus – not the way she'd got herself done up. But then again, if she hadn't made the effort to glam herself up, she needn't have even bothered looking for him in the first place. If there was one thing she'd learned from her time with Brendan O'Donnell – *that bastard* – it was that faces like him and Sammy Kessler had girls throwing themselves at them from every direction. So she had to be sure of standing out from the crowd to even hope of getting his attention.

She looked up at the sign above the door – here goes, another punt – unbuttoned her coat – sod the cold – and tottered up to the biggest of the three bouncers.

Please, let this be the place.

'Hiya,' she said, running a lavender-painted nail lightly across his chest. 'I'm meeting Sammy Kessler. He here yet?'

'Yeah,' the man said to her breasts. 'I'll take you through, darling.'

As they went inside, Carol saw him standing alone at the bar. She knew it was Sammy Kessler from the grainy photographs she'd seen in the evening papers, but he still wasn't really what she'd expected. Jewish blokes were meant to be all dark and handsome. Well, he was handsome, in a rough sort of way, and much more of a bloke than a chap – the type she liked, actually – but he had long curly hair, touching the collar of his jacket, and it was much fairer than she'd imagined it would be. He'd probably been a right little snowball as a kid. In fact, if he'd been wearing a long white frock instead of a black three-piece suit, he'd have looked exactly like the pictures of the angels they'd had on the walls of the hostel where she'd stayed when her mum had first chucked her out.

'The young lady you're expecting,' said the bouncer, handing her over like a package before heading straight back to his door duties. He was experienced enough to know that you only stood with the Kesslers if you'd been invited.

'Hope you didn't mind my little fib,' said Carol, swinging her shoulders in a parody of a shy schoolgirl. 'But I've heard so much about you, and I so wanted to meet you.'

'Aw yeah?' Sammy looked about him as if seeking out someone – anyone – more interesting.

This was going to be tougher than she'd thought. She moved closer. Still no bloody eye contact. What did she have to do, get her tits out or something?

'You're famous, you are.'

'Right.'

'I'm Carol Mercer. I used to be Brendan O'Donnell's girlfriend.'

There. Now the bugger was interested.

'But I walked out on him. Got bored.'

Why wasn't he offering her a drink?

'But I still keep in touch with Pete Mac.' Much too close in touch, unfortunately, the vile, greasy pig. 'He's told me a lot about you. Like you going out with Brendan's little sister, Catherine. And how terrible it was when she got shot dead by mistake, because of her dad and all that. That was so sad. Really horrible.'

A different look had come over him. Distaste? No, something stronger than that. It was real, deep-down hatred. She'd have to be careful what else she said.

Sammy put his glass down on the bar. 'Pete Mac? Why would I wanna hear anything that gobshite's been saying?'

'I suppose he is a bit thick.'

'Tell me something I don't know.'

She looked up into his eyes. 'At least he's only married to an O'Donnell. And I don't think he reckons them much, not when it comes down to it.'

'Look, darling, if you don't mind, I've got to –'

She took a gamble and stepped sideways, blocking his way as he attempted to leave. 'Don't be like that, Sammy. I only want to keep you company. And maybe there's stuff I could, you know, tell you about. Things about Brendan.'

He looked her up and down. She had some bottle, give her that. But she wasn't his type, not by a long chalk – too young and too cheap-looking for his taste. Although it might be entertaining to string her along for a while, if only to wind up O'Donnell. And who knows, maybe she might have picked up some interesting stuff. She seemed bright enough for a bird.

'I'll take you out for a drink. Next week.'

'Not tonight?'

'No. I'm busy tonight. Business.'

'Even for little me?'

'It's family business,' Sammy said, putting an end to it. He checked his watch, and started towards the door. 'See you here. Eight o'clock. Tuesday.'

Sod it. Now she'd have to spend the whole weekend in that miserable rotten hole that Pete Mac had got her over the tobacconist's shop in Bow. What was it with this lot and their families? They were hard as nails with everyone else, violent thugs who didn't give a shit, but have their mums snap their fingers, or their brothers phone them, and they jumped to and did as they were told like meek little bloody lambs. She was glad she didn't have a family to tell her what to do.

Really glad.

All she wanted was her little house back.

God, she missed it: all nice and clean and

everything in order. Mind you, if she played up the Brendan thing with Sammy, got him in a state where he was trying to outdo him, maybe she'd get something even better.

Chapter 10

It was just over an hour since Sammy Kessler had left Carol standing in the bar. Despite the biting frostiness of the night air, sweat was glistening on his top lip.

He and Daniel were standing behind their cousin Maurice outside the front door of a solidly middle-class, detached house in Surrey. A warm yellow glow was coming from the downstairs windows.

Maurice rang the bell.

Sammy swallowed hard, his mouth as dry as if it had been wiped out with a dishcloth. He pulled up his scarf, leaving only his eyes on show.

Daniel did likewise, covering most of his face with navy cashmere, and then flexed his fingers, ready to use the cosh in his pocket.

The door was opened by a man in his early forties. He was dressed casually – corduroy trousers, Aran sweater and Viyella shirt, yet his manner was as formal as if he'd been standing there in white tie and tails.

'Maurice,' he said, the slight quaver in his otherwise authoritatively clipped intonation betraying his apprehension. 'Tried to call you.'

'Did you, Charles?' replied Maurice, leaning up against the jamb.

Sammy and Daniel exchanged puzzled looks. These two *knew* each other?

'Sorry, old chap.' Charles let out a long, slow, sighing breath, as if deeply disappointed. 'Been a bit of a hitch, I'm afraid.'

'A hitch, eh, feller?' said Maurice, shoving the man to one side. 'I think we'd better come in and discuss it then, don't you?'

Maurice now had Charles pressed up against the sink in the kitchen at the back of the house.

'What d'you mean, feller?' Maurice's face was almost touching his. 'We can't get in there till tomorrow fucking morning?'

Charles gulped, lifting his chin to avoid Maurice's breath. 'Please, keep your voice down. Daphne's through in the dining room.'

Maurice leaned even closer to him, his chest pressing against him. 'Maybe it's time we joined her.'

Charles opened the dining-room door as if trying not to disturb a sleeping child. 'Daphne. A surprise. We have guests.'

A slightly faded woman, sitting at a bulbous-legged oak table, looked up. She was writing in a leather-bound book with a fountain pen. Standing behind her, in the bay window, was a long-haired, teenaged girl, wearing a smocked peasant blouse and flared, hipster jeans; she was decorating a luxuriant, ceiling-high Christmas tree.

Daphne smiled sportingly. 'How lovely. Can I make anyone a drink?'

Maurice plonked himself down on the table, right next to where she was sitting, making her start. He picked up the book and flicked through it before letting it fall from his fingers. 'What's this then?'

'A note I keep. Of people who've been for dinner.' Daphne glanced over at the girl, who was staring at the three strange men in their wide-lapelled, flared-trousered suits, a blue-and-silver glass bauble dangling from her hand on a gold thread. They were men of a type that Daphne and her daughter rarely came across, and especially not in their own home. 'And what they ate when they came,' she finished, distractedly.

'That's right,' said Charles. 'And that's why you're checking it now, isn't it, Daphne? Because we've got people coming tonight. In about an hour. Pre-Christmas drinks, then supper.'

'Don't give me that, feller.' Maurice snorted derisively. 'If you were having people round tonight, why isn't she all dolled up?' He grasped Daphne's chin, pinching her flesh, and turning her head towards her husband. 'Look at the state of her.'

'Charles? What's happening?'

'Mum!'

'It's all right, Fiona,' Charles said. 'Everything will be fine.'

'And it's already nearly nine o'clock. Everyone knows your sort are tucked up in bed with a cup of cocoa by ten. So don't fanny around with me, mate. Now, are you coming to the bank with me or what?'

'I promise you. This new time lock won't let me open the vault until six o'clock tomorrow morning.'

'Charles?' Daphne was now very close to tears. 'What's going on?'

Maurice levered himself off the table. He pointed to the girl. 'You, sit down here by your mother. And keep schtum.'

'Do as he says, Fiona,' said Charles. 'Sit down and be quiet.'

'Good advice, feller. I'd hate to have to hurt a pretty young girl like her.'

Daphne swiped her eyes with the back of her hand. 'Oh, my God, Charles, I've realised who they are. You must do as they ask. They're those people they were talking about on the news. The IRA kidnapping gang.'

Maurice, who had just walked out into the hall, burst out laughing. 'We're not the Irish, love,' he called over his shoulder, 'we're the frigging Jews.'

Sammy went out after him. 'What're you up to, Maury?'

'Blimey, feller, get a grip. I'm just going out to the car. I brought some ropes and gags along just in case.

130

Good job too if he's telling the truth and we've really got to keep them three quiet all night.'

'You never said there'd be a kid involved.'

'You never asked.'

'We never had a tree when I lived up in Manchester. Except over the park, like. But they didn't have balls.' Maurice laughed, amused at his own wit, as he stroked a finger down the girl's cheek.

'Leave her alone,' hissed Charles, straining against the rope that was binding his wrists behind his back.

'I'm all right, Dad.' Fiona shivered, despite the warmth of the room.

'Will you leave off?' snapped Sammy. He was looking down at the floor, and could have been speaking to any of them. He knew he shouldn't have got involved in this. It was Daniel who wanted the money for the property deal with the Baxters, not him. Now here he was holding three hostages, all trussed up like bloody oven-ready chickens ready for roasting, in a posh house somewhere in the middle of fucking Surrey. And if that wasn't enough, the woman looked as if she was about to wet her pants, the kid might well start screaming her head off at any minute, and the sodding bank manager looked the type to suddenly come over all like Batman and try to protect his family and his firm's dough. And they could all identify Maurice, because for some stupid fucking reason he wasn't even wearing a bloody mask. How had he been so totally brainless as to go along with Maurice and his foolproof fucking plan? Why hadn't he just taken the night off, and gone out with that bird of O'Donnell's? It couldn't have been much worse than this.

Maurice patted the girl's face, hard enough to sting. 'Now you behave, Fiona.' He said her name as if recounting a nasty smell. 'And nothing's going to happen to you. But you start getting difficult, like, and I can't guarantee you won't get hurt. All right?'

Daphne dropped her chin. 'I need to use the lavatory.'

Maurice nodded. 'Sure, I'll come with you. But you do just want a piss, don't you? I don't think I fancy watching you doing the other thing, love.'

Charles launched himself to his feet. 'Please, don't do this. How would you feel if it was your wife? Your child.'

Maurice turned down his mouth and shook his head. 'Haven't got a wife actually, feller.' He was grinning. 'But I reckon I've got plenty of kids knocking about the place.'

Sammy was beginning to panic. This was supposed to be straightforward, easy, now look at it. This was the sort of situation that could so easily get out of hand, especially with someone like his cousin around. 'Maurice, let her go to the lav, mate. I'll stand outside the door – make sure she don't try and run away or get out of the window or nothing.'

'I'll have to think about that one.'

'Maurice, please,' begged Charles. 'It's not her fault they installed that new timing device. I tried my best to let you know, but I couldn't get hold of you.'

Daphne turned to her husband. 'You *knew* about this, Charles?'

'Blimey, she's got a sour-looking gob on her, ain't she, eh, feller? No wonder you come up with this plan. Get you enough money to get away from her bloody moaning, eh? Got yourself a bird tucked away somewhere, have you? Some little sort who works at the bank?'

'This was meant to be just between the two of us. You gave me your word.'

'What, like I'm your best pal or something? Your mucker from down the golf club? Sorry, feller, you've got the wrong idea. This is the real world. But tell you what, I'll be fair and make you a deal. You stand up, I'll untie your hands, and you take your trousers off. Then I'll let her go and have a piss.'

Charles looked away. 'No.'

Maurice shoved him backwards knocking him to the floor. 'Don't be silly, Charlie boy.'

Sammy stepped forward to intervene, but Daniel stopped him, grabbing him angrily by the arm. Daniel wasn't happy about the way things were going either, but Sammy had to keep control of himself. Showing disunity looked weak. And that could be as dangerous as Maurice going off on one.

He watched, grim-faced, as Maurice loosened the knots and waited for Charles to slip his hands out of the loops of rope.

'Sensible feller,' he said, when Charles, his head hanging low, eventually freed his hands. 'Now, off with your kecks.'

As Charles stepped out of his trousers, Maurice shook his head and tutted loudly. He was pointing at Charles, but speaking to his wife and daughter. 'Humiliating that, don't you reckon? See, you'd have to rip my head off before I'd do something like that. And in front of your wife and kid . . .'

'I'll get you for this, Kessler.'

Maurice shook his head and slowly turned to face him. 'Don't be daft, Charlie. You're in no position to get anyone. Because if you so much as try it, I'll have to tell your bosses all about that raid we did back in '71.' Maurice grinned at his cousins. 'Cleared the bank right out an hour before the staff got to work. Single-handed, I was. Mind you, according to the story this feller gave to the law and his bosses, there were six of us did it. And every one of us was armed with a sawn-off shotgun. Like a bloody gangster movie.'

Now Maurice was staring at Daphne and Fiona, as he jerked his thumb over his shoulder at Charles. 'Bank gave you a reward for that, didn't they, Charlie? You lying fucking hypocrite. For you being so brave, like. Your old woman and kid here, they were away on holiday at the time, if you remember. It was only because they were gonna be here tonight that you said I'd need two people to help me. To make it look authentic, like. By holding the poor cows hostage. Then you could go boohooing to your bosses. Say how you had no choice in the matter – *they were holding my family, threatening to rape me wife and daughter, do all sorts of nasty things to them if I didn't do as I was told.* That's why I never bothered with a mask.' He giggled happily. 'I mean, he's hardly gonna risk grassing on us, now is he? He'd be out of the bank and into the nick quicker than a street-corner tart dropping her drawers. It's a shame really – it's his plan, but we get to keep all the dough.'

Charles lunged at Maurice, but Maurice batted him away as if he were nothing more than a bothersome fly at a Sunday-afternoon picnic.

'Now you really are being daft, feller.'

As Maurice began punching and kicking her father, Fiona vomited over the table, and Daphne began to cry softly into her chest.

Chapter 11

Pete Mac shut the door of the flat behind him and took a deep lungful of chilly, early-morning air. Like a sumo wrestler about to face his opponent, Pete Mac was preparing himself.

He was going home to see Patricia.

He'd been away for three nights now, staying at the flat with the red-haired sisters and nipping round for a quick visit to Carol Mercer in between, but, seeing as it was the day before Christmas Eve, Pat would be bound to expect him to at least put his head round the door. So he was going to do the right thing and show his face for a half-hour or so before going to the cab office to find out what was happening with Brendan.

Or should he say to get Brendan's orders for the day . . .

He had no choice on either point. If he didn't go home there'd be murders, and the last thing he wanted was another rucking from Pat. And if he didn't drop into work, Brendan would start leading off as well. And he was already feeling more than a bit pissed off.

It was the Liverpool girls. They were getting to him.

He liked the redheads all right, they were a right laugh, game for anything – he had no complaints there – but he was beginning to suspect that maybe they hadn't been entirely honest about their hoisting skills. Either that or they were having him over. They'd been in the flat for over three weeks now and there hadn't been a sniff of any of the gear they reckoned they were going to lift for him, which meant that they were getting to be an expensive hobby. Especially now he had Carol Mercer on the firm as well, even though the rooms he'd got her over in Bow were as cheap as piss. Perhaps he should give the pair of them the bum's rush, and concentrate on young Carol for a while. That'd be funny, that would, turning up at clubs and that with her. It'd get right up Brendan's nose. If he had the bottle to do anything that mad, and didn't mind having his head ripped off.

Maybe he'd just keep all three of them going for a while. Why shouldn't he treat himself? Not many fellers could say that they had three bits on the side at once. But then he wasn't any ordinary feller, was he? He was Pete Mac.

Even knowing that he would probably soon be facing one of Pat's famous silent treatments, and Caty's sneering dismissal of anything he had to say, he didn't actually mind that much any more. Because as he drove towards his house in Jubilee Street, Pete Mac was feeling rather content with the way the world was treating him.

He was a one-off, and he knew it.

*

Luke was sitting drinking coffee in the corner of the office that Sandy had set up in one of the bedrooms of her new home on Old Ford Road. He watched her as she copied notes from a rough pad into a formal ledger. He thought she looked happy. And he was right – she was, or rather as happy as she could be, knowing that Barry was banged up on remand in Brixton. But moving into the house had certainly done a lot to cheer her up.

From the moment Brendan had shown her the place – could it really be only a couple of weeks ago? – Sandy had loved it. She could still hardly dare believe that the high-ceilinged, three-storey Victorian house complete with a basement 'airy' on the Old Ford Road was hers. And that wasn't all. At the front it faced on to Victoria Park, with its big graceful trees covered in frost in the early mornings and dripping with rain in the afternoons. Then there was the canal with its swans and ducks and even the occasional barge, right there at the back. She could actually walk down to the water from the kitchen door.

It was all too beautiful for words.

And after the nightmare years of looking after Barry – cleaning up after he'd vomited or soiled himself yet again, and having to witness the last few things she owned disappearing as his cravings drove him to sell even their clothes – Sandy couldn't believe her luck. Now it was more like living in some wonderful dream.

She even liked the work. Admittedly, she hadn't been sure about it at first. Running an escort agency had seemed so sleazy, even after the horrors she'd been through with Barry, but she'd been surprised at how quickly she'd come to accept it. And it wasn't as if she had much contact with the girls. She interviewed them, and phoned them with appointments, and made the arrangements for Anthony to collect their money – having a constant string of girls coming to the house would have looked suspicious even in an area where, it went without saying, people didn't ask questions. But if she had been forced to have more direct, personal exchanges with the escorts, it would have been a small price to pay for the stability she was now enjoying and the comfort in which she was living. It was an odd feeling, but it seemed as if the past few years had happened to someone else, a sadder, more wary, probably more frightened person. A person she would never want to be. Not again.

She owed Brendan a lot.

The telephone rang. Sandy cleared her throat, and, in a fair imitation of a Home Counties accent, made an appointment for a Mr Lawrence to have a companion for tomorrow evening – no doubt a special Christmas Eve treat for himself. She flicked over her page of notes, put down her pen, and leaned back in her chair.

'All right, Luke, lovely as it is to see you here –

again – you do know how busy I'm going to be today, don't you?'

'You're getting that phone voice down to a fine art, San.' He swirled the dregs of coffee round in his cup, watching the thick sediment form into a muddy spiral. 'You know what I'm doing; I'm keeping an eye on you. I don't like you being involved with Brendan like this. And it's not as if there's any need. You can come and work for me. Start tomorrow. Today if you like.'

'What is it with you O'Donnells? Can't you get staff or something? Am I the only worker left in sodding London?' She paused. 'You're all beginning to make me feel like a bloody charity case.'

'Don't be daft, Sandy. We've been friends long enough for you to know that's not true. And for you to know I don't like what Brendan does. He tries to make out that I'm as bad as him, but we all know that's not true. I've never liked the life him and Dad thought was normal, and I've always done my best to steer away from it as much as I can. I'd hate to see you getting dragged down to his level.'

'What, you reckon I'm not capable of looking after myself, do you? That I can't make my own decisions? Thanks very much.'

'Don't be like that.' He was still studying his cup.

'If you must know, Luke, Brendan makes me laugh. Makes me feel like a woman again. Like I'm alive. And it's a nice thing, having my life back.' She picked up her pen and flipped open her book as if to start work again. 'It ain't easy living with a junkie, you know.'

He slowly raised his head and looked at her. 'Does Barry know about you seeing Brendan? Cos remand in that place can do a bloke's head in. Especially when he knows he's up for a right handful.'

She gave up the pretence of working, stood up and went over to the window. 'Do you want the truth, Luke? I really don't know. Because he won't see me. Won't see anyone. Almost Christmas, and he won't even let me visit him.'

'Mum was like that.'

'Yeah, so I heard. I suppose that's where the poor, daft sod got the idea from. But he even sends me letters back. Don't even open them.'

'I'm sorry.'

'I know. Now go on, piss off home and see Nicky, I've got work to do before Brendan gets here.'

He stood up with a sigh. 'So, what you doing for Christmas?'

She turned to face him. 'If the wish on my lucky star comes true, I'll be slobbing about in bed in my nightie: drinking tea, eating toast and Marmite, and laughing my head off at Morecambe and Wise. Why? Wanna join me?'

Brendan winced as he spotted Milo leaning against the wall in his usual place in the snooker club. Not that it was very difficult to spot him; he was, after all, the only one there with big, blond Afro hair and wearing a plum-coloured, crushed-velvet suit draped over his scrawny frame. But while he wasn't exactly hard to miss, looking as he did like a gift-wrapped, yellow lollipop, it wasn't his fashion advice that Brendan was after. He'd turned out all right, a good little worker, even if he did look a ponce.

'Oi, Flanagan,' Brendan called to him, jerking his thumb towards the bar.

'All right, Mr O?' Milo stood with his back to the bar, his elbows propped on the counter.

'You've done well shifting all that merchandise, Flanagan. You're a good lad. Discreet and fast.'

'I do me best.'

'Can't ask more than that of someone,' said Brendan, brushing away Milo's mimed offer of a drink. 'And I've decided this could be a useful little sideline, so we'll be getting another consignment for you to handle in the new year. In the meantime, here's a little Christmas bonus for you.' He winked as he handed over a wad of notes. 'I believe in showing appreciation where's it's due.'

Milo watched Brendan as he bowled out of the club, whistling a slightly off-key rendition of the Slade Christmas song that seemed to be playing everywhere you went. Milo knew he was watching a man who understood that all eyes were trained on him

– and who didn't give a flying fuck. This was his world. He owned it.

'What's up with him?' asked a short, pale-faced, middle-aged man standing behind the bar, his roll-up bobbing up and down from his bottom lip as he spoke. 'He usually comes in, growls, checks if Anthony's collected the week's takings, and then finishes off by threatening one or two of us with a bit of light GBH.'

'Must have had a bash over the head,' suggested a squinty-eyed youth chalking the tip of a very expensive custom-made cue.

'No, it's a lot worse than that,' said Milo. 'From the whispers I've heard, it seems like the hard man's gone and fallen in love.'

Brendan was still whistling the Christmas song when Luke, breathing heavily, caught up with him just as he was putting his key in the street door of the O'Donnell family home on the Mile End Road.

'Hang on, Brendan,' puffed Luke. 'Before you go indoors, I need to ask you something.'

'You wanna get yourself fit, mate. Look at you, wheezing like some old pensioner.'

Luke lifted his chin. 'I had to park right up there, and then I saw you at the street door, and I wanted to catch you to have a talk.'

'Well, come inside then, it's bloody perishing out here.'

He shook his head. 'No, I don't want Mum to hear what I've got to say. And before you say anything, nothing's wrong. Well, not really.'

'Come on, Luke, spit it out, or I'm going indoors and leaving you out here.'

'It's Ellie. You know she's camping out at mine. I was wondering if Mum would wear it, d'you think, if I asked if she could come over and have a bit of dinner with us all? I'd hate to think of her alone on Christmas Day.'

Luke considered for a moment, deciding whether he should go for broke and say what he really wanted to. What did he have to lose except for an increasingly annoying lodger? A lodger who – much as he loved the little mare – thought it was fine to drape her dripping underwear all over his bathroom, to leave her dirty plates all over the kitchen, and not to give him and Nicky a moment alone together.

And those moments with Nicky were becoming more important all the time; he knew he was going to really miss him when he went back to see his mum for Christmas – even though it was just for the one day.

He found himself smiling; he was bang in love with the bloke.

Here goes.

'And ask if she could stay for a night or two. Maybe three. What d'you reckon?'

'Cramping your style, is it, having our little sister

around?' Brendan grinned and punched Luke on the arm.

'No.'

'All right, I'm only mucking about. And who knows, Mum might even *ask* her to stay here, once I tell her my news.'

'What news?'

'Come in and listen for yourself.'

'Mum, I want you to hear me out before you go mad. I thought you should know that Ellie's over from Kildare. She's been staying at Luke's for the past couple of days, and I want you to let her come here for Christmas dinner. Maybe stay a night or two.'

Eileen, who was sitting in her now usual place in the easy chair by the old, disused kitchener, looked up from the knitting that had become almost obsessive – a way of keeping the world away because she was 'busy'. Her expression was calm, but her voice was anything but. 'You want me to have your father's bastard in my home?

Brendan flashed his eyebrows at his brother. 'Least she's speaking to me, eh, Luke?' Then he turned back to Eileen. 'Mum, Ellie's an O'Donnell. She dropped the Palmer from her name a long time ago. And Aunt Mary's raised her right. She's an O'Donnell through and through. A decent Catholic girl.'

'Decent?'

'Look, Mum, this is important to me. I am loyal to no one but my family, you know that. And that's why I've brought this up now. I know you're gonna be chuffed about this.' He winked at Luke, then turned back to his mother. 'I'm thinking about settling down, getting married and having chavvies and that. Some time in the new year. I'm gonna bring her round for Christmas dinner, and I want you, and Patricia and Ellie – my sisters – to meet her and welcome her.'

Eileen stood up. 'You do as you think fit. You always do. So why change now? Bring whoever you like.'

Luke waited for his mother to climb the basement stairs and leave them alone in the kitchen. 'Married? You? Does Sandy know about this?'

'Course not.' He went over to the wall cabinet and took out a bottle of Jameson's and two glasses. 'I ain't asked her yet.'

'You're gonna ask *Sandy* to marry you?'

'Bloody hell, give the man a fucking coconut. You didn't think I meant Carol, did you?'

'What, got Sandy pregnant, have you?'

Brendan ignored the sarcasm, and poured them both a drink. 'I'm going round there soon as I get washed and changed. She's expecting me.'

'But I bet she ain't expecting this,' Luke muttered.

'What's that?'

'Nothing, Brendan. Nothing at all.'

*

Brendan was in the sitting room of Sandy's new house, his big, muscular body almost spilling over the sage-green Draylon armchair.

Sandy sat facing him, on the very edge of her seat. She was looking at him as if he were speaking in some obscure language she'd never heard before.

'You've done this out lovely, San. You've hardly spent any money, but I can't believe how good it looks. I reckon Luke was right about this place, it's gonna be a good little investment. They won't knock these gaffs down, not like them on Grove Road. He's a clever little bleeder, give him that. Knows his property all right. Maybe I'll have to listen to him more often, eh?'

He paused to light two cigarettes, handing one of them to Sandy. 'He's even started talking about doing up old warehouses down the docks. Although fuck knows who'd wanna live in one of them. But they might be worth having a butcher's – see what the SP is, eh?'

'Brendan, will you stop going on about property? You've just dropped a right bloody bombshell in my lap, and now you're talking about flaming warehouses.'

He reached out and took her hand in a tender gesture that surprised them both. 'How many times have you said yourself that you've just been looking after Barry, like he was your brother or something? I can give you more than that, San, I can give you a good life. A really good life.'

'You're serious, aren't you?'

'Never been more so.'

'But your family, what would they think?'

'That I'm a lucky bastard, and you must be mad. I know I've had birds that'd make grown men weep, but I want something more than that now. And, let's face it, neither of us is getting any younger.'

'Jesus, Brendan, you certainly know how to turn a girl's head, don't you?'

'Well?'

'I dunno. I suppose I'll have to think about it.'

'Course you will. And by the way, Pat's doing Christmas dinner round mine and Mum's, and you're invited. Now get your coat, we're going up West to celebrate.'

The possibility that he and Sandy might not have anything to celebrate, because she might turn him down, hadn't occurred to Brendan, and he'd already booked a table in a restaurant in Greek Street complete with a bottle of chilled Dom Perignon.

Just half a mile away from where Brendan and Sandy were now sipping the champagne, Sammy Kessler was in bed with Carol Mercer, Brendan's very recent ex.

The hotel he had taken her to wouldn't have been Carol's first choice, but it was a damned sight better than that grotty dump Pete Mac had come up with. And sex with Sammy – boring as it might be – was a far more pleasant experience than it was with Pete. Sex didn't mean much to her anyway, other than as a means to an end. But if she didn't want to be stuck by herself above the tobacconist's, with only a visit from Pete Mac to look forward to over Christmas, she'd have to do something fast.

'What're you doing over the holidays, Sam?' As she spoke she ran her fingertips up and down the inside of his thigh. 'Or don't you take no notice? You being Jewish and that.'

'You are kidding, right?' Sammy chuckled, making his eyes crinkle. 'You'd think Mum'd had been taught by bloody nuns and blessed at birth by the Pope himself to see the way she goes to town. We have the lot. Paper hats, a tree, presents, decorations. It's a right schemozzle. And the food, she even does roast pork and crackling to go with the turkey. Lays the lot on for the family, she does. Same every year. And if all of us weren't there, she'd kill us.'

That sounded promising. 'What, *all* of us?' She moved her hand closer to his groin. 'Is that an invite?'

'Don't be silly, Carol,' he said, throwing back the covers. 'Now get yourself up and out of here.

Danny's coming to pick me up in half an hour and I wanna have a bath.'

Close to tears – of fury and frustration, mingled with a good dollop of desperation – Carol got up and stood naked beside the bed. She'd worked so hard to get herself a decent place to live, and now everything was slipping away from her again. Why did blokes treat her like this? It was so unfair. Other women got what they wanted, and it wasn't as if she was asking for much. A bit of love, being part of a proper family, knowing that she belonged somewhere, and that someone cared about her – really cared.

She'd have to sort something out soon or she'd wind up back in some rathole like that stinking hostel she'd stayed in, exhausted from walking the streets all day, but terrified to fall asleep because of what the other girls might do to her if she let her guard slip for a single moment.

She pasted on a smile, leaned on the bed and thrust her breasts towards him. 'So where's my present?' she asked, her voice husky and low, convinced he wouldn't be able to resist her.

'What? Aw yeah.' Sammy lifted his jacket off the dressing-table stool and took out his wallet without looking at her. He counted out eight five-pound notes and threw them on the crumpled bedclothes. 'You get yourself something nice. Now hurry up, will you, or Danny's gonna be here.'

'But when am I gonna see you?'

'I thought I told you to hurry up,' he said, striding over to the bathroom without so much as a backward glance.

He might just as well have slapped her face.

Chapter 12

Patricia, with Ellie's and Caty's goggle-eyed help, carried on serving the meal as if Brendan arriving with Sandy, and then announcing to them and to the rest of the family – Eileen, Luke and Pete Mac – that Sandy – whose hand he was clutching, like a school-boy with a crush – had agreed to marry him in the summer, was perfectly normal behaviour. And the fact that the O'Donnells' talk would more usually have been about the various family 'businesses' – even if it was Christmas Day and they were in the formal upstairs dining room – rather than about wedding dates and bridesmaids, and whether top hats and tails would be worn, was not so much as mentioned.

Even Pete Mac didn't make any smart-mouthed comments, although one about whether Barry was going to be invited to the do was bubbling along nicely on the tip of his tongue. But Brendan appeared not to notice the atmosphere and carried on speaking nineteen to the dozen, directing most of his comments to Eileen.

'You know, Mum, I'm so glad you're home, it wouldn't have been the same if you weren't gonna be there. And I've decided we'll have the full works, a church and that, cos I know you'd like me to do it right. It won't be Catholic though, cos Sandy's C of E, ain't you, San? But it'll still be religious and that.'

Eileen's only response was to pick at the mound of food on her plate, more food than she'd seen in years, and beautifully cooked by her daughter. But how could she eat when everything around her had gone mad? There was this girl, *her husband's bastard*, actually living under her roof as if it was normal, moral, nothing wrong with it. And her son was talking about marrying Sandy, the woman who had lived with Barry Ellis for fifteen years without being married – a man who had worked for Brendan doing God alone knew what for even more years. And all this was being done and discussed in front of Caty, her beautiful, innocent little granddaughter.

The world was no longer a place that Eileen either understood or liked very much. In fact, life in prison had made more sense than all this. At least there had been rules that had to be followed.

'Tell you what, Luke, I am gonna put on such a do. We'll find somewhere right swanky, and we'll invite everyone. Everyone. They'll never have seen anything like it.'

Pete Mac considered his question about Barry's possible invite, but thought better of it, and just contented himself with stuffing as much food and lager as he could manage into his face.

'Tell you what, San, I've been to some dos in my time, but I'm gonna surprise even meself. I can't wait to see the look on the Kesslers' faces, when they see how much I've spent.'

Pete Mac had to react to that one. 'The Kesslers?'

'Yeah, course. How could I resist? Mum gets on well with old Sophie, don't you, Mum?' No response, so he squeezed Sandy's hand and looked at her instead. 'And we've gotta show Danny, Sammy and Maurice how it's done, eh, girl?'

Sandy just smiled.

He turned back to Eileen. 'You know that Danny Kessler's got three kids, don't you, Mum, and he ain't even married to the bird.' Another squeeze of Sandy's hand. 'That wouldn't do us, would it, babe? Living together over the brush.'

If Brendan noticed Sandy's embarrassed discomfort, he didn't show it.

Eileen could have wept with relief. The meal was over. The food – some of it at least – had been eaten, drinks had been drunk, and crackers had been pulled, and she could escape at last. Get away from the noise and the sight of her husband's whore's child. Desperate as it had been to sit through it all, Eileen had forced herself, doing her best to look as if she were enjoying it, knowing that Patricia and Caty had made so much effort to make it nice for her. A special day to share with her family – God help her.

Eileen pushed back her chair. 'Patricia, that was a wonderful spread. Thank you. You and Caty worked so hard.' She stood up. 'I'll just clear the table then go and have a rest.'

Patricia nudged Caty to her feet. 'Don't be silly, Mum. Me and Caty can do that. You go and have your lie-down.'

'That was the best meal I've had in ages, Mrs O'Donnell,' Sandy said, smiling at Eileen, doing her best to join in without being pushy. 'And the least I can do is help wash up.'

'No, I won't hear of it.' This time it was Ellie, palms out to show she'd brook no argument. 'You stay up here, have a drink with the lads, and talk about wedding plans with your –' she paused '– *new fiancé*.' She wrinkled her nose at Brendan. 'And it'll give me a chance to get to know my little niece, now won't it?'

Only Luke and Patricia noted the look of horror on Eileen's face as Ellie took young Caty's hand and led her away to the kitchen.

Sandy looked at each of the three men as they sat there swallowing booze, and talking about deals she didn't understand and people she didn't know – all in the shorthand that had grown up between them over the years.

Brendan was looking pleased with himself, Pete Mac was beginning to look a bit pissed, and Luke just kept looking at his watch.

Sandy smiled at him. 'I can see you keep sneaking a look at the time, Luke. You missing Nicky, are you?'

Pete Mac and Brendan both swivelled round to stare at him.

'Blimey, Luke,' said Brendan, shaking his head and now grinning as ecstatically as if he'd just been given tickets to the Cup Final, with West Ham the guaranteed winners. 'I was right. That *is* why you wanted Ellie out of the way. You've got yourself a bloody girlfriend.' He turned to Sandy. 'Might even have a double wedding eh, San? What d'you think, girl?'

'Girlfriend? Him?' Pete Mac spluttered into his lager. 'Stop pissing about.'

Luke shot a look at Sandy, who turned away, her cheeks burning. 'Sorry, Luke, I didn't think.'

Brendan frowned then slapped his hand on the arm of his chair. 'Aw, fucking hell, Luke. It's a *bloke* kind of Nicky, innit? I should have known it was too good to be true.'

Sandy smiled feebly at Luke. 'You'll have to bring him to the wedding.'

Pete Mac's explosion of laughter could be heard all the way down in the basement kitchen.

There was no laughter – even of the sarcastic kind – in the large house set in its lovely gardens in Surrey. Charles, now an ex-bank manager, was alone, Daphne and their daughter Fiona having left as soon as Maurice had phoned through to say that the vault had been cleared and that Sammy and Daniel could be on their way. Charles was sitting at the dining table, facing the half-decorated Christmas tree. He had an almost empty bottle of vintage port in front of him and an empty pill bottle in his hand.

Having come to the conclusion that he had nothing left to live for, Charles had done something about it.

Out in rural Essex, Sophie Kessler was in her element. Despite her misgivings about Danny's 'girlfriend' Babs being the mother of her eldest boy's children without being his wife, she had to admit that it was wonderful having the little ones in the house, and seeing their faces as they unwrapped the mountains of presents that Father Christmas had left for them under the tree. Maybe next year they'd celebrate Hanukkah as well. She wasn't a bad girl. And the kids were like angels. Who knows, maybe Danny would even marry Babs one day. She'd like that. But for now, things were pretty good the way they were.

Sophie couldn't help thinking back to when her own boys were little more than babies, and how they'd be so excited and get up so early on Christmas morning that it was still dark.

Sophie Kessler was a happy woman. Blessed.

And her boys were also feeling pretty blessed –

there'd been a lot more in that bank vault than even Maurice had expected.

Carol poured yet another bottle of bleach down the lavatory she was forced to share with the other lodgers in the rooms in Bow. She didn't get it, the way people lived, like animals. But at least with them all disappearing – obviously having places to go to celebrate Christmas – she had the opportunity to clean the place up a bit, make it decent.

As the tears trickled down the sides of her nose and plopped down into the pan, Carol resolutely broke into a wobbly, gulping rendition of 'Silent Night'.

Chapter 13

It was half past eleven on a cold but bright January morning. It being a Saturday, and with no pressing business – but with definite signs of a hangover making themselves felt – Brendan had only just got up. He came down the stairs into the kitchen, tying his bathrobe and yawning, mouth wide open, and making no attempt to cover his mouth.

He stopped dead on the bottom step. 'Where the fuck did you get that?'

Eileen, who was standing at the sink, looked over her shoulder at him then returned to her washing-up.

Ellie, who was over by the table, glanced up at him even more briefly. She was bent double trying to fix a lead to the collar of a boisterous Dobermann puppy that was bouncing uncooperatively around her feet.

'That's a nice way to say good morning, isn't it?' she chirped at the dog.

'Don't play me for a mug, Ellie. I asked where it came from.'

'If you'll stop shouting at me for one minute, Brendan, I'll answer you. If you must know, Luke brought him round last night, after you'd gone out. He's for Eileen. Her Christmas present. Two weeks ite, of course, but that's Luke for you. Kind as anything but so distracted with his property deals and whatnot all the time . . .'

Eileen closed her eyes as she heard the affection in Ellie's voice as she spoke about Luke. She didn't quite know how, but the girl had managed to settle herself into the house, and into Luke's affections, as if she'd always lived there. As if it was the most natural thing in the world. If only she knew that Eileen tolerated her because every time she set eyes on the girl, God help her, it tore Eileen's heart to see how much like her darling Catherine she was – perhaps then she wouldn't feel quite so cosy.

Ellie pulled the puppy towards her and kissed his velvety head. 'But he is so *cute*, aren't you, Bowie? That's what I called him, when Eileen couldn't decide. And now I'm taking him out for a walk for her.'

'Fuck the poxy dog. I'm talking about that.'

'Brendan!' Ellie let the lead drop to the floor as he strode towards her. 'Don't talk to me like –'

'*The fucking coat.*' He flicked the back of his hand across the mink-lined, brick-red, suede trench coat that she had draped around her shoulders. 'Where did you get it?'

He stepped back, clipping the edge of the puppy's paw, making it dive under the table, yelping pathetically.

Eileen gripped the side of the sink.

Brendan now had Ellie by the shoulders. 'No show, don't you realise, you silly little tart? No flashy show.'

'It's only a coat.' Ellie sounded a lot braver than she was feeling.

'Yeah, the sort that someone with plenty of money can afford to wear when they're taking the fucking dog out.'

Ellie tried to shrug, but his fingers were digging into her. 'Or the sort that a dodgy chequebook can buy,' she said, her attitude an uneasy mix of wariness and cheek.

Eileen spun round.

'*What did you say?*' Brendan was shaking Ellie so hard she thought her head was going to fly off. '*Are you telling me you've been kiting?*'

'It was Milo.' Ellie started sobbing. She was terrified, no one had ever treated her like this, and now even Eileen was shouting. 'He took me to Knightsbridge. And we bought some clothes. So?'

'You stupid little idiot, you're taking a dog out, and you're wearing that?'

'I don't get it,' Ellie gulped between her sobs. 'You had me drive that horsebox, but I –'

'*But you weren't wearing a fucking hookey mink.*'

'Oh, Ellie, what have you done?' Eileen sighed, as she walked over to them, drying her hands on her apron. 'Brendan, leave the child alone. Right now. And, Ellie, you sit down and I'll make you some tea.

161

Brendan, you phone Luke and tell him to bring this Milo round here, whoever he is, and deal with him.'

The shock of hearing Eileen addressing them both directly had them obeying her more quickly than if she'd held a gun to their heads.

By the time Luke arrived with a chipper-looking Milo Flanagan, it was nearly one o'clock. Brendan was dressed in a pair of dark trousers, a black roll-neck sweater and heavy black shoes. And Ellie was no longer wearing the coat. It had been thrown across the table and was lying there like a carcass on a butcher's block.

Luke kissed Eileen on the cheek. 'Everything all right?' he said in friendly greeting.

'Luke,' she said, stroking the puppy that was now curled up asleep on her lap, 'I'm sure Brendan explained on the phone. So if you'll just take Ellie out for an hour, and have a chat with her about things, Brendan will deal with this . . .' she didn't raise her eyes from the dog '. . . young man.'

The 'young man' was now looking far more worried than cheerful.

'Sure,' Luke said calmly, despite his genuine surprise at hearing his mother not only saying more in one go than he'd heard her say in the whole two months since she'd been out, but that she had apparently started addressing both Ellie and Brendan by name.

162

He kissed her again then turned to his half-sister. 'Come on, Ellie, let's get going.'

Eileen waited until she heard the sound of the front door closing. 'Not here, Brendan,' she said, still without looking up.

Brendan snatched the suede coat off the table with one hand and grabbed Milo's arm with the other. His mother had asked him to do something. Something she knew Luke couldn't do.

And he felt the happiest he'd done in years.

Milo was sensible enough to listen without speaking as Brendan drove them through Stepney in the direction of the City. He just sat there and waited for the bollocking to start. And here it came.

'You never, ever get any of my family involved in any of your shit ever again. Got it?' Brendan began. 'And you never, ever go anywhere near Ellie unless I'm there or Luke's there. You never, ever do any kiting while you're working for me – *if* you wanna *stay* working for me. And now,' he drove down Cannon Street Road and pulled on to the Highway, 'I'm gonna teach you a lesson, Flanagan. And if you listen, and learn, I'm gonna let you carry on selling the gear for me. And if not, I'm gonna kill you. And I think you know my reputation to understand that I mean what I say.'

Milo wasn't sure what was going on, but he was glad he hadn't had anything to eat or he would now be sitting surrounded by a very undignified puddle of spew.

Brendan parked his car in sight of the Tower, in the shadow of the high, blind walls that surrounded the St Katherine Docks. Despite the cold of the bright winter's day, he didn't bother with a coat, but he did pull on a pair of leather gloves. 'Right, you, follow me.'

Having palmed a fiver to the watchman on the gate, Brendan led Milo into the once bustling docks that were now part smart new development and part building site. Being a Saturday afternoon, the building site was deserted, and that's where Brendan was heading.

Milo was so shocked by the first punch, that when Brendan swung round and whacked him in the guts for the second time, he still didn't try to protect himself. The blows from Brendan's leather-covered fists came one after another until Milo collapsed on the ground, bloody and semi-conscious.

If he'd been a bit less dazed, he might have been able to save his face from the worst of the kicking by curling himself into a ball. But violence wasn't usually part of young Milo's world – he'd always left that to others.

Little did Brendan realise that he was doing something that Milo Flanagan would find very hard to forgive.

*

While Milo was being taught his 'lesson', Ellie was sitting in the passenger seat of Luke's car, about to get a lesson of her own.

'I wouldn't mind but wasn't it Brendan who bloody introduced me to Milo in the first place, at that pub we went to for New Year. You should have seen him, Luke. He was like a madman. I really thought he was going to hurt me.'

'Being violent to get his own way – that's just part of the game for Brendan. Believe it or not, he don't mean anything by it. Well, not anything personal.'

'But I'm his sister.'

'I don't think he sees things that way. Not exactly. Family's important to him and nothing would ever change that, but in the end Brendan's a simple sort of bloke – people either do what he wants or they don't. And he treats them accordingly.'

He glanced in the rear-view mirror as he signalled to turn right. 'Now me, I do care about what happens to you, Ellie. I care a lot. So whatever else you do, you've gotta promise me you won't do anything daft like this again.'

'Why is it daft? I didn't get caught.'

'But you might have done. And just take it from me, it's daft to be doing two-bob stuff. Because you always risk getting caught and then people get nosy and that mucks up the big stuff. The stuff that's Brendan's life.'

She tried sulking for a bit, but couldn't carry it on for long. 'Where are we going?'

'Kilburn. A little flat I thought you might wanna see.'

'Kilburn? Isn't that where all the poor Irish live before they can afford something better?'

'You are such a snob, Ellie. I'm surprised you even talk to rough cockneys like me.'

'You're my brother, aren't you? Family.' She glanced sideways and was pleased to see she'd made him smile.

'All right, don't start getting clever. This is serious. Now you're living over here with us, it's important that you listen to me. That you understand how things work. When you're part of the world that Brendan's involved in –'

'And that you're involved in.'

'Okay, I put me hands up to that one, but it's not gonna be for much longer, Ellie. That's the difference between me and Brendan, he don't want anything else, never has. But me, I've spent most of my life working towards getting out of it.'

'But I still don't understand why he went raving mad about a bloody coat. It was okay for me to smuggle bloody guns for him. And if it was such a big problem, he could have just said.'

'The thing is, Ellie, that wouldn't have stopped you doing it again, would it? It's complicated. It's not just that you could have got caught, and given the law a reason to come sticking their noses in. It's that Brendan's got this thing, that it's a bad idea to be too showy about having a few quid, when you're out and about mixing with the mug punters. The ones who ain't part of our world. And he's right, I suppose. That's why he likes everything to be kept low-key. You act lairy, spend too much, and them people, they start asking questions. Where's that come from? How'd he get that? That sort of thing. Then people get jealous. It's the flashy ones, the idiots you see all over the papers, mixing with Lord and Lady this and that, in nightclubs and posh parties, they're the ones that get nicked. They're too visible, see. Showy.'

She raised her eyebrows only slightly as she did a quick price survey of Luke's superbly cut suit, his handmade shoes and his chunky gold cufflinks, not to mention the Daimler he was driving.

'Brendan even still buys a bit of gear on the book.'

'Sorry? Whatever you just said, made no sense at all to a little Irish girl like me – like most of everything else you say.'

'On the book. Hire purchase. Buy a telly – have it on the book, pay by instalments, just like all the neighbours.' He stopped the car on the corner of a nondescript side street off the High Road. 'There it is, halfway down the street. The one with the lamp-post outside. And before you ask, no I am not driving up to the street door in this thing.'

*

'You said it's important not to have anything "flash" or "showy", Luke, but this place is a bloody joke. It looks as if nothing's been touched since the 1950s. And I'm talking about 1950s back home, not in London. It's bloody awful. Who the hell lives here? Not one of your friends, I bet.'

'Dad liked it like this.'

'*Dad*?'

'Yeah. This was his and Rosie Palmer's place.'

'My mother lived here?' She ran a finger through the dust on the sideboard. 'So this was the place Aunt Mary used to bring me to, to see her and Dad before he . . .'

'Before he died. Yeah.'

Ellie looked about her, trying to remember.

'Do you miss your mum?'

She shook her head. 'It's sad really, I never knew her that well. I don't even know if she's still alive. Aunt Mary would never let me talk about her. But I wish I had known her. And Dad.'

'He was my dad too, remember. I can tell you about him.'

'It's all so weird, Luke. For years I thought I was an only child and now I've got you and Brendan and Patricia.'

'And Catherine. You'd have liked her.' He reached out and touched her hair. 'You look so much like her.'

'You all really loved her, didn't you?'

His chin dropped. 'Yeah.'

'And you really love Nicky too.'

He looked up and smiled ruefully. 'Unfortunately, I do.'

Ellie frowned. 'Why unfortunately?'

'Listen to you. You'd never think you were an innocent little Catholic girl from Ireland.'

'I think we're all agreed I'm not that any more.'

He stroked her cheek. 'Even if Nicky is the best thing that's ever happened to me it's not exactly easy having a boyfriend.'

'No, I suppose not.' She looked around again, trying to get a sense of what it had been like when she'd been a little girl. 'Why do you still keep the place?'

'Sentimental reasons,' he said flatly.

It didn't seem right to tell her that it was actually one of their slaughters, the places they kept to divide up and store any proceeds of jobs they did. A place to stash any money they needed to keep well away from their other businesses before it went over to Kildare to be laundered through the stud farm. The farm that had been Ellie's home for as long as she could remember. And nor did it seem right to tell Ellie that her mother, Rosie Palmer, had only been allowed to live in the flat because of Gabriel O'Donnell's 'generosity' and that she had been thrown out the very day after Eileen had killed him.

Ellie went to the window and stared out at the

grubby, down-at-heel street. 'Just think, I could have been raised here if Mum had wanted me.'

Luke put his arm round her shoulders, constructing the lies as he spoke. 'You never knew, Ellie – I don't know why we never told you – but your mum wasn't well for a long time. She wanted to care for you, but she couldn't. Soon as Aunt Mary found out how sick she was, she came over here to collect you like a shot. Her baby niece needed her.'

When she turned to face Luke, tears were streaming down her face. 'You've all been so good to me. And I've never shown any of you how grateful I am. I've acted like a bloody fool, and I am so sorry. And I am so sorry I upset Brendan. I didn't mean it. I've been just like a stupid spoilt kid.'

'Don't cry, Ellie. Here.' He gave her his handkerchief, and she blew her nose noisily.

'Do you think Brendan will let me stay here in London? And still be bridesmaid at the wedding?'

He hugged her to him, kissing the top of her head. 'Course he will, sweetheart. You're family.'

He could so easily have added – *God help you* – but didn't think it would be of much help, not in the circumstances. What he said instead was: 'And do you mind watching your *bloody* language? Cos it ain't very ladylike.'

Chapter 14

Butchy Lee, the middle son of a travelling family, who used to spend their winters in Canning Town, had earned himself a fair bit of money from some very simple schemes. Keep it simple was, in fact, his motto – provided by his wife – and probably a good thing too, as he wasn't the brightest of men. But he could perhaps be counted as being among the luckiest. Not only was Butchy's wife very beautiful, she was also very smart. When Butchy won just over £142,000 on Littlewood's pools, she persuaded him it was time to settle permanently, and to use twenty-nine and a half grand of his prize on buying a beautiful home in Hertfordshire, complete with a sizeable tract of land. The purchase meant they had a big imposing house in which to bring up their kids, and plenty of space for Mrs Lee's horses – she too came from Gypsy stock and loved the creatures. Then there were the outbuildings that they turned into guest cottages, a gym, an indoor pool, garages, and a suite of offices from which Butchy's accountant and his eldest daughter ran his businesses. One of the most 'interesting' of which was the illicit night-time sulky racing – another of Mrs Lee's winning ideas.

This activity involved the illegal blocking-off of a stretch of the nearby A10, on which single-seater, horse-drawn, two-wheeled vehicles were raced against each other at great speed. Large amounts of money, alcohol and pride were involved in these very popular events, and tempers were often frayed to such an extent that side bets were usually to be had on the outcome of the resulting bare-knuckle fist fights.

But to prevent excessive violence breaking out, Butchy's daughter – a young woman who took after her mother in both the looks and the brains departments – came up with an impressive addition to the proceedings. Holding a cine camera, and steadying herself with her elbows, she would kneel up on the back seat of an open-topped car driven by Butchy, filming the horses speeding towards her. Thus, in one go, she provided both a definitive answer to any disputes as to who had won, and a nice souvenir of the races for all concerned.

It was obvious to Brendan, when he'd enjoyed the odd evening attending such meetings, and had gone back to the house for a few drinks and a bit of supper, that Mrs Lee had been responsible for her husband investing that part of his winnings very wisely indeed. The attraction of the fine-looking house, and the proximity of the charming little Norman church in the meadow next door to Butchy's land – complete with a vicar willing to turn a blind eye to the fact that the happy couple didn't actually live within the parish, but who were prepared to donate handsomely to 'church funds' – had Brendan convinced that this was exactly the right place for him to make Sandy the new Mrs O'Donnell. It was perfect. Somewhere he could put on a show for his family, friends and assorted faces from the East End, all while avoiding the prying eyes and subsequent questions of the outside world.

The two hundred guests were welcomed into a marquee, in the field next to the church, by a solo saxophonist and by uniformed staff who had been hired in for the day – leaving several fancy hotels in the West End short-staffed due to a sudden epidemic of 'gastric problems'. The staff were, to say the least, a bit surprised by the sort of people they were greeting. But a pattern soon began to emerge – cauliflower ears, bent noses and gold teeth for the men, and bleached hair, plunging necklines and a surfeit of diamonds for their partners.

These definitely weren't the sort of people they were usually employed to wait on, but having been offered five times the rate they were accustomed to receiving per shift, who were they to argue? Even if they were told that if they didn't *keep schtum* about everything and anything that happened during the day, they would very definitely regret it. And from the look of the guests they had no reason to doubt the warning.

*

While the guests who were staying the night were being shown to their rooms and cottages, and the others sipped champagne or light ale and generally turned up their noses at the unfamiliar ingredients in the canapés, Sandy was getting ready upstairs in the master bedroom of the main house.

Mrs Lee had done Sandy proud. Fine Gypsy lace had been draped over the bed, early-summer flowers filled the vases that stood on either side of the dressing table, and white ribbons had been wound around the mahogany frame of the cheval glass, which had been set up to face the tall Georgian windows so Sandy could see herself in her wedding gown in the best possible light.

Mrs Lee was not in the room with her as she dressed, she'd left that special moment to the family – or rather to members of Sandy's family-to-be: Patricia, Ellie and little Caty. Mrs Lee had thought it a real shame when she'd heard that Sandy had no family there of her own, and that they'd turned their backs on her years ago when she'd moved in with Barry Ellis. She wondered at how times had changed. No one turned a hair about such things nowadays. Still, Sandy had the O'Donnells now; they were her family.

As she fussed around the bride, Patricia was doing her best to also keep an eye on Caty and Ellie, making sure that they didn't get anything on their bridesmaid dresses. If she had anything to do with it, today was going to be perfect. Not like her own farce of a wedding, when she'd been sick as a dog with morning sickness, and had still stood before the priest in a virginal veil and a dress that was too tight round the middle.

Sandy's dress was beautiful. Needing little persuasion from Patricia and Ellie, she had chosen a white Juliet-style gown, with a deep-scooped neck, dotted all over with tiny pink and pale green satin rosebuds. She'd drawn the line at the headdress and veil they'd wanted her to wear – after all, she wasn't sixteen years old any more – but had compromised by agreeing to wear a single string of pearls woven into her hair like a delicate tiara.

After giving the bride and her attendants a final once-over, Patricia was satisfied that there was nothing more for her to do.

'Right then, I'll get myself downstairs to Mum. Can't leave her alone for too long, can I? Not with all them people around.'

Sandy, dry-mouthed at what she was about to do, nodded. 'Thanks, Pat, you've been a real help. And, I don't know how to say this, but I think it's lovely of your mum coming today. With it not being a Catholic do and that.'

'Don't be daft. She wouldn't have missed it for the world.' Patricia kissed her on the cheek. 'You look beautiful, San, really beautiful.' She pressed her hand to her mouth and sniffed. 'I'll see you three in church,' she said through her fingers.

Her mother had barely left the room, when Caty stomped over to the looking glass and glared into it. 'I can't believe you made me wear this get-up. Look at me. Pink satin! I look like a flipping Sindy doll. I never wanted to be a bloody bridesmaid in the first place, but then Nan promised to buy me a new record player, and I thought I was at least going to have a bloody choice about what I'd wear. I mean, just look at me!'

Caty was just about to pull the garland of flowers from her hair when Sandy came up behind her and grabbed her by the upper arms.

'Ouch! You're hurting me!'

'Good. You might be able to get away with all this shit with that lot, you saucy little cow, but not with me, all right? And as for you –' She let Caty go and jabbed a finger at Ellie. 'You can get pissed and have it away with who you like, and whenever you like, you little scrubber, but not at my wedding. Got it?'

'I don't know what you're talking about.'

'Don't you? I was watching you. Down there.' Sandy pointed to the sash window at the far end of the room. 'Look for yourself. Go on. Down there.'

Ellie gingerly swished across the room and peered down. Bugger. She wasn't lying. You could look right down into the stable yard. She must have seen her with Milo.

'I saw you down there, when you said you had to go and speak to Luke. You were letting that hippie-looking freak practically rub himself off against you, your dirty little mare. And I can smell the gin on your breath from here.' She narrowed her eyes. 'You know, I don't get it. You two have been given so many chances in life, been brought up to be so nice, been to good, expensive schools, and had everything your greedy little grabbing hands ever wanted, and what do you do with all them chances? You act like sodding brats. But you've come unstuck with me, girls, because no one's gonna spoil this day for me. No one. I've bloody earned it after what I've put up with over the years.'

Caty's face was set in an expression of pure contempt as she stared back at Sandy's stony face, while Ellie had taken a sudden interest in her white satin pumps.

Earned, that's what Sandy had just said. Ellie realised that she'd have to watch herself with this one. She'd thought Sandy was a right 'yes woman', but here she was dictating the odds like she was her mother or something – or worse, like she was Aunt Mary. And she wasn't even an O'Donnell.

Sandy glared at them. She wasn't about to break the silence. Let the pair of them suffer.

They didn't have to suffer long.

There was a knock on the bedroom door and Luke's voice – unusually nervy, asked. 'You all right in there? The vicar's called the guests through to the church, and he's ready as soon as you are.'

'Thanks, Luke,' Sandy said, to the door, her voice now light and happy. 'We'll be one minute, okay?'

'Don't make it any longer, San, if I've gotta lead you down that aisle, you'd better do it quick before I bottle out and make a run for it.'

'You silly sod,' she said affectionately, then, spinning round, she pointed at each of the two young women in turn. 'Now, smile, the bloody pair of you,' she hissed under her breath. 'Or you'll have me to reckon with.'

Sandy rotated her shoulders as if she were about to go into the ring to do fifteen rounds with John Conteh, then, pasting on a bright smile, she said joyfully: 'Why don't you come in, Luke? We're all ready.' Then threw over her shoulder: 'Aren't we, girls?'

Chapter 15

With most of the guests thanking their lucky stars that it was a brief Church of England service rather than the full Mass they'd been dreading, they were all back in the marquee within the hour – primed and ready to eat and drink, and, of course, to pass judgement on the O'Donnells and all the other families present.

As they sorted out which of the large round tables they had been assigned to, the band, standing on a dais to the side of the long top table, struck up a syncopated version of 'I'm Forever Blowing Bubbles'.

'Do you know who's paying for all this?' said Daniel Kessler, as he examined a slice of smoked salmon that he'd speared on the end of his fork. 'We are, that's who.' He held it out in turn to each member of his family sitting at the table. 'Us lot. With the profits from all that gear they keep pushing on to us for the shops.'

Maurice, who was eating his salmon rather than waving it about, lifted his head briefly from his plate. 'You've got to admit though, feller, it's very high-quality merchandise they produce.'

He turned to Sophie Kessler. 'And 'scuse me, and all that, Aunt Soph, but they come up with films and magazines that surprise even me. I mean, I've not blushed since I was a nipper and I pissed me pants on me first day at school, but the films they've been getting hold of . . .'

Sophie ignored him. 'Harold,' she said, 'I see Eileen's got up, probably going to the Ladies. Think I'll join her. Go and have a word. Make sure she's okay. And,' she leaned in close to her husband, 'make sure that fool nephew of yours remembers there are children present.'

Harold shrugged – 'Sure' – then turned his attention back to his boys. 'Maury's right, and we're earning well out of the arrangement.'

'No,' said Daniel, 'we're earning what the O'Donnells say we earn out of it. And no matter what they say, I *know* it was them who had that Spanish load off of us. And do you know what, I've had enough of them fuckers. It's right back to how it was in old man O'Donnell's day. Us doing what that arsehole Gabriel told us to do.' He threw down his fork, making the three children sitting at the table – his three children – sit up straight and stare warily at him. 'And having to be grateful for the crumbs off their poxy table.'

'I wouldn't mind having a taste of that particular O'Donnell's crumbs,' said Maurice nodding towards Ellie, who was sitting alongside Luke at the top table.

'I can't believe how much she's like Catherine.' It was Sammy. He had hardly been able to take his eyes off her since he'd first seen her in the church. It was as if he was a boy again, sitting in his brother's car wondering how he was ever going to tell his family that he was in love with Gabriel O'Donnell's youngest daughter.

'Come on, feller,' said Maurice, 'cheer up. She's been dead for bloody years now, and anyway, I thought you were all cosied up with that Carol sort of Brendan's.'

'You kidding?' said Sammy absently, still staring at Ellie. 'I had enough of her weeks ago. She did her nut when I mentioned O'Donnell was getting married. Said it should have been her walking up the aisle. Well, he's welcome to her if he can be bothered to have her back.'

'I thought this do was gonna be a laugh,' said Maurice rolling his eyes. 'Come on, Sammy, at least we got all that dough from the bank, surely that makes you smile, feller.'

'I don't like it, you know.' Sophie linked her arm through Eileen's as they walked across the grass towards the house, in the warm afternoon sun. 'All these unmarried girls with babies. It's not right. My Danny's – what does he call her? *Girlfriend*. Girlfriend! She's got three babies with him.' She sighed. 'What must everyone think of us? They're

181

registered in his name, of course, so – officially – they're Kesslers, but as for any thought about their religion . . . Nothing. Not that I've ever asked her, but I bet the girl's never so much as set a foot in a *shul*.'

'*Shul*?'

'Sorry, a synagogue. It's so sad, Eileen, the old traditions all going.'

'I suppose it's like you said, Sophie, on that day you met me outside the prison. Times have changed. And the new ways are passing us older ones by. Believe me, the only reason I came here today was to see my little granddaughter. She was so excited about being a bridesmaid. But why they couldn't have had a proper Catholic service . . .' She snapped open her handbag and took out her handkerchief. 'It's all such a farce, I had to get out of there for a bit of air.'

Sophie stopped suddenly, pulling Eileen to a halt beside her. 'At last you're talking to me. This is more like it. Sometimes when I call you, I feel like I'm chatting away to myself, you're so quiet.'

She took Eileen's hands in hers, a gesture that had Eileen's eyes brimming with tears, reminding her how much she'd missed such human contact.

'It's important to talk about things, Eileen, to get things off your chest.'

Eileen pressed her lips together, her eyes fixed on their entwined fingers.

'I can't imagine what it was like in that place for you. With all those terrible women.'

'I'm no better than them, Sophie.'

'Yes you are, Eileen. You acted out of love for your children.'

'Maybe I should have loved them more, and my own beliefs a little bit less. I had a lot of time to think while I was in there. And I can't tell you how many times I wondered what would have happened if I hadn't forced Patricia to marry Pete Mac just because she was expecting. And then her losing the baby and everything. I went over and over how things might have turned out differently if I hadn't been so sure I was right.' She shook her head despondently. 'I just don't know what to think. It's like Sandy. She was never married to Barry Ellis. She just lived with him for all those years. And now she's married to my . . .' Eileen hesitated. 'My son. Brendan. And I can guarantee that getting married will make no difference to the way he carries on.'

Sophie took out her cigarettes and handed one to Eileen. 'Perhaps some people, and things, never change.' She sparked her lighter. 'Now, how about we have these, then have a wash and brush-up, and get back to the do?'

They continued their walk towards the house in thoughtful silence, until they got to the graceful sweep of steps that led up to the big front door.

'Young Ellie,' said Sophie, as if experimenting with the sound of the name. 'She's a very pretty girl.'

'She's Gabriel's daughter.'

183

'I thought she might be.'

Eileen blew a plume of lavender smoke high into the air, watching it rise. 'And she's the living image of my Catherine.'

'I thought that too.'

Eileen frowned in confusion. 'You met Catherine? When?'

'No, I never met her. But a few years ago, a long time after it all happened – years after – I went downstairs to the kitchen one night, for a drink of water, and I found Sammy sitting by himself at the table. He was looking through a stack of black-and-white photographs. It was the first time I'd seen him cry since he was a little boy. They were pictures of him and Catherine. Taken when they'd been out to the coast for the day. Larking around and grinning at the camera.'

Eileen nodded. 'I know the ones. She had her copies kept hidden in her bedroom. I found them there. After the funeral.'

'It must be so hard for you.'

'And for your Sammy. Luke said they really loved each other.' Eileen turned her head away. 'It doesn't seem possible, but she'd have been thirty last New Year.'

'Is Ellie's . . . Ellie's mother still on the scene?'

Eileen's head jerked round, and she looked into Sophie's eyes with a hardness Sophie had never seen before. 'Gabriel's whore, you mean? No. His sister

Mary saw to that. Chased her away good and proper.'

'Mary. Is she the, how can I put it politely, the very stern-looking woman on the top table?'

'That's her.'

'So she has some use other than frightening burglars then.'

The meal was over, and the guests were now mingling, looking considerably more relaxed as jackets and hats were thrown off, sleeves rolled up, and high-heeled shoes kicked under the tables.

Pete Mac was sitting astride a chair next to Brendan. 'Look at the state of him.' Pete gestured with his pint towards Milo Flanagan, a vision of glam-rock perfection – except for a jagged scar through his left eyebrow, a permanent reminder of the beating Brendan had given him.

'Typical of you, Pete,' tutted Brendan. 'You are looking at one of our brightest boys there. Very bright indeed. Needs to be kept in line, but he's quick to learn.'

Milo caught them watching him and raised his glass in salute.

'Aw yeah?'

'Yeah, he knows his own game, understands all the wrinkles and how to sort 'em out.'

'What, like Butchy Lee's stupid little brother Reuben did? He's doing a ten stretch for dealing.'

Brendan didn't bother to mention Pete Mac's own

particular, spectacular brand of stupidity, this was his wedding day after all, and he was in a good mood, for Christ's sake.

'That's cos he was old school, Pete,' he said, patting his brother-in-law on the back. 'Like the old man was. Didn't understand the future, modern ways and how they work.'

'That's easy to say, but –'

'Listen, and you'll learn something. I'll tell you how that silly bastard Reuben Lee got done, shall I? He bought a nice little load off the Moroccan police – straight from the donkey's mouth, so to speak. Handed over a right big bundle for it and all. Then what happens? The silly fucker's a sitting duck, i'n he? The law arrest him at the border, nick back the gear, take a massive backhander off him to let him go, give him a bit of the merchandise back as a gift – very kind, thank you very much – and then customs are waiting there ready to feel his collar when he crosses back through Spain. Moroccan fuckers have grassed him up for a bigger divvy of the gear with the mob in Spain. Fucking amateur.'

'So why bother with it if the law's got it all tied up?'

'Jesus, you really do sound like the old man, Pete.' Brendan leaned forward and tapped Pete Mac's forehead with his finger. 'Because, genius, it's the way forward, the way for the modern businessman. We ain't gas-meter bandits. And we don't want none of that fannying about going across the pavement, doing silly little smash-and-fucking-grabs and hiring petermen. No, *this* is the way forward. And the Kesslers are our route into all them lovely supplies of speed, and young Milo is its very weird, if pretty, public face.' He winked happily. 'Now, if you'll excuse me, Pete, I have guests to meet.'

As Brendan walked away, Pete Mac's eyes met Milo's, and for all his stupidity, Pete Mac recognised something in the boy's expression that Brendan had completely failed to see – pure burning hatred.

The only lesson that Brendan had taught Milo Flanagan was to despise the one who had taught him.

The first guest to get Brendan's attention was DI Bert Hammond, who was sitting with his wife, drinking a pint of weak lemonade shandy. Hammond was tapping his toes, and wagging his head cautiously to the band's version of 'In the Summertime'.

'Bert,' said Brendan, shaking his hand, 'thanks for coming and helping us celebrate our special day.' He turned to Mrs Hammond – as broad-beamed and rosy as her husband was slight and pale. 'And this must be your lovely lady.' He inclined his head politely. 'Welcome.'

Mrs Hammond blushed even redder. 'We really appreciated the invite to the wedding, Mr O'Donnell,' she said, her Birmingham twang as marked as her husband's. 'And we did enjoy our stay in Spain over Easter, we really did, didn't we, Bert?'

'We did indeed, my dear.'

'Good, good, I'm glad to hear it. You'll have to go over there again, Mrs Hammond. I'll fix it up for you. Me and Sandy are flying over for our honeymoon, but then it's all yours. Any time you like.' He treated her to a smile, and then pointed at DI Hammond. 'But not until after the first Thursday of next month, Bert, cos I'm inviting you to join me and the boys at a boxing do on Park Lane. I know you're partial to the fight game, so make sure you put it in your diary. Sixth of June. It'll be a good evening's entertainment.'

Brendan flashed his teeth once more and walked away.

DI Hammond took another sip of shandy. 'I'm partial to a fight all right, O'Donnell.'

'What was that, Bert love?'

'Nothing, Betty, just thinking aloud, my dear.'

Brendan did a bit more glad-handing, pausing every now and again to check on Sandy who was on the dance floor with a circle of blonde wives and girl-friends, bopping away to the band. Finally, content that he'd had a few personal words with everyone he needed to, he went back to the head table, and called the room to order by taking off his shoe and banging its heel on the table.

'Right, now I know I promised there'd be no

speeches,' Brendan hollered, slipping his foot back into his shoe, 'but I do just want to say a few words.'

There were slightly drunken cheers and catcalls from all parts of the tent.

'First of all, thanks to Sandy for being daft enough to have me, and to the bridesmaids for looking like a pair of angels.' He raised his glass to more cheers and whistles. 'And to Luke for being not only my brother, but the best man, and for standing in as father of the bride.'

Brendan beckoned him over. 'We got him cheap, as a job lot,' he said, patting him on the cheek to loud applause.

'To Mum and Patricia for looking so beautiful.' All eyes turned to Eileen, as a chorus of 'Hear, hear's rippled round the crowd. 'And thanks to all them people who have been so loyal to me over the years. As you all know, I don't take kindly to people who disrespect me or my family.' There was a ripple of nervous laughter. 'But I do like it when we are able to do such profitable business with another family – the Kesslers.' He stared for a long, challenging moment at the Kesslers' table. 'And what a pleasure it is supplying them with all the merchandise for their specialist shops.'

Daniel half rose to his feet, but his father stopped him.

'Leave it, boy,' said Harold Kessler, grinding down on his cigar. 'Not the time or place.'

'So, I'll raise my glass to a full and happy future for us all.' Brendan swallowed his drink in one go and raised the empty glass. 'Now get dancing. The band's costing me a bloody fortune!'

As the singer launched into a Tamla Motown medley, Milo walked past Brendan on his way to join the dancers, but Brendan hooked him round the neck and drew him backwards.

He put an arm each around Luke and Milo's shoulders. 'I'm a very happy man, lads,' he said, the slight slurring of his words showing the first signs of all the drink he'd taken. 'And I'm gonna be even happier. Because what them Kessler fuckers don't know is that I'm gonna take over all their import trade. Every last bit of it.'

He sighed contentedly. 'Not straight away, mind, because I'm gonna wait till the time's right. Gonna surprise 'em when they're least expecting it. We don't wanna have to bother with none of that fighting lark no more, we ain't fucking cowboys and Indians, not like in the old days.'

Brendan pinched into Milo's shoulder and shook him. 'You've done good work for me, Flanagan, been a good servant. But it's time we expanded. And the money'll come in just right for some plans I've got to do a few more deals with the chaps over in Ireland.'

Good fucking servant? Milo Flanagan swallowed his desire to kick Brendan O'Donnell right in the balls, because there were other ways for a bright young bloke to get the better of a loud-mouthed pisspot like him. And Milo was nothing if not young and bright.

And screwing O'Donnell's spoilt little mare of a sister, Ellie, hadn't been a bad place to start.

Patricia was sitting with Eileen at one of the tables.

Ellie waved to them from the dance floor, but they didn't seem to notice, so she made her apologies to her partner – a flat-nosed thuggish-looking man who might have been surprisingly light on his feet but gave Ellie the creeps – and went to join them.

'Isn't it about time you had a dance, Pat?' she said, dropping down on a chair next to her. 'I don't know why you're sitting here like you're waiting for a bus.'

She followed Pat's gaze, and saw that she was watching Pete Mac talking and laughing with two young blondes. 'Oh, you're keeping an eye on that husband of yours, are you?'

Eileen took a gulp of her drink. Why had she come here today? She could have just waited and seen the photographs of young Caty.

'No, Ellie,' said Pat flatly, 'I'm not keeping an eye on him, I'm just being disgusted by him. And by those two. Look at them. Acting as if they don't care who sees them, touching and pawing another woman's husband. Christ knows where their own blokes are.'

'Drunk somewhere, I suppose,' said Ellie, looking

around at the increasing number of men slumped back in their chairs.

The two young women hanging around Pete Mac were well aware that Patricia was watching them, and were playing up to the fact. Everyone knew that Peter MacRiordan lived by his own marital rules and that he responded well to a bit of flattery.

'That wife of your'n performing again, is she, Pete?' said one of them in a breathy little voice. 'Poor you. Don't let you out of her sight, by the look of it. And everyone knows how good you are to her.'

That you're an overgenerous idiot, ripe and ready to be conned, was what they really knew, she thought.

The girls glanced at one another. 'And I've heard all about them two sisters you set up in that right nice flat an' all. They're having you over, did you know that?'

Pete Mac's dumb grin faded. 'How d'you mean?'

'It's obvious, innit? There's all that dosh they should be earning for you going out hoisting, but what are they doing? They're sitting around all day on their lazy arses doing bugger all, while you're keeping them.'

'You sure that's a definite?' Pete Mac had been having trouble making sense of what the redheads were playing at. They reckoned they were top shoplifters, but so far he hadn't seen much evidence of it – in fact, he'd seen bugger all. 'They really are hoisters then?'

'Take my word for it. Best in the north of England, that pair. And they're taking advantage of you, Pete. I don't get it, I really don't. Good bloke like you being taken for a ride by them scheming scouse tarts.'

'And you know what else,' said the blonde lookalike standing next to her. 'I reckon that Carol Mercer's taking you for a mug an' all. She's the sort who wouldn't think twice about having it away with someone else behind your back. And all while you're picking up the bills.' She put a hand flat on his chest. 'You know why, don't you? You're too good to 'em. You are. I'm telling you, Pete, if you had someone like us two in that flat them sisters are in, we'd make sure we looked after you. Really well.'

Pete Mac's grin returned. 'Yeah?'

'Yeah.' She licked her finger and ran it across his lips. 'Come outside and we'll show you.'

As she watched her husband leave the tent with his arms wrapped round the blondes who were walking on either side of him, Patricia rose to her feet. She was shaking. 'Look at him. The bastard. That's it. I've had enough. There are going to be some changes made, or he can sling his bloody hook.'

Eileen closed her eyes, unable to bear her daughter's pain.

Ellie's attitude was far more sanguine. She folded her arms across her chest and leaned back in her chair. 'Good for you, girl. We'll have you burning your bra next.'

As the band struck up the opening chords of 'Tie a Yellow Ribbon', Ellie took hold of Pat's hand. 'Come on, let's have a dance.'

Pat stood up and Ellie winked at Eileen. 'They can't keep us O'Donnell women down for long, can they, Eileen?'

Brendan had also been watching Pete Mac. Even though he'd promised himself that nothing would go wrong today, and that he would keep control of his temper come what may, he couldn't let this one go. Couldn't let his moron of a brother-in-law get away with treating Patricia like that. Not in public, he couldn't. It reflected too badly on him. Made the family a laughing stock. And whoever had brought the birds along weren't gonna be exactly thrilled when they sobered up either.

He stormed outside after the three of them.

It didn't take Brendan long to find them. Pete Mac was leaning back against a tree with his trousers bunched around his ankles. One of the blondes was on her knees with his penis in her mouth, while the other one was standing over her with her top off, leaning forward so that Pete Mac could fondle her breasts, while she kissed him full on the mouth.

Brendan grabbed hold of the standing blonde's hair, and yanked her backwards. Her yells causing the kneeling one to stop her ministrations to Pete Mac, and to look up to see what was going on.

Mistake.

Brendan struck her – whack! – across the face with the back of his hand.

Then he started on Pete Mac. He used one hand to pin him by the throat to the tree and balled the other into a fist that he pulled back ready for action. But, much to Pete Mac's relief, he hesitated.

'You are this close to getting a good hiding, you stupid, fat fucker. And the only reason I'm not gonna beat your brains to a pulp is that you're family. And fighting in the family is a sign of weakness. And I ain't gonna make even more of a show with all these people around. But you just remember that I can have you any time I feel like it.'

'Brendan, you've got me wrong, mate, I love Pat.'

The girls were scrabbling around to tidy themselves up and to back away before Brendan noticed.

'Yeah, course you do. And so long as she puts up with you, you're all right, you ponce.' Brendan spun round and faced the girls. He jabbed a finger at them as he spat out his words. 'I don't for one minute suppose I'd ever recognise either of you manky pair again, but if you've got any sense whatsoever, don't you ever make yourselves known in my company again. Now piss off before I get really upset.'

With that he turned back to Pete Mac, shaking his head contemptuously. 'Put your fucking prick away, and get back in there to your wife. You wanna fuck about, at least be a bit fucking subtle about it, you wanker.'

Neither Brendan nor Pete Mac noticed DI Hammond standing behind the flapping entrance to the tent, watching and listening to their every word.

A few moments later DI Hammond was sitting with his wife back in the marquee, tapping his toes to the band's thumping rendition of 'Signed Sealed Delivered'.

'You know the old saying, don't you, Betty, my dear,' he said, his eyes fixed on Sandy who was still enjoying herself on the dance floor along with most of the other women. 'Marry in May –'

'– and rue the day,' Mrs Hammond finished for him with a pleased and happy smile.

'Exactly. Well, I think it won't be long at all before this particular new bride is going to rue this day very much indeed.' He sighed contentedly. 'And I must say, I am looking forward to witnessing the repercussions.'

Chapter 16

Brendan and Sandy were driving back from Gatwick airport to the Mile End Road. They had spent their honeymoon at Brendan's villa in the hills high above Estepona on the Costa del Sol, and were looking tanned, healthy and prosperous – a handsome couple in every sense. The contrast between hot, sunny Spain and the miserable, overcast skies and grey, grimy streets of east London couldn't have been more pronounced.

Sandy sighed loudly as they pulled up outside the house, but Brendan didn't notice the shabbiness. All he saw was his family home – the place where Eileen now lived, not with him any longer, not since the wedding, but, by some unspoken agreement, with his half-sister Ellie.

Brendan used the key that he still kept on his chain to let them in, and Sandy followed him down the stairs to the kitchen.

Eileen was sitting in her usual chair, Ellie and Patricia were sitting at the table, and Caty was kneeling on the floor playing ball with Bowie – no longer a pot-bellied puppy, but a fit, sleek young dog.

Sandy put on a smile and handed Eileen a flat, red

leather box. 'It's a little present, Eileen. From Brendan and me.'

Eileen took it with a nod, opened the lid and took out a row of pearls. 'They're lovely,' she said quietly.

'Let me see, Eileen,' said Ellie. 'Oh, they are so beautiful. Here, let me fasten them round your neck for you.'

Sandy forced another smile. She'd never had much to do with Eileen O'Donnell in the days when Gabriel had still been around, but on the odd occasion when they had met up, Eileen had always been kind to Sandy, and she'd appreciated it. But in the run-up to the wedding she'd made it very clear that she disapproved of Sandy and Brendan getting married.

It was strange, being disapproved of by a woman who had actually killed her husband. But it was as though, regardless of what she had done, Eileen was like most other women of her generation. She knew her place, and thought that others should know theirs too.

And Sandy's place, according to Eileen, should have been supporting 'poor old Barry' as he had come to be known over the years.

If only Eileen knew the truth about his drug taking and all the associated madness, perhaps then she'd have understood why Sandy had married Brendan; why she had been prepared – no, more than that, *keen* – to do something that would give her a good life after everything she'd been through. And perhaps then she'd be more sympathetic than critical, and it wouldn't be like talking to a brick wall whenever Sandy tried to speak to her. But then ten years inside could do strange things to a big, tough man, let alone to a frail-looking, middle-aged woman, who'd done little more in life than raise her children and look after her man – before her moment of madness had turned her entire world upside down.

Sandy was only glad that Brendan had agreed to move into the house on Old Ford Road. No matter how she tried to sympathise with Eileen, she really couldn't have stood living under the same roof with a woman who she felt was continually judging her.

Especially when that someone was a murderess.

'Did you get anything for me, Auntie Sandy?' It was Caty, the voice and face of an angel in her neat little convent uniform – and the mind and cunning of a she-devil. 'And for Ellie?'

'Course we did, sweetheart.' Sandy found another smile. 'And for your mum.'

'Really?' said Patricia. 'For me? I didn't expect anything.' She went over to the sink to fill the kettle. Brendan followed her.

'You look really happy,' she said to him.

'I am, Pat. I only wish you were an' all.' He stood back so she didn't splash his pale cream, linen flares. 'You don't have to stay with him, you know,' he said, lowering his voice.

'I'm beginning to realise that.' She half turned to

face him. 'Must be Ellie's influence, with all her women's-lib talk.'

Brendan frowned, clearly not impressed. 'He still going to the boxing tomorrow night?'

'Boxing?' She looked blank.

'I got the tickets before me and Sandy went away. Charity do, up the West End. And make sure he remembers it's dinner suits. And, sorry, Pat, it's lads only.'

Patricia raised an eyebrow. 'Of course.'

He looked over at Sandy, who was showing Ellie the fringed lace shawl she had brought back for her.

'Sandy's persuaded me to let Luke bring some mates with him,' he said, scratching his stubbly chin.

'Right.' Patricia said the word slowly, with a lift of her chin. 'Mates. That'll be nice for him.' Then she burst out laughing.

'What?'

'You. It is 1974, you know, Brendan.'

Brendan might not have liked what she was laughing about – or her women's-lib nonsense, for that matter – but at least it made a nice change to see her without the usual downtrodden scowl on her face.

The next morning, as Pete Mac scoffed down his bacon, beans, eggs and fried slice, Patricia reminded him about the boxing do, but there was no need. He was looking forward to it.

He just hoped he could get all the things he had to sort out done and dusted before it was time to get ready.

Number one on Pete Mac's list was the sisters from Liverpool, and that was why he was now standing in the bedroom of their flat, looking at the half-dozen handbags that could have come straight off a cut-price stall in the market. The sisters were standing on either side of him, heads bowed as if they were being scolded by the headmaster for running in the corridor.

'Is this it?' he said, picking up one of the bags and tossing it straight back on the bed. 'I told you after that fucking wedding that if you didn't stop trying to con me, you'd be out on your pretty little arses. Now I wanna see some top-quality gear in this flat, or that's it. And while you're at it, you can get me a watch. From Bond Street. One of them new digital jobs, or whatever they call 'em.'

After a further ten minutes of admonishment, Pete Mac left them to think about what he'd said.

Waiting until he closed the front door behind him, one of the sisters said to the other: 'S'pose we'd better stop flogging all the stuff off to that Milo one. Cos we don't wanna lose the flat, now do we?'

'No,' said the other girl, 'not till we've got enough cash together to get somewhere nice.'

*

Feeling he was on a roll in this laying down the law business, Pete Mac's next stop was Bow and a visit to Carol Mercer.

She opened the door in a tiny baby-doll nightie, her big blonde hair gently tousled, and wearing full make-up. She'd been expecting something like this for the past few days, and had made sure she was ready.

His eyes widened, but he was here on business, not for a quick tumble. But then again . . .

'I'm a fair man, Carol,' he said, walking through to the bedroom. 'I told you after the wedding – you had two weeks to find yourself somewhere else. No argument. Done deal.'

'Don't be like that, Peter.' She came up behind him, leaned her head on his back, and put her arms round him. They didn't meet because his belly was in the way. 'You don't know how hard it is for a young girl like me. Men take advantage. I go and look at a horrible room somewhere, and the landlord thinks that I'll –'

'Cut the crap, Carol,' he said turning round to face her. 'You know what I like. Just show a bit of appreciation and I'll see what I can do.'

Carol was down on her knees with his trousers unzipped before the dozy-arsed lard bucket had a chance to change his mind.

When she had finished the job, Carol hurried through

to the shared bathroom on the landing and spat into the sink.

Christ, she despised him. Almost as much as she hated Brendan. And as for his going on and on about the poxy wedding. Why the hell did Pete Mac think she had any interest in how 'beautiful' and 'lovely' that rotten cow Sandy looked, and that he liked women to look 'feminine' like that? Why should she care that Brendan O'Donnell was married?

And the way Sammy Kessler treated her wasn't a lot better.

How had it come to this? She'd have to get her life back in order soon or she'd go off her head.

She lifted her chin and looked in the mirror. Pete Mac was standing behind her – stark naked. His face ruddy and slicked with a film of sweat.

Oh God, surely not again?

He confused her by tossing her his car keys. 'I'm gonna have a wash. Run down to me car and get me dinner suit out of the boot. And don't be long, Cal, I'm in a hurry.'

Milo stood in front of the full-length mirror in the bedroom of his flat in the tenement block in Poplar, checking out his profile.

'What d'you think, babe?'

'Gorgeous,' Ellie breathed into his ear. She was standing behind him, completely naked, having watched him, fascinated by his easy, self-confident beauty, as he'd bathed and dressed, making himself ready for his boys' night out at the boxing do.

'You'll have to get going soon, Ellie,' he said, looking straight ahead at her reflection. 'I'm being picked up and I don't think it's time to tell Brendan about us yet.'

Ellie grabbed his wrist and stared at his watch. 'Bloody hell, Milo, I had no idea it was that late.'

She ran around the room picking up her scattered clothes, pulling on her underwear and swearing softly to herself.

'Time goes so quickly when I'm with you,' she said, pulling up the zip of her boot. 'One last kiss then I'm off.'

Milo pulled her to him and almost crushed her in his arms. He could hear her breath coming faster as the excitement flooded through her.

'Come on, Ellie, give me a break, or I'll never get out tonight.'

'Would that be so bad?' she whispered into his ear.

'Yes. Brendan's expecting me.'

He took her by the hand, picked up her bag and led her through the hallway to the front door. 'I'll call you tomorrow.'

'Promise?'

'Promise. Now go!'

Milo listened for the metallic clang of the lift door then went back to the bedroom and picked up the phone.

'Good evening,' a snooty-sounding woman answered, '*Sunday World.*'

'Dave Seymour, please.'

'*David* Seymour?'

'Yeah, that's the bloke.'

He listened to a series of clicks and crackles, then heard: 'In-Depth team, David Seymour speaking.'

'Hello, Dave, it's me, Milo.'

'Problems?'

'No, I'm just checking you've done the legwork getting yourself well in with that little fruit, Nicky Wright, and that everything's in place for this evening.'

He smiled very happily at David's reply.

The inside of the flat above the Moulin Bleu in Frith Street always surprised new visitors. And that pleased Luke O'Donnell. In contrast to the streets and clubs below, it was light, airy, clean and contemporary, with a few large abstract paintings spotlit on plain white walls. He liked living in Soho, it was a place where you could be yourself and no one bothered you. Even if you were 'different'.

Luke was in the bedroom getting ready for the boxing evening, fiddling around unsuccessfully with his bow tie, while Nicky was in the bathroom, gurgling along to the Rubettes on the radio as he brushed his teeth. He was far more relaxed than Luke.

'So, who's this friend you're bringing tonight?' Luke called through to him.

'Not jealous, are you, sweetie?'

'Don't you dare pull any of that camp crap tonight, Nicky.'

'Would I let my lovely boy down?'

Luke ripped the tie from round his neck. 'Do this bloody thing for me.'

'Temper.' Nicky padded through from the bathroom. He was wearing trousers, but his smooth and tanned chest, and his immaculately pedicured feet, were bare. He took the tie, looped it back over Luke's head, and then moved round behind him. Then he put his arms over Luke's shoulders and began tying it into a bow.

'I am going to behave beautifully. You told me I should bring someone, so I'm bringing along a very nice boy called David. And, before you ask, he's not queer, he's just a friend. A customer at the record shop. Very grown up, only buys jazz, knows how to conduct himself. And nice and butch to impress your Brendan. Like you said, as far as anyone needs know, we're all just blokes out together, eh, Lukey?' Slowly he ran his knee up the back of Luke's leg.

Luke gulped, looked at his watch, and undid the tie again.

'We've got twenty minutes,' he said, pushing Nicky on to the bed.

As Luke kissed Nicky, his mind whirled with what

had happened to him during the past year since they had met in the poky little record store where Nicky worked in Old Compton Street. Luke had known almost right away, had never been surer of anything in fact, that his future was going to be with Nicky – that whatever else happened, he was going to spend the rest of his life with him.

Chapter 17

Sitting with Brendan at the table for eight in the plush hotel on Park Lane were Pete Mac, Luke, Luke's boy-friend Nicky Wright, Nicky's new friend David Seymour, DI Bert Hammond, DC Jim Medway and Milo Flanagan.

At the centre of the massive, chandelier-lit room was a raised boxing ring, around which all the tables had been arranged, with just enough space left between them for the waiters. These evenings were always popular with those who wished to be seen doing their bit for charity – regardless of what the cause might be – and to have the opportunity to treat their guests to a night out, a way of either saying thanks for services rendered, or to oil the wheels of future deals.

And tonight Brendan was doing both.

He ordered four bottles of champagne, and three each of whiskey and vodka, then took off his jacket and set about making sure everyone was introduced.

DI Hammond raised an eyebrow as Nicky was pointed out to him. 'So, you're Mr Right, eh?' he said. In other circumstances, his Birmingham accent would have been enough to have earned him a punch on the nose, never mind what he'd have got for the sarcasm. But not tonight.

Brendan turned to DC Medway, hurriedly changing the subject. 'Remember our gaff down in Limehouse, Jim?

'Do I? We had some nights down there, all right,' said Medway, the alcohol he'd already consumed in the upstairs bar at Brendan's expense making him forget the presence of his boss. 'Bare-knuckle fights, plenty of booze, and birds with big thrup'nies taking the bets. What more could you ask from a night's entertainment?'

'You're right there, Jim,' said Brendan, then added pointedly, 'Shame you missed it, Bert.'

Luke leaned back while the waiter set down a prawn cocktail in a leaf-shaped glass dish in front of him. 'It'll be unrecognisable round there soon.'

'There he goes again.' Brendan waved his spoon at his brother, mentally totalling the number of vodkas that Luke had already swallowed. Still, who could blame him? He was probably finding the situation as uncomfortable as Brendan – sitting there with his *friend* in a public place. And Christ alone knew what part the other bloke – *David* – played in it. Jesus, he didn't want to even think about it.

'Property,' he went on. 'That's all you hear out of him. Reckons that the docks are gonna be a gold mine one day. But who'd wanna live and work round that shithole unless they had to, I don't know.'

Pete Mac scraped the last of the pink sauce from his dish, shoving the shredded lettuce to one side. 'Unless they had access to the bonded warehouses, eh, lads?' He licked his spoon clean. 'Gear we used to have out of there, eh.'

'How do you mean?' asked David, speaking for the first time since he'd said hello to everyone.

Brendan's forehead creased almost imperceptibly. 'Ignore him, mate. Here, have another drink and eat up. They're already bringing in the main courses.'

David noted Brendan's discomfort. He took a small mouthful, thinking as he chewed, and then put down his spoon. 'And what do you do, Milo? You look like you should be in a pop group. Playing in the clubs.'

'Funny you should say that, David, it's not a bad guess. I do spend a lot of me time in clubs, as it happens.'

'Really? What sort of line are you in?'

Brendan leaned across the table and tapped his butter knife on the side of Milo's glass. 'Now that'd be telling the man, wouldn't it?'

Milo tossed down his spoon and leaned back in his chair. He didn't like being shut up. He'd thought it might be a laugh coming along tonight, seeing David pumping them for information. But he was beginning to wish he hadn't bothered. There had to be easier ways to have the O'Donnells.

Luke was also beginning to wish he hadn't come.

He felt sick. Maybe he should try and eat something.

The waiters came round and placed a great slab of bloody steak, adorned with little sprigs of watercress and a grilled Vandyked tomato in front of each of them.

Luke tasted the bile rising in his throat. ''Scuse me, chaps,' he said, standing up. 'Gotta go to the Gents.'

'You're mad,' Pete Mac called after him. 'Look.' He jabbed his knife towards the boxing ring. 'The comedian's coming on. He's brilliant this feller. Remember, we saw him at that stag do we went to with Kevin and Anthony?'

'Yeah, all right, Pete,' said Brendan, smiling reassuringly at DI Hammond and flashing a warning glare at Nicky to stay put. 'Think Luke's feeling a bit rough. I'll go and see to him.'

With the audience roaring at the comedian's joke about a virgin, a Welshman and a pound of ripe peaches, Brendan wove his way through the crowded room, acknowledging people's greetings. As he came to the table where the Kesslers were sitting with their guests, he paused briefly.

'All right, Sammy,' Brendan said, studiously keeping his eye on where Luke was heading. 'I hear you're scraping up them crumbs from my table again.' He shook his head in mock sorrow. 'Schtupping Carol Mercer, eh? Still, I don't mind someone having my leftovers. Wouldn't do for me, of course, but I ain't like you, now am I?'

Milo, who had been watching Brendan, waited for him to move on, then he too rose to his feet.

'Think I'd better go before the fights start and all,' he said, before he threaded his way across the room.

He too stopped at the Kesslers' table, taking just a moment to drop a piece of folded paper in front of Danny before carrying on towards the Gents at the far end.

'Now what's *that* all about?' asked Sammy, still clearly rattled by Brendan.

Danny squinted at the paper. 'It's a note,' he said. Then a smile spread slowly across his face. 'That weirdo's got the right arsehole with the O'Donnells. Reckons he's ready to have one over on 'em.'

He carefully refolded the paper and put it in his top pocket. 'Interesting.'

Luke and Brendan finished up in a quiet lavatory way up on the third floor next to a small bar area. After the ordeal of sitting among all those men with Nicky, knowing that Brendan didn't approve, and only being able to imagine what ninety-nine per cent of the rest of them there tonight would have to say about his and Nicky's relationship, Luke really didn't feel like having to be pleasant to strangers.

'You know, I don't get you, Brendan,' Luke said, throwing cold water over his face. 'You carry on alarming about not drawing attention to yourself, and then you go inviting all those people to your wedding, spending all that money. Now you've got us all here tonight, spending even more money and, according to the programme, O'Donnells' Cabs are even sponsoring one of the bloody rounds.'

'That, Luke,' said Brendan, positioning himself in front of the urinal, 'is because we're among our own. Or I thought we were meant to be. That David bloke's asking enough questions.'

Luke leaned forward, pressing his forehead against the cold glass of the mirror. 'He don't understand. He knows Nicky from the fucking record shop, for Christ's sake, not from Borstal or the nick.'

'Well, perhaps you'd better explain to him that it's not right for someone to be so fucking nosy.' Brendan zipped his fly and went to the run of sinks to wash his hands. 'If you're sober enough.'

He threw his used towel into the basket and draped his arm round Luke's shoulders. 'Just be careful, eh, Luke. Just be careful, mate.'

With the tables cleared of any evidence of dinner, cigars lit, glasses charged, and with both the comedian and the final item in the charity auction over – only fifty quid for a pair of Ali's signed gloves! Brendan doubled it – the fights, all amateur bouts, and all billed as being fought in strict accordance with ABA rules, were under way.

The place erupted into yells, whistles, cheers and jeers. Bets were laid, wads of money changed hands, more drinks were drunk, and blood and sweat sprayed over those 'lucky' enough to be sitting close to the ring.

Come eleven thirty, the final bout was over. Very few jackets were being worn, and not many of the audience could lay claim to any degree of sobriety.

Brendan showed out to a waiter. 'Another three bottles of Remy,' he said, before pulling the man down by the shoulder and whispering something in his ear.

The waiter looked at the money that Brendan had pressed into his hand. 'Of course, sir,' he said with a bob of his head.

A few moments later, the curvy teenaged girl, who had held up the cards announcing the rounds, came over to the table, still dressed in the silver bikini she'd been wearing as she strutted around the ring.

'Right, chaps,' grinned Brendan, wrapping his jacket around the girl's shoulders. 'I'm off. So, anything else you want, just tell the waiter. Luke'll see to the bill.'

David, one of the few men in the room who had carefully paced his drinking, watched Brendan steer the girl towards the big sweeping staircase that led up to the main reception area. 'Didn't I hear Brendan say he'd arrived home from his honeymoon yesterday?'

'That's right,' said Pete Mac, belching loudly.

'Surely that's not Mrs O'Donnell?' said David innocently.

214

Luke, now very drunk, looked at him as if he were thick. 'Course it's not. Sandy's a lovely woman. Wouldn't see her acting like a trollop.'

David glanced at Nicky. 'Sorry, I don't understand.'

Luke stretched across the table for the last of the vodka, knocking over a line of empty tonic bottles. 'Brendan might be totally in love with Sandy, but he don't live by the same rules as other people.' He drained the liquor into his glass. 'He can go with who he likes, and, to him, he's doing no wrong. He's not betraying Sandy, cos she don't know what he's getting up to.' Luke considered for a hazy moment. 'This is his private life. Nothing to do with her.'

Pleased with his explanation, Luke leaned in close to Nicky.

DC Medway and DI Hammond both muttered something about finding the lavatories, and excused themselves.

Luke paid them no attention. 'You'd never do that to me, would you, Nicky?' he slurred. 'Cos it's only me you want, innit?'

Nicky slipped his hand under the table, and cupped it over Luke's crotch, making him smile with pleasure. 'Get us a room upstairs, Lukey, and I'll show you who I want.'

David, flicking through the souvenir programme – three pounds for thirty-two glossy, black-and-white, sponsored pages – was wondering, not for the first time in his career, about the powers of alcohol to loosen tongues, banish inhibitions and to destroy supposedly strong men's will.

God bless it.

He was also wondering when he would get to talk to Milo again. They'd had their meetings and phone calls, of course, setting the whole thing up – David getting in with Nicky had taken time and care – but now, after seeing them all together tonight, he was really intrigued by how someone like Milo fitted into the O'Donnells' set-up.

Milo's own thoughts weren't a lot different. He himself was wondering how he fitted in with these bullying pissheads. Since Brendan had shut him up, he hadn't said anything other than answering the odd question as briefly as possible, but he had been taking in every little thing that had gone on. And they all confirmed why he didn't like the O'Donnells. Why he didn't like them one little bit.

And that most of all he didn't like Brendan – the cocky, big-mouthed whoreson, who had made him look a fool in front of everyone by interrupting him and as good as telling him to be quiet.

The time had come for Brendan O'Donnell to be taught a lesson for once.

If only he knew what Milo had in store for him.

Chapter 18

The sky was the colour of the lead nicked off a church roof; it was humid as a swamp, and Carol Mercer could feel the sweat trickling down her back. She was standing in a baking hot telephone box just along the street from her miserable rooms. She now hated those rooms almost as much as she had hated the childhood home she had shared with her mother until she'd been thrown out on to the street.

She was in the phone box because she couldn't stomach using the filthy phone she was supposed to share with the other tenants. As with the rest of the place, its dirtiness disgusted her. But at least she'd had a temporary reprieve as far as money was concerned: Pete Mac had stumped up for another month's rent after the 'favour' she'd done him last night.

The thought of what she'd had to do for that money made Carol shudder. She still had the taste of him in her mouth, and if it hadn't been unladylike, she'd have spat on the floor. Although looking down at her feet, it seemed that plenty of people had far fewer qualms about such behaviour.

Carol puffed out her cheeks in a weary sigh and rang yet another number.

''Lo?'

At last, a result. Sammy Kessler had answered in person.

Okay, Carol, she urged herself. Concentrate, girl. Be bright and cheerful. There's a lot riding on this. This could be the way to get somewhere decent to live, and to get shot of that animal Pete Mac.

'Sammy! How are you?'

'What? Who is this?' Sammy Kessler was straining to hear her over the babble of excited male voices echoing behind him. The chorus of shouts erupted into excited whooping as the men urged on the favourite as it moved closer to the winning post.

'It's Carol, of course. Who'd you think it was?'

'Look, darling, I'm busy right now.' Sammy snorted air down his nostrils as a vision of Brendan's smirking face came unbidden into his thoughts. 'Really busy.'

She bit back what she wanted to say, deciding it would be wiser to carry on with the little-girl act. 'But you're always busy, Sammy. And you know what they say about all work and no play –'

'I don't give a fuck about what anyone says, d'you hear me? But since I've got you on the line, I might as well tell you now, I'm gonna be a whole lot busier. So don't bother phoning me again, all right? Phone O'Donnell if you want a fucking night out.'

Carol heard the click of him cutting her off.

She let the phone drop from her hand, leaving it to swing wildly from its cord.

Someone tapped on the glass. 'It's gonna pelt down out here in a minute,' yelled an elderly woman, pointing at her shopping trolley as if it were somehow a deciding factor in her argument. 'You finished yet?'

'No, but he fucking will be,' snarled Carol as she barged out of the booth past the now open-mouthed woman. 'They all fucking will be once I start talking.'

'Bowie'll be just fine, Eileen,' said Ellie. 'I left him some extra Bonio by his basket, and a fresh bowl of water.'

Eileen nodded absently. She was sitting in the passenger seat, while Ellie drove them through the West End traffic in her new pride and joy – the bright yellow Hillman Imp that Luke had bought her. 'Thanks.'

Eileen hadn't wanted the puppy at first, had baulked at having responsibility for a dog after so many years of having all her decisions made for her. And she'd been more than happy when Ellie had taken over caring for the creature, but she'd soon realised that he could provide a useful alibi, a reason for refusing to go out, and for not doing things that scared or worried her.

She stared out of the window at the packed pavements and the lines of crawling traffic. If she valued being left alone so much, what did she think she was doing going out shopping? And with Ellie of all people.

And yet here she was, with Ellie chattering away to her as if this were the most normal thing in the world. But for Eileen it was anything but. Not only was the world so strange and so busy, so full of noise and bustle and bright colours, and crammed with people rushing everywhere, there was also the unexpected problem of having to see Ellie every single day.

When looking at her was just like looking at Catherine.

She wasn't like her in her ways, of course. Not at all. Her temperament was far more like Brendan's. No fear or shame, bold as brass and twice as determined. But when Eileen looked at that lovely face of hers, it was as if she'd been blessed with having a second chance with her beloved daughter.

The frightening thing was, as time passed by, the differences between their two faces – Ellie's and Catherine's – were blurring, becoming hazy, as they gradually merged into one. It was unnerving. As though she was losing Catherine all over again, but getting her back at the same time. Even when she dreamed about her, her face became Ellie's.

It had been the unsettling similarity between the two that had been the key to Luke persuading Eileen to let her to stay in the house in the first place. If she'd shown her the door it would have been just like turning Catherine out on to the street.

And it was also the reason why Eileen had finally given in and agreed to come out shopping with Ellie.

Life and everything about it was so confusing.

Ellie flicked the indicator stalk, and turned off Oxford Street, easing the Hillman into the short queue of cars waiting to go down into the underground car park below the big, leafy square.

'Thanks for coming with me today, Eileen,' she said, pulling forward on to the ramp. 'You know, I was saying to Patricia, I feel like a country bumpkin walking around in the clothes I brought over with me from Ireland. Don't get me wrong, they're fine for Kildare, but once I saw myself in the outfit that Patricia helped me pick out for the evening do after the wedding, well, I knew I had to do some proper shopping or go around looking like a fool.'

Eileen couldn't let that one go. 'So why ask me to come with you? Sure, I've no more idea about fashion than the dog. Why not ask Patricia? Especially when you two seem to be getting along so well together.'

Ellie smiled, her cheeks folding into the dimples that made her look even more like Catherine, and that made Eileen's senses almost leave her. 'All right, Eileen, you've seen through me. I'll be honest with you.'

Her smile faded as she turned to look Eileen directly in the eye. 'Patricia was busy today. Because of me. I persuaded her to go and get something done with her hair. Get some layers put through it. Buck it up a bit. She's a good-looking woman, and it'll take ten years off her. Give her a bit of style and some new confidence in herself, so she can show that eejit Pete Mac that she's still got it, and what he risks losing if he doesn't stop playing his stupid games.'

Eileen's eyebrows lifted slightly. Good girl, she thought. But then came the blow, the one that deep down she had been expecting ever since Ellie had first set foot in the house.

'And I wanted her out of the way because I wanted it to be just the two of us today, Eileen. I wanted you to myself, with no chance of anyone interrupting us. Because I want you to tell me something. The truth. About why you killed my father. I've asked the others but they tell me everything except what I really want to know. Skirting round things, claiming they're not sure about this and about that. So it's down to you, you're the only one who can tell me why you did it. And I think you will, because you understand that I've got a right to know. And because now I know you better, I'm positive you had a reason to do what you did. And that it's got to be something more than him having an affair with my mother.'

'Quite a speech,' said Eileen, displaying no emotion.

'Quite a situation,' said Ellie.

The car behind them started honking, but neither of them showed any sign of hearing it.

'I guessed this was going to happen,' Eileen said to

her lap. 'That if you stayed in London, the time would come.' She considered for a moment before turning to Ellie and saying: 'If you're sure you want to know, then, all right, I will. I'll tell you.'

'Jesus, Eileen, you really are one for surprises. I never thought it'd be this easy. I thought I'd at least have to get you a bit pissed.' She slapped the steering wheel. 'What the hell. Let's get this thing parked and go and have a drink anyway.'

Ellie pulled forward at speed, bouncing the car forward in a series of amateurish leaps, watched with knowing disdain by the driver of the car behind them.

'There used to be an Italian place in James Street,' said Eileen, steadying herself with a hand on the dashboard. 'Not far from here. I used to have lunch there with Sophie Kessler, years ago, after we'd been shopping. It had little booths that made it cosy – and private. It might still be there.'

They emerged from the car park, just as fat summer raindrops the size of two-pence pieces started splattering down on to the hot pavement.

'You up to running?' asked Ellie, taking Eileen by the arm.

Eileen nodded and Ellie hurried her across the parched grass to the cover of an overhanging canopy at the back entrance of a big department store.

'You'll be all right here for a couple of minutes,' said Ellie, noting how Eileen nervously distanced herself from the huddle of shoppers doing their best to protect themselves and their bags from the worst of the cloudburst. She obviously preferred to risk getting wet than stand close to them. 'I won't leave you for long, I'll just nip back and fetch my umbrella from the boot.'

With that she sprinted back to the car park, holding her handbag over her head in a futile attempt to keep her hair dry from the now teeming rain.

Ellie was just about to slip the car key into the lock, when a rough hand clapped over her mouth. 'Give us your bag, bitch.'

In a single fluid move, Ellie spun round as she ripped the hand away from her face and twisted it up the back of its owner – a scruffy-looking teenager – making him yelp with pain. In her other hand Ellie had her car key, which she touched to the side of his neck. 'You picked the wrong fecking one with me, you cheeky little bastard. You dare move and I'll rip your bloody throat out for you.'

The boy held his head as still as he could, not knowing that all she was holding to his flesh was a key. 'Listen, darling, I –'

'No, if you've got any sense *you'll* listen. I come from a very scary family, a family who would really hate it if anything nasty happened to me. But today must be your lucky day, because I'm the nice one. So I'm going to let you go. But first I'm going to give you a warning. You never, ever come down here again, or you might just be unlucky, make a mistake, and pick on me again. And next time perhaps I'll forget my manners and have you on your back with my heel in your face before you know what's hit you. Or maybe worse, I'll get one of my big brothers to do it for me. Do you understand me?'

He risked the briefest of nods.

'Okay.' She took a breath and let him go.

Let him go? Was that the stupidest thing she had ever done?

Ellie could have wept with relief as the youth zig-zagged off towards the shadows of the stairwell. She dropped her head and closed her eyes, concentrating on nothing but being still, the way she did when she fell from a horse and had to calm herself before getting back in the saddle.

'Ellie?' It was Eileen. She was standing by the lifts, her hair glistening with raindrops in the dull glow of the fly-dirt-encrusted strip lighting.

Eileen started running towards her. 'What's wrong? Are you all right? Is everything okay?'

'Sure, everything's grand. But look at you, you're all wet.'

'I couldn't stand there with all those people any more, I . . .'

Her words trailed away. 'But never mind that. That scruff you were talking to, was he bothering you?'

'No! The eejit thought I'd *lend* him some money,' she said, rolling her eyes as if nothing of any account had happened. 'Can you believe it?'

'This isn't Ireland, you know, Ellie.' There was now something that looked almost like motherly concern on Eileen's face. 'People in London can be very dangerous.'

Ellie, her mouth open and her brow lowered, turned away from Eileen on the pretext of opening the boot to search out the umbrella.

London can be dangerous?

Was the woman being sarcastic? It was genuinely hard to tell. But, whichever way you looked at it, it was a bit rich coming from a woman who had killed her own husband. Still, she'd have to swallow those feelings if she was to have any hope of finding out the truth about her father's death.

This was going to be some drink.

While Ellie and Eileen were joining the early-lunch crowd in the trattoria in James Street, Patricia was standing in the doorway of a very expensive hair stylist's in a square at the back of Regent Street. She was looking up at the sky. The rain was still pouring down and the clouds were low, dark and heavy, threatening a long, wet, muggy afternoon.

From the corner of her eye, she caught the image of a well-dressed man, hurrying along the street, holding a copy of the *Daily Telegraph* over his head as a makeshift umbrella.

'I'd go back inside for a while, if I were you,' he smiled at her over his shoulder as he trotted past.

'Don't want to spoil that hair of yours, young lady. Very pretty.'

Patricia looked at him as if he'd lost his mind.

Pretty? No one had called her that in years. She turned and considered her reflection in the plate-glass window of the salon.

Maybe she didn't look too bad after all. And maybe Ellie was right – perhaps Pete Mac had better watch out if he didn't want to lose her.

Eileen broke a bread stick in two, was about to eat a piece of it, but changed her mind and placed the bits side by side on the pink tablecloth.

'When I went in that place, you know, the prison, I was so cocky.'

'You, Eileen? Cocky? I can hardly believe that.'

'What I mean is, I thought all the women and the girls in there were ignorant. Beneath me. Despite what I'd done – killing my own husband – I felt superior to them. But the thing I hadn't worked out, not back then, was that you can cure ignorance. You can learn, find out how to change things. Make them better. But what you can't change is stupidity. No, that's another thing entirely. If you're stupid you're stuck with it. And that wasn't only a problem for a lot of those women in there, I soon realised it was my problem too. I understand that I'm as stupid as hell. I chose to do what I did because I honestly thought it would be best for my children. That it was the way to make it all stop.'

Ellie leaned forward, her expression and body language challenging whatever Eileen had to say. 'I know my father wasn't exactly a saint – I remember, Aunt Mary always used to make the joke: my brother Gabriel, he was no angel – but I don't understand what was so bad about him for you to kill him.'

'Now you're showing your ignorance, Ellie. Well, I hope it's ignorance, and not stupidity.'

'What do you mean?'

'Too many women stay with men, bad men, because they think they have no choice. They put up with them, and suffer at their hands just because they're married to them, when what they should be doing is protecting themselves and their children by getting them as far away from them as they can.'

'So why didn't you leave?'

'Because women like me don't do that.'

'That makes no sense.'

'I know.' Eileen looked around as if seeking help. 'Look, there was this woman, she came to the prison to give us a talk one day. She was an "expert" on wife battering – if you can believe such a thing exists. She came in to help us poor souls by giving us the benefit of her wisdom. She was a small-minded do-gooder in lots of ways, talked down to us, acted much the same way as I'd acted towards the other women when I'd first gone in there, I suppose. But she did tell us one incredible thing.'

She sipped at her drink, wanting time rather than

the taste of the wine. 'Every single week, two women die at the hands of their own men. Can you believe it?'

Ellie shrank back in her seat. 'Are you saying my father used to beat you?'

Eileen lifted her chin and stared up at the ceiling. 'No. But I am saying he was a violent bully. And it was his fault that Catherine died.'

'No, that can't be right.'

'Believe me, it can. There was trouble with the Kesslers. He told the boys to sort it out, made them take a shotgun to frighten them. But what none of us knew – apart from Luke – was that Sammy Kessler was seeing Catherine. She was in the car with Sammy when the gun went off. It hit her in the neck. She stood no chance.'

'No!'

'Yes. If Gabriel hadn't made the boys take the gun, my baby, your sister, would still be alive today. I couldn't take any more. When Catherine died, I knew I had to stop him. Stop him from destroying the rest of my children.'

'And you want me to believe that's why you killed him?'

'It's the truth.'

'But I don't understand. Luke and Brendan both told me that Catherine died in a car crash.'

'That's what they wanted everyone to believe.' Eileen unfolded and refolded her napkin. 'But it wasn't true. The truth is, it was Gabriel's fault. Simple as that. Trouble is, I know now – too late – that my killing him was all a stupid waste. Regardless of anything I did – or can do – the boys are going exactly the same way as their father.'

'As *my* father.'

Eileen didn't comment on the correction. 'Even Luke. No matter how he tries to convince me – and himself – otherwise, I know he's not the innocent he pretends to be.' Eileen pressed her fingers to her lips. 'And look at yourself, Ellie, caught up with Brendan. Impressed by his madness – and don't try to pretend otherwise. Because I know how it is. Their world is a mad, bad place, and they're spiralling down into its vile and rotten depths. Luke as well as Brendan. And you have to think about whether you want to go with them.'

'Aren't you being a bit –'

Eileen ploughed on as if Ellie hadn't spoken. 'Maybe if I'd not done it, if I'd not killed him, but had just stayed at home, maybe then I might at least have been able to have some influence over Luke.'

Eileen moved the pieces of the bread stick around, placing them back together as if it was a single whole again. 'I don't know. I don't know anything any more.'

Ellie took a big gulp of her Chianti. 'Sure, you're not alone there, Eileen.'

Chapter 19

Less than a mile away from the restaurant where, a couple of days ago, Ellie had sat listening to Eileen, and even closer to the hair salon where Patricia had begun to realise that she might actually have some value as a woman, the Kesslers were in the back room of one of what they referred to as their dirty bookshops. Though books were only a part of the merchandise they had on offer.

In the front of the shop, Bug Eye, the peeping Tom who worked the public counter, was eavesdropping rather than spying for a change. Ignoring his smattering of Monday-morning customers, he was lurking by the door to the back room, curious to know why the young man with the blond Afro and the extravagant dress sense was in there talking to Danny, Sammy and Maurice.

'Like I say, I don't know anything about any of your past arguments with the O'Donnells, that was all before my time,' Milo was saying, leaning in his usual casual way against a wall full of shelves stacked with Super 8 cine films. 'Except what I've heard from that trappy git, Pete Mac, of course. But I'm just here to let you know what I do know – that Brendan

O'Donnell is intending to have all your trade off you. Every bit of speed you bring in, he's planning to have it.'

He offered round his cigarettes. Only Maurice took one.

'And how do you know that then, feller?'

'He wants me to handle it all for him.'

'*You what?*' Danny lunged forward, but Maurice stopped him before he could actually grab hold of Milo.

'And,' Milo went on, apparently not fazed at all, 'before you think you can just go round there team-handed and stop him with a bit of well-placed violence, you ought to know that he's well in with the Irish.'

'Do us a favour.' It was Sammy, he looked knowingly at Daniel. 'Now we know you're talking a load of bollocks. Course O'Donnell's in with the Irish. He *is* fucking Irish. Just like your family are – *Flanagan.*'

'I mean the grown-up Irish.' Milo took a moment to light his and Maurice's cigarettes, letting his words sink in. 'The very bad, political boys. The ones with the fucking bombs and that. Which means that not only have you got to be careful, but I have too. Because I intend to do up Mr O'Donnell like an 'alf-rotten kipper, and I definitely don't want that lot on me back.'

'Aw yeah?' Sammy still sounded sceptical. 'Why would you do that then?'

'Because that bloke has got right up my nose lately, and I ain't having it. And that's why I came here today – with the information about the speed – because I thought that might make you feel the same way about him as I do.'

'We already do, thanks, feller,' said Maurice. 'We take all the risks selling the merchandise in the shops and he takes the majority cut. We might as well be running a fucking supermarket for him.'

'You finished talking about our private business, have you, Maury?' Daniel said flatly. He sat down on the corner of a packing case and folded his arms. 'Look, Flanagan, much as I'd like to think I could trust you, I don't know the strength of you, do I, mate? First of all, you shove that bloody note under me nose at the boxing, like a kid in the fucking playground, then you come bowling in here like you was our best friend or something. But how do I know this ain't a set-up? That you ain't doing this for the O'Donnells. Sticking your snotty Irish nose in our business.'

'I won't take offence, Danny, cos I understand your concerns. But I'm gonna prove myself. I guarantee it. See, I've got a way to have them bastards. Then you, and me – all of us – we'll all be laughing.'

'At least listen to him, feller,' said Maurice, pointing to Milo with his cigarette. 'I know that I for one would very much like to keep all this fucking gelt we're earning. You've seen the figures on that calculator thing of your dad's, Daniel, seen them with your own bloody eyes. The tills are overflowing, fivers bursting out of the bastards. And what happens, we have to clear them out to pay them fuckers for their sodding *merchandise*.'

'Maury.' Danny's voice was warning his cousin, but he paid no heed.

'How about you, Sam?'

Sammy shrugged. 'You know Danny's always made these decisions.'

'Okay, Danny,' said Milo, totally businesslike, not a sign of the cheeky cockney always up for a laugh. 'Like I said, I'm gonna have the O'Donnells, so hear me out and just say if you're interested.'

'You've got five minutes.'

'Fine.' Milo grinned. 'Now, d'you happen to know anyone in Brixton who owes your family a favour?'

'Why?'

'Because we are gonna send a message to Barry Ellis.'

Ellie and Patricia were in the communal changing room of one of the many fashionable boutiques on Kensington High Street. Patricia was looking around self-consciously. Despite the fact that it was a Monday morning, and that she and Ellie were the only two women in there, Patricia still felt horribly awkward.

It was the first time she'd ever been expected to take off her clothes in such a public space before – face it, she just wasn't the sort of person who did that kind of thing. These days, she wasn't even used to taking them off in front of Pete Mac.

'Are you okay, Pat?' Ellie asked, clearly amused by her half-sister's discomfort.

'Yeah, course I am. And I'm really glad you persuaded me to come today. Especially when I see your'n and Sandy's clothes. I mean, I'm not exactly a fashion plate these days, am I? Not that you knew me when I was younger of course,' she babbled nervously.

'I wish I had known you,' said Ellie, suddenly serious.

Patricia was too caught up with trying to keep herself decent to notice. 'This is nice,' she gasped, struggling to pull up the straps of the halter-neck dress from somewhere deep down in the neckline of the brown-and-cream patterned blouse that Ellie had insisted Patricia should borrow from her. 'I'd never have chosen this on my own. It was bad enough going to that hairdresser's by myself, but I just know I wouldn't have had the courage to come into a place like this without you.'

'Good thing too,' laughed Ellie. 'Carrying on like that by yourself, they'd have called security. You look like you've been let out for the day.'

Ellie stepped forward and, with a few unceremonious tugs and jerks, hoiked the blouse right over

Patricia's head, leaving her in just her bra and the unfastened dress.

'Ellie!'

'What? Sure, you've still got your undies on.' She looked at it critically. 'And doesn't that look like it was made before the war? Even Aunt Mary wears less scaffolding under her bosoms than that thing you've got on there.'

'It's comfortable,' Patricia said, straining to pull up the dress and secure the straps behind her neck without exposing too much flesh. 'And anyway, what does it matter? Who cares about the state of my underwear?'

'You should care, that's who,' said Ellie firmly.

'There.' Patricia turned to look at her reflection in the mirrored walls. 'What do you think?'

'Hang on.' Without comment, Ellie unhooked the fastening of Patricia's now exposed bra. 'Let's get this thing off you and have a proper look.'

Patricia checked guiltily about her, as if she'd just been caught trying to stuff a stolen frock down her knickers, and then eased the bra straps down over her arms.

'So, tell me, have you ever thought about having your tits made bigger, Patricia?'

'*What did you say?*'

'I saw an article about it in a magazine. *Cosmo*, or *Nova*, I think it was. They can do it, you know. Lift 'em high and blow 'em up like balloons. It's a grand

236

idea. Especially for a woman of your age. Sure, it'd give you a new lease of life.'

'You cheeky mare, I'm only thirty-seven.'

'First mistake, Patricia. Never admit to being more than twenty-nine.'

Ellie turned sideways on to the mirror and studied her own reflection as she cupped her breasts in her hands.

'Milo reckons mine are perfect.'

'Milo?'

In reply, Ellie flashed her eyebrows and her breasts – lifting her cheesecloth shirt up over her face – making Patricia snort out loud.

'You are so rude, Ellie.'

'No I'm not. I'm just my own woman. Like you're going to be when I finish with you.'

'I don't know about that.'

'Well, I do. Because no one treats my sister the way that that Peter MacRiordan treats you.'

Patricia avoided Ellie's gaze, busying herself searching through the mound of garments that Ellie had insisted they take into the changing room.

'What was Dad like, Pat? Did he treat Eileen the way Pete Mac treats you? Is that why you put up with it? Because it was what you got used to when you were a kid?'

Patricia clutched the embroidered velvet pinafore dress she had selected from the pile to her chest. 'This is a bit out of the blue.' She sounded flustered.

'Not for me, it's not. I think about it all the time. What he was like, why Eileen did what she did. Even about Aunt Mary putting up with Uncle Sean. He's an eejit, that one. He'd drive a saint to murder, let alone a bitch like Mary. But there's your mam, quiet, respectable even, and she goes and does something like that. I'm telling you, Pat, I've heard her version of it, but it's still all a bloody mystery to me. And getting to the bottom of anything in this family's worse than breaking in a bad-tempered colt – you never know when you're going to get a kick up the arse.'

'Mum hasn't been herself since . . . Aw, you know.'

'I understand that. But Eileen's told me stuff about my dad, and Catherine, and how she died. But it's nothing like Luke and Brendan have told me. I'm sure Luke knows more than he's letting on. But will he say anything? Will he feck. And as for Brendan, there's no point even considering asking that one. It's like they're all talking in code, hiding things, protecting one another. But I'm bloody family, for God's sake.'

Patricia dropped her hands from her chest, letting the dress fall to the floor. 'If I tell you the truth, Ellie – the truth that I know anyway – about Dad's drinking, and his temper, and his womanising, and . . .' Her throat flushed red, as her words staggered to a painful halt.

'I promise I won't tell anyone. You don't have any

worries there, Pat. And, to make it fair, you're not to tell anyone about me and Milo.'

'By anyone, I presume you mean Brendan.'

'Of course I mean Brendan. Finding your way with that one is like dealing with Aunt Mary in a bloody three-piece suit.'

Chapter 20

Despite it being only eleven o'clock, DI Bert Hammond was drinking whiskey with Brendan in the O'Donnells' Bella Vista club in Shoreditch. Or rather he was holding a full glass of the stuff, which he hadn't so much as sniffed at, let alone tasted. He left the heavy boozing to Brendan, who was making a good job of finishing his second refill, only just drawing the line at knocking it back in one go.

DI Hammond looked about him, as if checking for eavesdroppers – even though there wasn't a single customer in the whole place, and the barman had, very sensibly, put himself far away enough from them so as not to be accused of the punishable offence of sticking his oar in where it wasn't welcome.

Hammond leaned towards Brendan and said in low, confidential tones: 'I'm glad you could meet me this morning, Brendan. You see I've had a troubling weekend. Very troubling. The good lady and I were meant to be going home on a little trip to Birmingham to see her mother, but I was – unfortunately – otherwise engaged, having to have meetings with some very objectionable people.'

He made another, slightly more dramatic check

around the still-punterless room. 'Thing is,' he went on, rubbing his stubbly, salt-and-pepper moustache with the knuckle of his index finger, 'there are a lot of very unpleasant rumours flying around.'

'Aw yes, Bert?' said Brendan, only half listening, his real concern being that the barman should fill the now empty glass he had just set down on the counter. 'And what sort of rumours would they be then?'

'I'm afraid to say they're about your brother Luke.'

Brendan was immediately on the alert. He didn't like people talking about his family, and he especially didn't like it when people had things to say about his brother, but most of all he didn't like it when people said smart-arsed things about his brother being 'different'.

'Aw yeah, Bert. What sort of things would they be then?'

'That he's started running knocking shops.'

Brendan snorted with aggressive, dismissive laughter.

'Oh dear, Brendan, I don't think that's the right attitude to take at all. I know I wouldn't find it funny, if I were you, because that's not the half of what they're saying.' That stopped the flash, cockney git in his tracks. 'In fact,' Hammond went on, noting with pleasure every tiny twitch on Brendan's face that showed the policeman had hit the target, 'there are so many rumours flying around about all manner of things to do with your family – and the Kesslers, as it happens – that it would have me rather worried if I were in your position. Silly little things, admittedly, in some cases, but from people who, although they don't know that much, know enough to start some very nasty aggravation if they feel like it.'

Brendan *really* didn't like this. The Brummy wanker was acting as if he was the one calling all the fucking shots. He knew plenty of senior coppers who played the potentially dangerous game of socialising with the very people they were supposed to be nicking. And, usually, it suited them all: wheels were oiled and everyone got on with their business, and enjoyed the backhanders, thank you very much all round. But there was something about this bloke that was starting to get on Brendan's nerves.

He slammed down his glass. 'Who? Just tell me the bastards' names, and I'll show 'em fucking rumours. I'll shut this crap down right now.'

'Don't go getting yourself all agitated, Brendan. It's no one who needs matter. Not for now, anyway.' Hammond was really enjoying himself, stirring things up with his invented stories that could – oh so easily – be true. Carry on at this rate, and he'd not only have all the evidence his superiors wanted about corruption in the force, but he'd have a very tasty bonus, the East End jackpot – plenty of solid gold dirt on the O'Donnells and the Kesslers.

He looked at his watch. 'But I'll make sure I keep

you informed if there are any further developments. That's all I have to say for now, as I'd better be on my way.'

But Brendan had plenty more to say, and he wanted Hammond to hear every word of it. 'No, hang on a minute. About Luke. On my life, Bert, he's a fucking landlord, nothing more. We all know how things have changed round here. And he's taken advantage of it and he's gone legit. I swear he has. He's got all these respectable building contracts, and . . .'

Brendan was casting about wildly, he couldn't let Luke get pulled in over something like this – over anything – he wasn't strong like Brendan. He'd crack like cheaply laid tarmac if they got hold of him.

'I'm telling you. Contracts with local authorities and everything.'

'What, like that Mr Paulson we've all been reading about in the newspapers? He's been a very naughty boy according to those reports. Bribes, dodgy contacts, and who knows what else he's been up to. And I know it's getting him into a whole lot of trouble, having dealings with local authorities. You don't mean to tell me your brother's involved in that sort of business, do you, Brendan?'

'I told you, on my life, Bert, he –'

'Listen to me, Brendan, I'm getting in very deep here, letting you know the score on all this, but I'm warning you: there are people who don't like outsiders running toms round there. You . . . People should know that and take note. All right? Now, I really do have to be on my way.'

The moment Brendan saw Hammond steer his car out on to Folgate Street, he rushed back into the club, reached across the bar and snatched his car keys from the hook under the counter.

'If any of the boys want me, I'm shooting round Luke's. And I'll be back at the cab office early afternoon.'

Brendan drove to Frith Street in less than fifteen minutes, ignoring the abuse from other drivers as he cut them up, jumping red lights, and narrowly missing those pedestrians who were daring enough to use zebra crossings in front of him. And when he slammed to a halt and parked outside the Moulin Bleu, he didn't even bother to look for someone to mind his car. He just locked it up and left it to the mercies of Soho.

After leaning on the bell for a good thirty seconds, Brendan was about to leave and try somewhere else, when the door opened and Luke stood there in front of him, wet-haired, barefoot, and wearing only a pair of faded, flared jeans.

'Sorry, Brendan,' he said, 'you caught me in the shower.'

'You're gonna be even sorrier when I've finished with you, you prat. Now get upstairs.'

Brendan followed his brother up to the top of the nondescript stairway, and then into the narrow lobby and through the door into Luke's large, bright living room.

'Hammond's tipped me the wink,' Brendan said, pacing up and down like an expectant father in a hospital waiting room. 'He knows what's going on in your properties.'

He spun round and jabbed a furious finger in Luke's face. 'This could blow everything, you stupid, fucking hypocrite. Once they start nosing around your so-called respectable stuff, we'll all be dropped right in it. The clubs, the escorts, the drugs, the films, even the fucking minicabs. There'll be no excuse to keep them out. And they'll just keep digging. And digging. And you don't even wanna know what the Irishmen'd do if the law start sniffing around over them guns.'

'No, this Hammond, he's got it all wrong, Brendan.' Luke's face was screwed up as if having to explain things to his brother was causing him great pain. 'I don't have anything to do with the girls.'

'So why have them there in the first fucking place? It's not even our sodding patch. People – them bastard Kesslers for a start – are gonna get the hump with you, with us, operating out that far east. You know we gave them our word that they could have that territory if they wanted it. And it's us who's meant to have the fucking hump with them, not the other way round, you moron. This could make us look stupid, Luke. *Stupid.*' Flecks of saliva were bubbling in the corners of Brendan's mouth.

'We did them a favour, acted like big men, let them have that area – the scraps off our table – and now we're creeping back there like two-bob merchants nicking it back. And I don't fucking like it.'

'Don't go getting narky with me, Brendan.' Luke had his chin in the air, a man wronged by his brother's accusations. 'It's not like I'm pimping for 'em or nothing. All them girls work for themselves. They just pay me for the rooms, that's all. I get a good day rate off 'em. And cos they don't care what state the places are in, it's an ideal set-up. As soon as I get enough money to buy up a few more places, I'll be able to invest in the first of them warehouses down the docks.'

'For fuck's sake, Luke.' Brendan threw up his arms, totally exasperated, then pulled off his jacket and threw it over one of the low-slung leather and chrome armchairs. 'I think we'd better have a proper talk about this, with you explaining exactly what you think you're up to, mate. Come on, let's sit down and have a drink. No, hang on.' He swiped the back of his hand across his mouth. 'I've already had a fucking skinful. Let's have a cuppa tea instead.'

Brendan started walking towards the kitchen door at the far end of the room.

'No, Brendan, please, sit down. I'll make you a cup and bring it through.'

But Brendan was already walking through the kitchen door.

As he stepped inside Brendan did a double take that wouldn't have shamed the Keystone Kops. 'What the fuck is he doing here?'

Nicky Wright, sitting at the breakfast counter wearing just a T-shirt and a pair of underpants, shrugged. 'Having a bit of a late breakfast.'

Brendan turned round and banged straight into Luke.

He smacked him flat up against the kitchen wall. 'I don't believe this, Luke. I've been through there saying all sorts of fucking private things about the business, and this little prick's been sitting here listening. Why didn't you fucking tell me he was here?'

Brendan didn't wait for Luke to reply. He shoved his brother to one side and pushed past him back into the living room. He snatched his jacket off the chair and headed for the door. 'You are beginning to seriously fucking annoy me, mate,' he said without looking round.

He paused in the doorway, still staring straight ahead, unable to look his brother in the eye. 'I just hope, Luke – really, genuinely, seriously, fucking hope – that that little slag back in there ain't more important to you than your family.'

'Brendan, he won't say anything, I –'

That was as far as Luke got before Brendan slammed the door on him and raced down the stairs out into the streets of Soho.

Chapter 21

'Brendan shouldn't be long now, Luke,' said Sandy, her neck stretched out as she peered wide-eyed at her reflection in the mirror stuck inside the lid of her make-up bag. She was stroking a crescent of plum-coloured shadow on to her eyelids, getting herself ready for an evening out on the town.

She lowered the silver quilted bag a few inches and looked over it at Luke, who was sitting across from her at the new farmhouse-kitchen table that she'd had delivered just the week before. The table that made *her* kitchen, overlooking *her* garden look even more beautiful than it already did, if that were possible. It was hard to take it all in at times – that this was really where she was living, that this was really all hers. That this was how her life was now.

'But you know what Brendan's like,' she added lightly. 'He said we were going out for something to eat at half eight, and it's already, what?' She glanced up at the wall clock. 'Nearly ten past already. Looks like something's come up, and if it has, he could be hours.'

She put the little brush back in its case. 'You sure there's nothing I can help you with?'

'No, you're all right, San. Long as I'm not in your way.'

'You're fine,' she said, but from the tension in his face, and the way he was fiddling with his car keys, she couldn't help feeling that Luke wasn't fine at all.

And she was right. Since Brendan had stormed out of Luke's flat yesterday lunchtime, warning him that he should put his family first, and that his loyalty was to them and not to Nicky, Luke hadn't been able to think about very much else. He'd wound up getting himself in such a state over it that he'd rowed with Nicky about whether they were going to spend the evening watching *Kojak* or listening to Nicky's latest Elton John album. It had got that ridiculous.

As a result of Luke's shouting and hollering, Nicky had stomped out of the flat saying he never wanted to see Luke again. And he hadn't come back all night, although Luke was sure he'd be home soon. They loved each other too much to let something as stupid as a row over whether or not they were going to watch the telly separate them.

Nicky was the one he wanted to spend the rest of his life with, and Nicky knew it. Luke only wished he had the courage to admit it to Brendan. But if he could unravel this mess with his brother, then he would at least have started moving in the right direction. He couldn't let things stay messed up, not when he was so close to getting his life the way he wanted. He was going to run a strong, legitimate business that had nothing to do with the family. And that was why he'd come to talk to Brendan. Luke was going to explain that he'd thought about what Brendan had said, and he'd decided to give all the girls six months' notice. That would let him rack up a nice chunk of rent, which, added to the profit he'd make when he sold the houses, would leave him laughing. He'd have a good lump of that stake he needed to buy his first warehouse. It would be the beginnings of his property empire, and of his and Nicky's new life together.

'Talk of the devil,' said Sandy, getting to her feet, as the doorbell chimed. 'That'll be him now. Probably got his arms full of goodies and can't manage the key, the silly bugger. Honestly, you should see the things he brings home for me, Luke.'

She was talking to him over her shoulder as she walked out to the hall. 'He's so generous. Been that way ever since the wedding. Treats me like I'm some kind of a princess or something. I'm telling you, it takes some getting used to after what I've had to cope with over the past few years.'

But it wasn't Brendan.

When Sandy opened the door she was confronted by Anthony, who almost blocked out the light with his massive bulk, and – as far as Sandy could make out – Amber, as she called herself, one of the escort girls. Because, despite the warmth of the summer evening, Anthony was wearing a voluminous black

251

mac, and he had the girl tucked away in its folds under his arm, shielding her from view.

Sandy didn't say a word, she just leaned back against the wall and let them pass her into the hallway.

For Anthony to turn up unannounced or uninvited with one of the escorts there had to be something very wrong.

'Go through to the kitchen, Anthony,' she said, then added hurriedly before he went in: 'Luke's in there.' She didn't want anyone saying anything out of turn because they thought they were speaking in private. That could start all sorts of trouble. And she didn't want that – not in her newly decorated kitchen, she didn't.

Anthony raised his head towards Luke in silent greeting and, surprisingly gently for such a big man, unwrapped his billowing coat from around Amber's shoulders.

Luke drew in his breath so loudly that Sandy turned to look at him rather than at her unexpected guests.

'Bloody hell,' murmured Luke, rising to his feet in almost cartoonish slow motion. 'What the fuck's happened to her?'

Sandy followed Luke's gaze to where Amber was standing, or rather bending over the table. She was gripping it for support, her chest heaving as she tried to surf across the pain. Almost the entire front of her body-hugging, ivory satin catsuit was stained with blood, her hair was soaking wet, and the side of her face that had been hidden by Anthony's coat looked as if it had been repeatedly smashed in with a house brick.

'Sorry for bringing her round here, San, but I didn't know what else to do. Couldn't take her to the hospital in this state, could I?'

Anthony pulled out a chair and eased Anber slowly down on to it. 'She didn't want to do what the punter wanted,' he said, his big face creased into a deep, angry frown. 'So he decided to *punish* her, the fucker. Doing that to a woman.'

He turned to Sandy. 'Sorry for the language, San, only it gets to me, how a so-called man could do something like that to a woman. He smacked the hell out of her, then he pissed over her – can you believe that? You should smell the poor cow's hair. Then he cleared off and left her in the hotel room. If you really think she does need the hospital, I could run her down there.'

Sandy very calmly walked over to him and put a hand gently on his massive forearm. 'No, not the hospital, you were right in the first place. That wouldn't be a very good idea. Too many questions. I'll see to things here now, Anthony. Amber did the right thing calling you. Just like she'd been told if there was ever any trouble, cos you're a good bloke and you handle these things well. Now you go and get yourself a drink. The cabinet's in the living room. Up on the first floor. Luke'll show you where.'

Glad of any excuse to get away from the upsetting – bewildering – sight of a battered woman, Anthony and Luke shot up the stairs in pursuit of the numbing effects of a large glass of anything containing alcohol.

'I couldn't believe it,' mumbled Amber through her torn and puffy lips. 'The things he wanted to do to me, Mrs O'Donnell. Wanted to put these things inside me. Said he'd read about it in these magazines. He had them with him. In his briefcase. Sharp things. Big things. Said he wanted me to look at them with him. Then do it. He seemed so decent at first. Nicely spoken and everything. And the hotel was lovely.' She started crying. 'I think he broke some of my teeth. It was horrible, really horrible. I thought he was going to kill me. It was only when I started screaming that he ran away and left me.'

Sandy put a cork place mat on the table then fetched a Pyrex bowl full of warm salt water and a clean tea towel from one of the drawers. She dampened the cloth and wiped it across Amber's cheek. Amber moaned pitifully. 'That really hurts, Mrs O'Donnell. Please, be careful.'

Sandy straightened up and took a deep breath. 'Stop whining, darling,' she said, dabbing again at the girl's bloody face. 'It's how we earn our living, giving blokes what they want. And do us a favour and stop wriggling about, will you, you're getting blood on my new table.'

On the other side of the kitchen door, Luke – holding a glass in each of his hands for Sandy and Amber, and a fresh bottle of whiskey under his arm – was listening with a baffled frown on his face. *How we earn our living*? He'd never heard Sandy talk like that before.

He waited long enough for her not to think that he might have overheard her, and then knocked quietly.

'Okay to come in?' he called.

'Sure, and tell Anthony to come down as well, while you're at it. These cuts are not half as bad as they look. He can get her off home once he's finished his drink.'

Much as he would have liked to have got out of there – although preferably without a beaten and bruised woman in tow, who, if anyone saw them, would no doubt raise eyebrows as well as questions about whether he was the culprit – Anthony didn't get the chance, because at a quarter to nine, and without a word of explanation for his lateness to Sandy, Brendan arrived home.

He ruffled Sandy's hair – messing up the carefully tousled look she'd created especially for their evening out – and threw his car keys on the new table, making her cringe. Then he turned to Luke and Anthony. 'Glad you two are here.'

He reached for the bottle of whiskey and poured himself a large measure into one of the glasses, apparently not caring that someone had already been drinking from it.

'Get her out of the way, San,' he said, acknowledging Amber's presence for the first time. 'Stick her in a minicab or something. I wanna talk to the boys in private.'

Sandy didn't have to ask if she too was being dismissed.

Brendan drained his glass and refilled it, while he waited for Sandy to remove Amber and herself from his presence, then he began.

'I've been contacted by the Irishmen. Been asked to get another consignment ready for shipping over there. A big one. We've got to fund it from our end, but then they're gonna as good as double our money soon as we deliver.'

'How's the delivery being done?' Luke didn't really need to ask.

'Same as before. Ellie driving the horsebox. That worked well.'

'Brendan, you can't get her involved again. Once was bad enough, but –'

'*Don't even think about questioning me, Luke.*' The sound of Brendan cracking his glass down on the table was drowned out by the volume of his voice. 'Because after that fucking *surprise* you sprung on me in your flat yesterday – with that little tosspot sitting there looking at me like he had every right – I don't think you're in any position, do you?'

Anthony kept his gaze fixed firmly on the glass in front of him. He was beginning to think that taking Amber home hadn't been such a bad proposition after all. Brendan in this sort of a mood wasn't a pretty sight.

Brendan topped up all their glasses to the brim. 'This is a great opportunity,' he said, as if he hadn't just been shouting like a maniac. 'Good as printing money, plus the Irishmen are the right people to have on our side. And while we're at it we're gonna take over the Kesslers' speed business and all, set ourselves up as sole distributors and importers. Cos that sort of money's gonna come in handy to fund these Irish deals.'

Anthony and Luke watched him drain his glass and pour himself yet another drink.

'And I've been thinking about what Hammond said to me the other day about your property, Luke, and, d'you know what I realised? We've been too generous with them Kessler bastards. For far too fucking long. We've been so soft with 'em, they've started taking our kindness for fucking silliness.'

He stretched an arm around Luke's shoulders. 'I dunno about you, brother, but I feel just about ready for a fight with them cunts.'

Chapter 22

It was Sunday lunchtime, and the Rose and Punchbowl pub in Stepney was packed with regulars enjoying a drink as they tucked into the roast potatoes, prawns and cockles set out on the tables and the bar by the landlord's wife.

The snacks were always regarded as a treat, a generous gesture, with nobody minding that they were also there to encourage a healthy thirst among the customers. It wasn't as though they were the type of punters who needed to have their arms twisted up their backs to encourage them to sup a few more pints, anyway.

Brendan, Luke, Pete Mac, Anthony and Kevin Marsh were sitting at a table in a far corner, close to a door marked 'Private', which led to the upstairs living accommodation. It was a place where they presumed they wouldn't be disturbed.

Brendan was floating his scheme for the job that would supply the balance of the cash to fund the arms deal with the Irish, and that would pump-prime the rest of his plans – the plans that would increase the O'Donnells' trade in every existing sector, and in a few, very profitable, new ones. And if it all went the way he hoped it would, there would also be enough cash left over to make up the shortfall for the stake Luke needed to start his new property business over in the docks. If he really had to, and if he still thought it was a sensible idea.

But, best of all, it would put the Kesslers right back where they belonged, and where they deserved to be – at the bottom of the stinking heap, just like the snivelling two-bob merchants they'd been before the O'Donnells had been so generous to them.

Brendan's scheme was simple: they were going to take out a security van.

The others heard him out politely enough – they weren't stupid, this was Brendan O'Donnell – but when he'd finished they were all left feeling distinctly unconvinced.

As usual, it was Pete Mac who blundered in at the front of the queue.

'Nah, Brendan, that'll never work. It's no good, not nowadays. They've got all them radios and that, ain't they? We'd never get away with it.'

'And that, genius,' Brendan said, rapping his knuckles on Pete Mac's forehead, 'is why I've planned it and not you, you pudden.'

Pete Mac's lips turned down in a petulant snarl. He knew the rest of them agreed with him, it was a barmy idea, but, of course, it had been him who'd been brave enough to say so. And him who'd been made to look like the prize idiot. Again.

It gave him the right hump. Perhaps Brendan thought it made him look big, humiliating his own brother-in-law in front of other people.

The cunt.

He swallowed down his pint in two gulps, and held up the empty glass without even bothering to look towards the bar.

A smiling, late-middle-aged woman appeared beside him. 'Yes, Pete? Same again?'

He stared ahead of him. 'Yes *the same again*,' he said in a mocking imitation of her voice. 'But it's Mr MacRiordan to you, you saucy mare.'

'Right, sorry, course it is. Sorry.' The woman flushed a deep, embarrassed shade of red. 'Mr MacRiordan. And can I get you other gentlemen anything?'

'Yes, please, darling,' said Brendan. 'Same again all round and stick it on the tab.' He palmed the woman a fiver, and winked at her. 'And have one yourself, love.'

'Thanks very much, Mr O'Donnell,' she said carefully.

'What's all this Mr O'Donnell lark?' Brendan asked with a pained frown. 'How long have we known each other, Ivy? Since I was a nipper with the arse hanging out of me trousers, that's how long. And if you can't call me Brendan, now who can?'

She smiled, just grateful to get away from the

table, and not giving a flying fart about what she was supposed to call the nasty bastards.

Brendan bent forward and jabbed an accusing finger in Pete Mac's face. 'Can't you get it into that thick nut of yours, *Mr fucking MacRiordan*, that you have to keep things nice? Not only is it ignorant treating an old girl like that, but you're drawing fucking attention to yourself. And to me. You dozy-eyed bastard.' He shook his head and reached across for one of the packets of cigarettes littering the table. 'Just keep things subtle, Pete, eh? Discreet. Try and remember, for fuck's sake. Or we might as well just put an advert on the fucking telly about what we're up to.'

With very inopportune timing another woman appeared at Pete Mac's side. And this one didn't need Pete Mac's rudeness to get anyone's attention. She was the sort who immediately had the eye of everyone in the bar trained right on her. And it wasn't because she was fetching drinks.

She was in her early twenties, with white, bleached-blonde hair piled up on top of her head, and curling down in tendrils around her neck and heavily made-up face. She was wearing a mid-calf, halter-neck cotton dress that, even if it hadn't been flapping open showing off her thighs, would have been just as revealing, as it was made as good as see-through by the brilliant, early-afternoon sunlight streaming in through the windows that had been flung open to let some air into the fug of alcohol and cigarette fumes. But perhaps the most striking thing about her – well, as far as the other customers were concerned – was that she'd come into the pub carrying a dinner plate full of Sunday roast, complete with sploshing gravy that had made its mark down her very ample front.

She smacked the plate down in front of Pete Mac, treating his shirt and tie to their very own share of the gravy.

'You like it here that much, do you, Pete? Well then, you stay here, you bastard!' Her voice came out as an alarming, croaky growl. It was very loud.

'One o'clock you said you was coming round mine for your dinner. One o-fucking-clock. Now it's ten past poxy two. And do you know how many boozers I've had to go to looking for you?' She turned about her, making sure she had the full attention of her audience. 'Cos he obviously wouldn't have been indoors with his old woman, now would he?'

With that she marched over to the door, accompanied by a chorus of appreciative cheers and whistles. But she hadn't finished yet. She stopped in the open doorway, jammed her fists into her waist and spun round to face Pete Mac.

'Aw yeah, I meant to say. You might as well stick with them two red-headed slags of your'n, you tosspot, cos me and Rhona don't wanna know about moving into your flat no more. In fact, you can stick your bleed'n flat right up your hairy arse.'

The effect of the now direct sunlight coming through the open door on her gauzy cotton dress had the whistles being drowned out by an enthusiastic round of applause.

Brendan puffed out his cheeks. 'So much for keeping things subtle, eh, Pete?' He closed his eyes and dragged his fingers down his face. 'Now, who the fuck was that?'

'Dunno her name,' said Pete Mac, picking up a slice of roast beef from the plate, tossing back his head and feeding it into his mouth. 'I met her and her mate at your'n and Sandy's wedding,' he went on, his mouth full of food. 'Nice girls. You slapped one of 'em, remember? I ain't sure, but I think she was the one what gave me the blow job.'

Brendan shook his head, clenching his fists under the table, just *this* short of punching him. 'You are so classy, Pete. D'you know that? Very classy indeed, mate.' He was barely able to spit out the words. 'You don't know how proud I am to call you my fucking brother-in-law.'

Pete Mac grinned, surprised to be the object of such praise.

There were strings of beef stuck in his teeth.

Carol Mercer was stretched out on the pristine white sheet she had bought from a stall down the Lane to cover the stained, lumpy mattress, which stank out the room in her stifling lodgings. She was flicking through an ancient copy of *Woman's Own* which she'd lifted from the family-planning clinic when she'd gone to renew her prescription for the pill. Not that she actually had any need to take the bloody thing. Sammy had made it more than clear that he had no intention of having anything more to do with her, and even Pete Mac had gone among the bloody missing.

And the sodding rent was due at the end of the rotten month.

She tossed the magazine to one side. She really had to get her head round what she was going to do about her situation or she would be left so deep in the shit that she'd never be able to claw her way out of it.

But what she wanted to do first, what she *needed* to do first for her own pride and satisfaction, was show the arseholes who'd pissed her off that they couldn't mess around with Carol Mercer and get away with it.

She might have looked, and even acted, like a sweet, dumb blonde, but she hadn't been forced to look after herself since she was just a little kid without learning a thing or two.

It was almost five o'clock on the following Friday morning, when the security-van driver changed lanes, and entered the northbound core of the Blackwall Tunnel.

'I love it these summer mornings,' he said, narrowing his eyes as he tried to accustom them to the suddenly dim lighting inside the tunnel. 'No traffic about, no rain or fog to stare at and give me a headache. And knowing I'm going to get all the deliveries done nice and early, then back home and out in the garden with a can of lager in my hand, and the paper on my knee till teatime. Then a little stroll down the boozer, and all knowing it'll still be light for hours. You can't whack it, can you?'

'No traffic? Well, how about them two cheeky buggers?' His mate nodded his head towards a family saloon and a post-office van that had cut in front of them and sped their way into the tunnel. 'They must be doing bloody seventy.'

'Ignore the idiots. Let them be the first ones in the cemetery.'

'I wouldn't have thought a mail van could go that fast.'

What happened next meant that neither of them noticed the third vehicle, a builder's truck pulling into the tunnel behind them. They were too busy trying to figure out what was going on ahead.

The first of the speeding vehicles, driven by Anthony, had skidded sideways, and come to a halt, blocking the exit to the north side. Anthony got out, opened the bonnet and started fiddling about with the engine as if he were dealing with some kind of fault.

The second vehicle – a mock-up of a Royal Mail van – driven by Brendan, and with Luke in the passenger seat, had stopped a third of the way into the tunnel. It was now parked diagonally across the lanes, forcing the security van to come to a stop – which it did twenty yards behind it.

The builder's truck had also stopped, and was now pointing sideways, blocking the entrance from the south. Kevin Marsh and Pete Mac had jumped out of it and were busily erecting the police signs they'd taken from the back of the vehicle, declaring the tunnel closed due to a serious accident.

'Get on the radio,' shouted the driver.

His mate grabbed the hand-held mike and started twiddling knobs on his side of the dashboard. 'Can't get nothing 'cept a load of crackling. There's no contact.' He fiddled a bit more. 'Aw fuck. It's being in the tunnel.'

'Keep calm,' said the driver. 'They can't get us while we're locked in here, and soon as other drivers realise what's going on, they'll get help for us.'

'Don't want to worry you, but look in your wing mirror.'

The driver looked.

'You might be able to tell me I'm wrong, but, far as I can see, there is no other traffic. They must have blocked the entrance somehow. But . . . Aw sweet Jesus.' The driver's mate pointed at the windscreen. 'What I *can* see are two great big blokes wearing overalls and masks coming straight towards us. And one of them's carrying a fucking shotgun.'

Brendan rapped on the driver's side window, and

gestured for him to lower it. 'Give us the keys,' he shouted through the glass.

The driver shook his head, his eyes fixed on the gun. 'They don't open the back,' he shouted.

'We ain't thick, moosh. We know that. We just don't want you getting any ideas about trying to drive off, or running us over, or doing anything else silly.' He raised the gun and pointed it directly at the driver's face. 'The bullets in this thing can cut through armour plate,' he lied. 'And you don't even wanna know what it would do to your head after it's shattered this window.'

'Give him the keys,' said the mate. 'I ain't gonna be a dead hero, not on the wages we get paid.'

The driver took the keys out of the ignition, wound the window down a crack and let them drop down into Brendan's outstretched hand. 'We don't want any trouble, all right?' he said, his stomach gurgling as threateningly as if he'd just followed a night in the pub with a double-strength vindaloo. 'We'll do as we're told, but just do us all a favour and put that thing away.'

'Carry on acting sensible and you'll have nothing to worry about,' said Brendan, putting the keys in his overall pocket.

Without lowering his gaze from the driver's face, he said to Luke. 'Tell 'em they can get started.'

Luke trotted off back down the tunnel to the builder's truck, and he, Kevin and Pete Mac started unloading the oxyacetylene cutting gear that they needed to get them through the skin of the van and into where the strongboxes were held.

'All them years working for your dad in the scrapyard finally paid off, eh?' said Kevin, carefully pushing back his protective visor without disturbing the mask concealing his face. He looked at his watch. 'Twelve minutes. Not bad.'

He stepped back, a man pleased with a job well done. 'There you are, lads. I'll get this gear stowed back in the truck, while you start unloading.'

With the strongboxes secure in the back of the mail van, Brendan told Luke to get the engine running, and for Kevin and Pete Mac to draw the truck round to the front of the security van ready to leave the tunnel.

While they did as they were told, Brendan tapped on the driver's window again. 'One last thing,' he said, opening the driver's door with the keys. 'Now don't panic and no one'll get hurt.'

He pulled two sets of handcuffs from his trouser pocket. 'You,' he lifted his chin towards the mate. 'Right arm.'

The mate did as he was told.

'And you,' Brendan said to the driver, 'left arm.'

He handcuffed them together with one set of cuffs then looped the other pair through them and fastened them to the steering wheel. Brendan then relocked the door and put the keys back in his pocket.

*

The car, the mail van and the builder's truck left the tunnel at a discreet distance from one another, and at a sedate thirty miles an hour. Three vehicles and their now unmasked drivers going quietly about their early-morning business. Meanwhile, the queue at the south end of the tunnel was beginning to lengthen as furious drivers honked their horns and tried to do U-turns to get away from the jam, while those at the front slapped their hands on their steering wheels and swore loudly as they stared at the police signs telling them of the closure.

Fifteen minutes later the three vehicles, all stolen the previous week and decked out with false plates, had been wiped clean and dumped on a parcel of scrubby wasteland behind the railway goods yard in Stratford.

Brendan, Luke, Pete Mac, Anthony and Kevin had transferred the cash boxes to two anonymous Ford saloons and were now heading – via different circuitous routes and two more changes of vehicle – to the slaughter, Rosie Palmer's old flat in Kilburn, where they were to meet up in a couple of hours' time to divvy up the takings.

Kevin lit a cigarette and handed it over from the back seat to Brendan who was driving. 'Amount of boxes we got, we could do the deal with the Irishmen and still have enough left over to buy a bleed'n mansion in the country somewhere.'

'You'd be surprised, Kev, them places ain't that

dear, you know,' said Luke. 'It could buy us a whole row of mansions.

'But why waste it on property, eh, Kev?' said Brendan, winking at Kevin's reflection in the rear-view mirror. 'When there's booze, women and motors out there?'

Chapter 23

While Brendan and the boys were busily breaking into the security boxes that they'd taken over to Ellie's mother's old home off the Kilburn High Road, Ellie herself was with Patricia in a swish West End restaurant in James Street.

The restaurant was a couple of doors along from the Italian place that Ellie had gone to with Eileen a few weeks previously. Ellie had noticed it at the time, and she'd thought how modern and sophisticated it looked, just the like ones she saw in her magazines. She'd also noticed all the expensive-looking cars lined up outside, and had been surprised that there'd been so many. According to the news, times were hard, and the country was struggling to find its way out of some sort of economic crisis. But there wasn't much sign of it on this particular street.

Maybe all the restaurant's customers were in the same sort of 'business' as her family, and didn't have to concern themselves with money the way that – in Brendan's words – ordinary mug punters had to.

Whatever the explanation, it had certainly made an impression on Ellie. And telling Patricia that she wanted to have a girly lunch with her – so that they could get to know each other properly, as real sisters should – had proved to be the perfect excuse to go there.

Ellie sighed appreciatively as she and Patricia walked through the beautifully furnished dining room, with nothing to disturb the sophisticated murmur of conversation except the sound of heavily expensive silverware on elegantly simple white china. Regardless of what Eileen had done – and, in truth, the woman gave Ellie the creeps – and the admitted strangeness of the rest of the O'Donnells – with the exception, of course, of her darling Luke – Ellie loved her new life in London. And she was determined to visit as many of the fancier parts of the city as she could.

Ellie had also decided that there was no real hurry to do so, as she had every intention of staying in London for good. Not with bloody Eileen, that was for sure, but in a nice little flat of her own – somewhere chic and expensive.

Despite her preconceptions, Ellie couldn't help but be impressed by Patricia's behaviour, as they were shown to their table. Contrary to what she had expected from someone who had practically had a fit when she had had to use a communal changing room – and who put up with so much crap from Pete Mac – Patricia's attitude to the two waiters who attended them was remarkable.

As the young men pulled out their chairs for them,

and expertly flicked napkins from their folds, draping them across Ellie's and Patricia's laps, Patricia acted as if it were all commonplace to her, as if she did this sort of thing every day.

It was like seeing a different woman.

'Don't you look like you own the place,' Ellie whispered, leaning across the table, once the waiters had left them to consider the menus.

Patricia shrugged. 'I've been to places that'd make this gaff look like Kelly's Eel and Pie House,' she said, looking around at the other diners. 'And night-clubs like you wouldn't believe.'

'Really?' Ellie was intrigued. Perhaps it really *would* be nice to get to know her sister better. 'You go out much, do you?'

'When I was a younger, I did. Not so much now, of course. But you should have seen me a few years ago. The clothes I had then. You wouldn't have recognised me.'

Ellie watched Patricia's face as she scanned the menu, while at the same time polishing the cutlery on the edge of the tablecloth, occasionally pausing to check that each item was clean enough for her.

Again, Ellie couldn't help but wonder: how could this be the same person who put up with that pig of a husband of hers? Who let herself be treated like dirt.

Ellie slapped her menu down on the table. 'Okay, Pat,' she said, all smiles and encouragement. 'Let's get the ordering done with, then we can have a proper chat.'

'So you only married Pete Mac because you were expecting?' Ellie was working her way through a plate of chocolate profiteroles, while Patricia toyed with a tiny cup of coffee.

'No, I never said that. I said I was *forced* to marry him because I was expecting.' Patricia caught the waiter's eye and pointed to the empty Chablis bottle with a nod and a smile before turning back to Ellie. 'But I lost the baby.'

'So it wasn't your Caty you were expecting?'

'No. It was a little boy.'

'I'm sorry.'

Patricia shrugged. 'What's that Frank Sinatra song that Brendan loves?' She thought for a moment, the alcohol slowing her thinking. "That's Life", that's the one: you pick yourself up and get on with . . .' Another moment to think. 'It. The race.'

'I'm no Frank Sinatra expert, Pat, but are you really saying that you think you just have to put up with things? Make do? Accept second-best? Worse, bloody *third*-best with that pig.'

'No, you don't understand. I've got my life. It's what I've settled for. I don't have much of a choice any more, now do I?'

'Don't be stupid, Pat. Course you do. Look at you, you're gorgeous. And with your new clothes and your lovely hair . . .' She lifted her chin towards the table by the window. 'And look at him over there; sure, he can't keep his eyes off you.'

'Don't be daft.'

'I'm not being daft, I'm being angry. You're worth more than this. You ought to have a bloody affair. That'd show him.'

'Ellie, you don't know –'

'Yes I do, I know that your man's doing his bit for the contraceptive industry, so isn't it about time you had a go too? Show the bastard what you're made of.'

Patricia snorted rather than swallowed her mouthful of wine and started coughing uncontrollably. 'For goodness' sake, Ellie,' she spluttered.

'Aren't I only speaking the truth? Why not have some fun?'

'Because Brendan would go mad.'

'*Brendan* would go mad?' Ellie stopped with her spoon halfway to her mouth, intrigued by the idea. 'You aren't worried about what Pete Mac would have to say? But you wouldn't want to upset your brother?'

'Brendan has standards – for me, anyway. But Pete Mac? He wouldn't notice if I was stretched out stark naked on the carpet in front of him, doing the business with the bloody milkman.'

'So if you don't want to have an affair, and you can't stand the eejit, why don't you leave him?'

'Can I tell you something without you laughing at me?'

Ellie had trouble swallowing her last mouthful of pastry. 'I'm not mocking you, Pat. And if you think I am, I'm sorry.'

Patricia reached out and took her sister's hand, and smiled, a genuine, warm smile. 'Don't you dare. There's far worse than that to be sorry about in our family. And plenty to be ashamed of.'

Ellie returned her smile. 'I like you saying that – our family.' Although for the life of her, Ellie couldn't understand how Pat could say she was ashamed of them, when she seemed more than happy to stay with them and do what they told her. Probably more of that *we all share the same blood* stuff that Brendan was always going on about.

There was a lot she had to learn about being an O'Donnell.

'So, what was it you were going to tell me?'

Patricia looked shy, almost furtive. 'When I was a *lot* younger I was a good-looking girl, and –'

'You still are.'

'No, I mean really good-looking. I'm not bragging or anything, just stating the truth, like saying I've got dark hair. And I used to have this dream. About going into modelling. Not that Dad or Brendan would have let me, of course. But I used to read all the magazines and, like I say, dream that I'd do it one day.'

'That's so sad.'

Patricia shrugged. 'If I hadn't drunk all this wine I'd never be saying this, Ellie, but instead of getting yourself caught up with Brendan – and before you say anything, Luke told me about you driving the horse-box, because he's worried about you – why don't you consider it? Modelling?'

'This is me we're talking about. A bloody farm girl.'

'Come on, Ellie, I've seen you, you've always got your nose in *Nova* and *Cosmo*, and the way you dress now . . . Look at you. I know you're my sister, but I mean it, you're gorgeous. You could make a fortune for yourself. And be safely away from Brendan's *businesses*.'

Patricia was totally taken aback as Ellie burst into tears.

'Modelling?' she sniffed into the hankie that Patricia hurriedly stuffed into her hand. 'Me? I can't even keep a boyfriend. Even when I let him do what he bloody well likes with me.'

'What d'you mean?'

'Milo Flanagan. I wasn't meant to be seeing him. *Brendan forbade it*. But I was. And I was so happy, Pat. But then he just stopped calling me. That was it, no explanation.' She blew her nose loudly. 'Perhaps my time with him was good training. Let men do what they like with me. But in pictures rather than in real life.'

'I'm not talking about the grubby sort that you get in those blokes' magazines. I'm talking about fashion, and proper photographic work. But never mind all that. Tell me something, have you called him?'

'No.'

'Why not? Don't you want to be happy? Go on, go and call him now. Say you're sorry, even if you don't know what for.'

As Patricia watched Ellie walk between the tables to the telephone mounted on the wall by the cloakroom, she closed her eyes. Was she really the right person to be giving advice about men?

After several false starts, Ellie finally dialled Milo's number.

'Y'ello?'

'Milo, it's me, Ellie. I wondered why you haven't called me.'

'I'm bored with you, sweetheart, okay?'

He felt a small pang of regret as he put the phone down. He'd actually liked the bird. But for all her education, and her nice way of talking, and her stories about living in the country with her horses, she was no better than a brass. But then what should he have expected, she was an O'Donnell, wasn't she? And they were a whole family of alley cats. And she'd been the last tie to be cut. Now he'd have no regrets about what he was going to do.

Ellie sat back in her chair and shook her head in answer to Patricia's questioning smile.

Patricia felt her face drain of colour. Why had she interfered? 'Sod him, sod the lot of them.' She beckoned to a waiter. 'Two brandies please.'

'So,' she said to Ellie. 'You're definitely tall enough; you're slim, and you've got a cocky enough attitude to do it.' She sipped at her brandy. 'The way you walked back from that phone, even though you were upset, you were gliding like a princess. And as for looks, if that bloody Penelope Tree can be in *Vogue*, then I'm sure you can.'

'Thanks very much.' Ellie muttered the words into her chest.

Patricia reached out and took her sister's hand. 'Ellie, I've no idea what that fool just said to you, but believe me, you're much too good for him. And, if you want this you can have it. I'll make sure you can. I'll sort it all out.' She fumbled around lighting a cigarette, trying to think what was needed. 'We'll have to get you a portfolio. I know you have to have one of them. And I'll get you to see all the right people; protect you from the bad ones.'

Ellie's head was still bowed.

'I really mean this, Ellie. I've got the money, I know people – well, people I'd have to look up again, but people I know wouldn't refuse me. I can make this happen for you. You can live the life I had snatched away from me.'

'Hang on, Pat, are you doing this for you or me?'

Patricia pulled her hand away. 'I'm sorry, I'm being silly.'

'No, you're not.' Ellie looked up and grabbed her hand again. 'That just came out wrong. You're so used to people telling you what to do, and Pete Mac being mean to you, that you don't recognise when you're just being teased. Pat, believe me, I know I'm not acting like it, but I couldn't think of anything I'd like to do more. It'd be fantastic.'

She leaned forward and smiled through her tears. 'Tell you what, let's go and buy Caty something really trendy.' Ellie held up her hand. 'And before you say anything, nothing too grown up or tarty. And then we go home and spend the evening watching telly with her, painting our nails, and having slimy mud face packs.'

'You are so like Catherine. And I am so drunk. But I'd like that, Ellie. A lot. And modelling, babe, that's what you're gonna do. You are going to be the best there's ever been.'

It seemed that Ellie's fantasy of leading a glamorous life in London was going to be made real by the person she'd have least expected could do so. And she wasn't going back to Kildare now – that was for sure.

'Thanks, Pat, and doing it together, with you, it'll be fantastic.'

*

By the time the two of them had finished their second brandy, Ellie's career and her new cosmopolitan existence had been mapped out in front of her. And Patricia was going to make sure that not one man was involved, who might hurt or spoil things for either of them.

Well, not unless he had a camera in one hand and a modelling contract in the other . . .

Chapter 24

Brendan arched his body backwards, stretching his neck and kneading his fingers into his kidneys. His back ached and his shirt was sticking to him where he'd been sweating from the efforts of the afternoon. First, he and the others had worked at jemmying open the cash boxes that they'd 'liberated' from the security van; then they'd had to open up the void under the kitchen floorboards hidden beneath the fridge so they could stow the bundles of banknotes; finally, they'd had to restore the floorboards and drag the fridge back in place to cover their handiwork. After being up since before daybreak, Brendan was well and truly exhausted.

But he couldn't remember feeling so pleased with the world in a long time. Even taking the piss out of the Kesslers at the wedding hadn't been as good as this.

'That's more than a tidy few quid,' said Kevin, offering round his cigarettes.

Brendan took one, tossed it in the air and caught it in his mouth like a performing seal with a fish. 'And we'll have the bunce off the Kesslers for this month's consignment of films and magazines in a few days to add to the pot,' he said with a victor's grin, the cigarette bobbing up and down between his lips.

Anthony turned on the single cold tap that supplied the deep butler sink, stuck his shaven head under the water and let it run down his neck. He then angled round so he could drink from the cool, gushing flow.

'I don't get this,' said Pete Mac, leaning back against the draining board, watching Anthony as if he were barmy. 'After all that work, all we get is a bloody swig of water. Remember when your dad was alive, Brendan? Rosie Palmer used to lay on a proper spread for us after a job. She used to do sandwiches, Scotch eggs, pork pies, and plenty of booze. That was the right way to celebrate after working your nuts off. Not sticking your bleed'n head under a tap.'

Brendan ran his hand over his five o'clock shadow. 'I dunno about you, Pete, but after I've been home and had a bit of a kip, then a shower, a shit and a shave, I'm gonna get meself changed into some nice clean clothes and go out for the evening and celebrate more than properly.'

He bent forward and checked his reflection in the side of the stainless-steel kettle. 'There's a very nice little brunette started at the Bella Vista last week. Tits like coconuts, she's got. And no trap on her at all. Just what I need.'

Up until then, Luke had hidden his lack of enthusiasm for having had anything to with the job.

He had just got on with speaking when he was spoken to, smiled in the right places, and done what was expected of him. He had only been tempted in the first place as it was a quick way of getting the wedge he needed for the warehouse – a step forward to setting up his new life with Nicky, and getting away from the family business for good. But Brendan's attitude turned his stomach. He couldn't stand the thought of what his brother was about to do, and he knew he had to get out of there before a row started.

He had really hoped that Brendan would settle down now that he and Sandy were together. Or that Brendan might at least be a bit – what was it he was always telling Pete Mac he should be? *Discreet*. That was it. But he should have known there'd be no chance of that, not with Brendan. It was always the same – one rule for him and the rest of them did as they were told.

Maybe Sandy had come to realise early on that that was how Brendan operated, and that was why she'd said what she had to the escort who'd been beaten up – that there was a price to pay for having a nice life.

Maybe.

But whatever the explanation, Luke wasn't in the mood to care very much at the moment. It was a terrible thing to admit, but his own brother disgusted him, just as his father had done before him.

'I'll be getting off then. Back home.' Luke

couldn't hide the look of disapproval on his face as he left them standing in the kitchen.

'He right makes me laugh, he does,' Luke heard Pete Mac saying as he opened the door to let himself out on to the street. 'He can get stuck in like the rest of us, no trouble, do a man's job, and do it well, but he can't stand it when you talk about enjoying the company of a few birds. I just don't understand that geezer, Brendan. I don't understand him at all.'

Luke paused in the doorway, listening.

Kevin and Anthony exchanged glances. They knew how Brendan's temper could erupt if anyone even thought about mocking his brother.

'How are you celebrating then, Pete?' asked Kevin, slapping him harder than was friendly across the shoulder, and widening his eyes in warning.

'Oi! That fucking hurt,' said Pete Mac, rubbing his flabby, stinging flesh. He sniffed noisily. 'I might pop out for a bit.'

'A bit of what, I wonder?' muttered Luke, slamming the door behind him.

'What did he say?' asked Pete Mac, his face screwed up as he tried to figure out what Luke had said, and whether or not it was an insult. 'I thought he'd fucking gone.'

'I never heard nothing, Pete,' said Anthony, stubbing out his cigarette in the sink. 'Come on, it's been a long day. Why don't we all get going?'

Anthony and Kevin went through to the sitting room to collect their things.

Pete Mac was about to follow them, but Brendan barred his way.

'Do yourself and the rest of us a favour, Pete, and learn from what just happened there. Always make sure you know who can hear you before you open that big gob of yours. All right?'

'Wasn't my fault the nosy bastard was listening,' he said, and skulked off to the sitting room.

If only Pete Mac had realised that Brendan was reminding himself as much as Pete about the risks of people eavesdropping, he might have put up a bit more of an argument.

Sitting in the single greasy armchair, in her grotty rooms, Carol knew exactly what she was going to do: she was going to have the whole bloody lot of them. Every single one of the men who'd treated her so badly – as if she was nothing more than a thing to be used and thrown away. And she was going to start with Peter MacRiordan.

What did she have to lose? She couldn't stomach staying in this dump any longer anyway – even if Pete Mac did decide to be 'kind' enough to let her stay another week. No, she would use some of the money she had put away to get herself somewhere decent. It was okay, she'd worked it all out. Soon as she was back on her feet, she'd find someone who'd treat her the way she deserved to be treated for once. Like a lady.

She went out on the landing to the payphone, wiped the receiver with a disinfectant-soaked cloth, and then found the number for the local police station in the dog-eared telephone book hanging from a chain fixed to the wall.

'Hello,' she said, speaking more clearly and slowly than usual. 'I want to talk to someone.'

'Can I ask what it's about please, miss?'

'There are things I know about someone. Bad things. He's tied up with a very bad local family.'

'Yes, miss, of course. Thank you. I'll make sure your message is passed on.'

Carol stared at the receiver. *He'd put the bloody phone down on her.*

The young constable on desk duty shook his head with the wisdom of someone who had been in the force for almost a whole year.

'Another loony been reading the Sunday papers, Sarge. All of these stories about gangsters on every street corner in the East End bring 'em out like a rash. This one reckons she knew all about a very bad local family.'

The sergeant put down his mug of tea on the counter, and picked up a pen as if to write. 'Nothing about Al Capone?'

'Not that she mentioned, Sarge.'

He went back to his tea. 'She wants to be careful,'

287

he said, 'or she'll wind up holding up a flyover somewhere.'

'Don't, Sarge, you're scaring me.'

A full hour passed before Carol stomped into the police station in person. It had taken her about a minute to get over the shock of having the phone put down on her, and another to decide what she was going to do next.

For starters, she was going to target someone too stupid to move quickly enough to cover himself before the law were on to him. Then, when they had him, and he started blabbing – he wouldn't be able to help himself – she was going to stand back and watch it all unravel.

It then took her about another forty-five minutes to get ready. On the whole, no mean feat considering the temper she was now in. The rest of the hour was taken up walking, or rather half running, to the police station.

When she got there, her temper hadn't improved, but the treatment she was offered certainly had.

The sight of the gorgeous young blonde striding up to his counter had the immediate attention of the constable who had earlier dismissed her so abruptly.

'Yes, miss? How can I help you?'

'You wouldn't listen to me on the phone. So I've got something else for you. Here's the names and the address of a bloke and two birds. Go round there first thing, while the lazy tarts are still in bed, and you'll find the pair of them with enough nicked gear to open another branch of John fucking Lewis. Now don't tell me that ain't good enough to interest you.'

Sandy stepped out from behind the screen, head down, as she fastened the top button on her shirt. She felt so tired. She'd had to leave home before eight o'clock this morning to make sure she got here for her appointment, and on top of that Brendan had got in really late last night and his boozy snoring had kept her awake until the early hours.

And the surroundings didn't improve her temper.

The dark-panelled offices, with their gilt-framed paintings, thick, sink-in-up-to-your-ankle rugs, and parquet flooring weren't what she'd been used to when she went to see the doctor. But when she'd told Brendan that she hadn't been feeling too well, he'd insisted she'd gone up to Harley Street. She could only thank God that he'd been too busy to come with her. He could be so touchy if people said something he didn't like, and the last thing she wanted was a scene in front of people like these. Even the nurse spoke like she was a bloody duchess.

'Please, take a seat, Mrs O'Donnell,' said the doctor, gesturing to the wing-backed armchair on her side of his wide partners' desk.

Self-consciously smoothing her hair, and then her

skirt, Sandy sat down. It felt more like having an interview than being told you had to take the tablets three times a day until it was all cleared up – whatever *it* was.

'Well?' she asked, quietly.

'Well, indeed, Mrs O'Donnell. First things first. You do appear to have a slight infection.' The doctor looked knowingly at his nurse, who answered with no more than a slight, but equally knowing, lifting of a single eyebrow.

'What d'you mean? What sort of infection? Is it bad?' Sandy's reticence had been wiped away at the very mention of the word 'infection'. 'Is that why I've been feeling so rough?'

He paused. Then he began speaking very slowly to Sandy, making sure that he avoided any direct eye contact with her.

'There's really no need to worry, Mrs O'Donnell.' He had – for a very fleeting moment – thought about suggesting that she might want to speak to the nurse about making an appointment for her husband to come along for treatment. The correct procedure. But after thinking about his most recent meetings with Brendan O'Donnell, he had swiftly reconsidered his recommendations for arranging a visit. O'Donnell was, after all, a man whose previous appointments with the doctor had included a very late termination for a girl who was clearly not legally of age, and a man who had the larger part of a pint glass imbedded in his cheek – and an extremely angry disposition.

The doctor smiled down at his desk. 'Nothing to worry about at all. Tube of cream. Apply when required. Problem'll disappear before you know it. But,' he lifted his chin a little and gazed over his glasses at the tips of his steepled fingers, 'I do have something else I need to discuss with you.'

Sandy gripped the arms of her chair. The bloke had looked up her fanny, tested her wee, and had taken about two pints of her blood last week, and he'd done the first two all over again this week.

An infection was one thing – everyone got a bit of cystitis now and again – but what the hell was wrong now?

It was now half past nine and Carol Mercer was standing outside Eileen O'Donnell's house at the Stepney end of the Mile End Road. She'd got there early because she didn't want to risk running into Brendan – not while she was telling Eileen all the things she had to say about her son, and definitely not afterwards either.

All the time she'd been with Brendan, Carol had never known him get out of bed before ten. Well, not unless he was on business of some kind.

That was a point. She nibbled nervously at her bottom lip. Say he had been out working somewhere, and had thought he'd just pop round to see his mum on his way back home?

She checked along the street. Not a single motor that he would have been seen dead in.

Good, he wasn't there.

Probably.

But say he'd borrowed a car like he had before?

Aw shit . . .

But if she didn't do it now, she really didn't think she'd have the courage to go away and come back later. She was shaking like a leaf as it was. But she was also determined that it was about time the bastard got what was coming to him. Let the big man know what it was like to be on the receiving end for once.

Carol fiddled with the mousy-brown curly wig that, along with the frumpy pleated skirt, white nylon blouse and make-up-free face, made her look unrecognisable as the Carol Mercer that Brendan had thrown out on to the streets with nothing more than a bit of shopping and a red face. Then she took a deep breath, lifted her chin, and marched boldly up the front steps to the street door.

Carol was more than a little surprised when it was opened by a very pretty, dark-haired young woman in a housecoat. She'd heard Brendan had got married recently and had moved over to Old Ford somewhere. But surely even he wouldn't have the bollocks to move his bit on the side into his own mother's place.

Well, not so soon, he wouldn't.

'Can I help you?' asked Ellie, her cultured Irish voice another surprise for Carol.

Irish? She could be family.

No, she wasn't the sort of scrubber who'd be a relative of the O'Donnells.

She had to be his bird. But fancy having her staying with his mum. She knew he was a bastard, but this took some beating, this really did.

What a fucking family.

But maybe she was the new wife? She was certainly young and beautiful enough for Brendan.

Carol lowered her gaze. 'I'd like to see Mrs O'Donnell, please. Eileen O'Donnell,' she added hurriedly, and did a quick flip through her mental index box of all the things Pete Mac had moaned on about when he'd talked about his *murdering witch of a mother-in-law*.

Got it.

'It's about church business.'

Ellie might just as well have closed her eyes and started snoring, so pathetic was her effort to hide her boredom. No one was going to spoil her plans for this morning. She was starting her new beauty regime, getting herself all polished and primped and prepared for the photographer who was going to take her pictures next week for her portfolio.

'Sure. Come in.' She gestured for Carol to step inside. 'I hope you won't think I'm being rude, but I was just going up for a bath.'

Carol smiled, but it only reached her lips. *Going up for a bath*. Lucky bitch. She'd had a bathroom once. In her lovely little house. All new, and tiled, and full of matching fluffy towels and flannels. 'Of course I won't think you're rude,' she said pleasantly. 'You go up and enjoy a nice soak.'

'Right. You'll find her down in the kitchen. The stairs are at the end of the hall.' Ellie called over her shoulder as she started up the stairs: 'Eileen, you've got a visitor.'

Then she high-tailed it up to the bathroom before anyone tried to include her in any talk about priests or Mass or bloody flower-arranging rotas.

Carol found Eileen down in the basement kitchen standing by the sink. She was switching on the electric kettle. Old habits died hard, having a guest meant making a pot of tea. There was a Dobermann sitting expectantly at her heel.

Carol wasn't keen on dogs. She wasn't scared of them, it was just that they got hair over everything. Spoilt things, stopped them looking nice.

'Who are you?' asked Eileen with a more defensive than aggressive frown. It felt wrong, this stranger in her kitchen, especially a stranger who had the advantage of knowing who she was.

'I'm somebody who's going to tell you the truth,' said Carol, more boldly than she felt. 'Don't suppose that happens much in a family like this, does it, Mrs O'Donnell?'

'I don't know what you're talking about, and I really don't think I want you in my home. So if you don't mind –'

'But I do mind.' Carol walked across the room and stood right in front of her. She'd have to be quick in case that Irish trollop decided to come down after her bath. If Eileen got nasty, Carol was sure she could take her as easily as snuffing out a candle, but she really wasn't sure about the other one. She looked as fit as a bloke. And if she was tough enough to put up with being married to Brendan O'Donnell she probably had the guts to put up a good fight as well.

'I've come to tell you about your son. About Brendan.' She held her chin high in the air – defiant. 'How he makes filthy, disgusting films. And makes women do things that would have you –'

'No.' Eileen took a step towards her. 'I don't believe you. Why are you saying these things?'

'Because he's making films with women who are too scared, and too drugged up, not to do as they're told. He's a brute, a bully, and he lives off filth and violence, and you should be ashamed to call him your son.'

Eileen turned away, and fussed around with the kettle, checking if it had boiled. 'I won't listen to you.'

'Well, I think that's a pity, because if you don't stop him –' Carol moved closer '– then perhaps I'll have to tell the law. And I've got plenty to tell them all right. Things about your whole bloody witch's brood. Things that they're into right up to their poxy necks. And you're no better for letting them get away with it.'

She hadn't planned to say that bit about the police, it had just come out of her mouth. But it wasn't a bad idea. Why shouldn't she grass the bastard the same way as she'd done with Pete Mac? If she'd been left with nothing, why shouldn't he lose everything as well?

Eileen's chest was rising and falling as if she'd just run round the block carrying a sack of spuds in each hand. 'I'm warning you,' she breathed, staring at the bulbous reflections in the kettle. 'If you don't get out of my house – right now – it'll be me who calls the police.'

'An O'Donnell calling the law? I don't think so, do you, love? But I'm ready to leave anyway. This place stinks of that filthy bastard son of yours.'

Eileen gripped the edge of the sink, trying to control her breathing. She felt as torn, confused and worn out as she had all those years ago when she had tried to put a stop to things in her own, sinful way. But all that had turned out to be was a stupid, misguided waste of so many things that it haunted her every waking and sleeping moment – knowing that she could have done things differently, better.

She felt totally exhausted by it all.

Carol was now so close to her that Eileen could

feel the heat of the girl's body as surely as the heat from the kettle. It was as if they had both been fixed to the spot.

Then there was the spell-breaking sound of someone clomping down the stairs. They both turned round.

It was Ellie.

'Eileen, I wondered if you'd seen my nail-varnish remover. Oh, sorry to disturb you, I didn't realise you still had company.'

'Sorry?' Carol shook her head as if she didn't understand the words. 'Your kind are never sorry. It was me Brendan should have married, not you.'

'What did you say?' Ellie strode across the room towards them. 'Eileen, who is this?'

Eileen would spend the rest of her years wishing that she had had acted differently, but as Carol grabbed the kettle, yanking it from its socket, and throwing its boiling contents into Ellie's face, she just stood there, screaming in horror.

Chapter 25

Despite his late night, Brendan was still exhilarated from the security-van job, and had been up and out only minutes after Sandy had left for Harley Street. He had now popped home to see how she was after her doctor's appointment.

He pulled up outside the house and looked across at the park, as he always did, to make sure that no little toerags were playing football too close to the fence. He wasn't about to have his motor dented by some budding Georgie Best aiming a goal shot too high.

Satisfied that the only games he could see being played were way over the other side by the lido, he pocketed his keys and turned to the house.

As he did so, his forehead pleated into a deep frown and he began walking very quickly, breaking into a run. Sandy was standing waiting for him in the doorway.

She never did that. Never.

This had to be important. And not in a good way.

'What is it?' he said, seizing her by the shoulders. 'What did the doctor say?'

'Oh, Brendan, I can't believe it.' Sandy's mouth

was so dry, her tongue was sticking to her teeth. 'I don't know how it happened.'

'What, for Christ's sake? What happened?'

'You know I had to go back to the doctor's?'

'Yeah, that's why I'm here. What did he say?'

'I'm pregnant.'

Brendan's expression immediately transformed into one of disbelieving joy. He wrapped his arms around her and kissed her tenderly on the top of her head. 'You have made me the happiest man alive, Sandy O'Donnell.'

'You're pleased then?'

'Pleased?' He kissed her passionately, holding her to him as if he would never let her go. 'That answer your question?'

'Do you think we can go inside?' she asked, now grinning as broadly as Brendan. 'All the neighbours'll be watching.'

'Good.' Brendan ran down the steps to the pavement and shouted along the terrace. 'I'm gonna be a dad!'

It took Sandy some minutes to persuade Brendan to come indoors, but nothing could dampen his mood.

He made sure she was sitting down, and then he pulled the phone over to the table.

'I'm gonna phone Mum,' he said. 'Believe me, this is gonna blow her away. She loves kids, San. Really loves 'em. And then I'm gonna call the rest of the family. And everyone I know. Then we are gonna start planning the biggest fucking party anyone's ever seen. It's gonna make the wedding look like it was put on by bloody pikeys.'

'I thought your mates who did the wedding were pikeys,' she said, laughing.

'Yeah, well . . .'

He joined in her laughter. And then he put the phone down, walked over to her chair, and stood there in front of her. 'Do you know, I love you, Sandy O'Donnell.'

It was the first and last time he would ever say those words.

When Brendan eventually rang his mother, the ambulance had just arrived to take Ellie away.

When the police turned up at the address Carol Mercer had so thoughtfully written out for them, Pete Mac was in bed with one of the two redheads. The other one had got up to answer the door. And with little more than the hand towel she'd grabbed on the way, the police hadn't had much difficulty in persuading her to let them in – *it's that or out here in the street, miss* – and that they were just making enquiries.

The bedroom, in fact the whole flat, was stuffed to bursting with all the gear that the sisters had finally hoisted over the past three weeks. If Pete Mac hadn't been cursed with such a dangerous mix of always claiming he was too busy and actually being bone idle, he might have organised the fencing, and wouldn't now be completely surrounded by incriminating evidence.

The sight of the uniformed officers coming into the bedroom full of hookey gear had the other sister bawling her head off, and in all the confusion – what a touch of luck – no one had so much as mentioned anything about them producing a search warrant.

'Please, don't blame us,' wailed the one still in bed. 'He made us do it.'

Pete Mac's mouth fell open, and he threw back the covers to get up, making the female officer present wince and avert her eyes at the sight of his wobbling, boozer's belly. 'Now hold up a minute.'

'Let the lady finish, sir.'

'Don't pretend you didn't,' sobbed the other one, throwing pathetic little-girl-lost glances at the two male officers. 'We had no idea who he was, we're down from Liverpool, see. Just trying to make a living – getting jobs in London and that. It's so hard up there. And we met him and he was really nice. But then he turned nasty. We were really scared of him. Then we found out he's part of this really horrible family – the O'Donnells. It was terrible.'

'Are you saying this man held you here against your will?'

The girls looked at one another then nodded.

'Both of you?'

This time the nods weren't so assured.

'Perhaps we'd better discuss this down the station.'

Carol was sitting smoking nervously in an interview room at the police station. The door was ajar as she waited for the WPC to come back with a cup of tea for her. So far she had only told them about Pete Mac, but at least they were now interested in what she had to say.

Thank God. Now she'd thrown that kettle of water over Brendan's wife – *why the hell had she done that?* – she was going to have to make sure she told the law everything, so that they got the bastard off the streets as soon as possible. Before he got to her.

She'd spent last night in a bed and breakfast, too terrified to go back to the rooms where Brendan or one of his goons might find her, but how long could she hide from him?

Carol heard a noise in the corridor and looked up hopefully. She hadn't had anything to drink since she'd got up and was gagging for some tea. But it wasn't the WPC. It was Pete Mac being led past between two big burly coppers. Behind him, weeping and snivelling, were the two red-headed sisters.

Pete Mac spotted her and spat on the floor. 'You just wait, you bitch,' he snarled.

It was rapidly dawning on Carol that Brendan O'Donnell was probably going to kill her.

She snatched up her bag, leaving her burning cigarette in the ashtray, and slipped out into the corridor.

'Everything all right, miss?' asked the now very interested young constable at the desk.

She flashed him one of her best smiles – teeth, the lot. 'Fine, thank you. They've asked me to come back this afternoon. Hope to see you then, eh?'

With that she was out of the door, down the front steps and running through the traffic towards Mile End tube station, thanking her lucky stars that her money was in the bank and not under the bed back in her rooms. She had no intention of going back to that place ever again.

But perhaps she should just make one more phone call, before she jumped on a train and went off to start what she could only hope would be a new life.

'Pat, it's me, babe. Pete. I'm in trouble. You've got to help me, but I don't want Brendan to know.'

'What sort of trouble this time?' Pat's voice was flat, without emotion.

'I'm down at the nick. I need you to call a brief, but, please, don't use the usual bloke, I don't want him telling Brendan.'

'Would this have anything to do with the fact that you were caught with two red-headed sisters – red-handed, should I say?'

'What?'

'I know all about it, Pete. Another one of your whores just phoned me. And do you know, I'm not sure if I can be bothered calling a solicitor or not. I mean, *three* whores?'

'Pat –'

'I'll have to think about it.'

Patricia put down the phone and picked up the piece of paper on which she'd written the solicitor's number that she'd looked up immediately after Carol Mercer had made her anonymous call to her.

She thought for ten long minutes about what she should do. Then picked up the phone and instructed the solicitor as Pete Mac had asked.

But after she'd made the call she still wasn't sure, not in all honesty, why she'd bothered.

This was pushing your luck a bit far, even for Pete Mac.

When Brendan eventually found his mother and brother on the fourth floor of the hospital, Luke and Eileen were standing staring through the glass wall of an isolation ward. They were watching Ellie, who was stretched out on her back, her face, shoulders and chest swathed in bandages. She was attached to drips in both arms, and was surrounded by flashing machines and monitors.

'How is she?'

Luke just kept staring at his sister, the beautiful girl who had looked so much like Catherine, and who had

had a whole, wonderful new life mapped out in front of her. A life that had now been ruined.

'How is she?' Luke's voice was low, restrained.

'Her face is destroyed, Brendan, that's how she is. And it's all your fucking fault.'

'My fault?'

'You're just like Dad. You wreck everything and everyone you go near.'

Eileen turned round to face him; she wanted to look her son in the eye as she spoke to him.

'A woman came to the house,' she breathed. 'She said things about you, things about films you're making in her house, and about things you're doing to young girls. Then,' she gulped back the tears, 'she did that to Ellie.'

Eileen drew back her hand and slapped her son as hard as she could.

Brendan ran down the four flights of stairs, barrelled across the hospital reception and snatched the pay-phone out of the hand a woman who was in the middle of a call.

'Fuck off,' he growled, punching out the number of the cab office. 'This is private.'

The woman, horrified, hurried away.

'Paula, it's me,' he spat through gritted teeth. 'I want you to get a message to Anthony. Tell him I want Carol Mercer found, and then I want her gone. Got me?'

Chapter 26

It had taken very little effort on the Kesslers' part to set the wheels in motion for Milo Flanagan's plan for revenge on the O'Donnells in general, and Brendan O'Donnell in particular. It needed only a few promises, very little time, and even less effort. It seemed that there were more than enough people in HMP Brixton who would be only too pleased to do the Kesslers a favour, especially if it meant having one over on the O'Donnell family. Of course, there had to be a nice bung in it for them as well. That, plus a guarantee that Brendan would never find out who had helped them.

And today, the day after Ellie had been scalded, and Brendan's own mother had slapped him, was the day it all began to slot into place.

Barry Ellis, with his thin, scratchy towel draped around his neck, was shuffling along in his prison browns – no longer conscious of the sickly, musty smell they gave off, after the months he'd spent on remand – heading towards the recess to empty his pisspot.

It was a stiflingly hot morning, the sort of July

weather when even if you'd just stepped out of a luxuriously scented cool bath, and were wearing, a soft, fluffy bathrobe, you would still feel immediately sticky and unclean again. But, surprisingly, Barry wasn't feeling too bad. In fact, he was feeling calmer now than he had done in months – probably in years. The medication they'd put him on was helping, and, apart from smoking a bit of draw, he was clean, and proud of it. There were still a surprising number of opportunities for him to get hold of any kind of gear that he might have fancied – and an amazing number of people who seemed all too keen to supply him – but he'd decided he didn't want it any more. He'd had enough.

Barry Ellis had taken back control of his life.

And now he was enjoying a feeling of relief, a feeling that he was genuinely relishing, a feeling that he appreciated more than anything else.

It was all down to the simple fact that Barry knew he was never again going to do any more harm to the people he loved.

He'd cut himself out like a cancer. His mum, his sister, her kids – he'd never be in touch with them again, so he wouldn't be able to hurt them.

But most of all he wouldn't be able to hurt Sandy.

He'd had a lot of time to think about things during the hours he'd been banged up in his cell, and it had come to him like a flash of glorious inspiration, when he'd remembered how Eileen O'Donnell had managed to handle her time when she'd been away. And he'd decided, there and then, that that would be how he could pay Sandy back for everything she'd done for him during those terrible years. The years he'd lost since the day he'd seen the dogs ripping Stephen Shea's body apart in the O'Donnells' scrapyard.

And now he was proud of himself. More proud than he could ever remember.

Barry Ellis had set his loved ones free.

Too many blokes expected too much of their wives and families while they were inside. But not him. No. He'd done the right thing. And he knew it.

Another few steps forward, closer to the echoing chatter coming from the tiled recess.

It was then that Barry first saw the big black man loping along the corridor, making his way straight to the front of the queue.

No one said a word, because he was the man who ran the wing, the one who even gave orders to the POs.

Originally from over Notting Hill way, he'd worked for the Kesslers since he was a schoolkid. He was one of the mob of heavies they'd brought back with them when they'd returned to the East End, thinking they could muscle in on the O'Donnells' turf without so much as a discussion on the matter.

Barry dropped back in the queue, hoping to make himself invisible. All he wanted was a quiet life – that would do him. The most he'd got involved in since he'd been inside was trading for his bit of dope. Keeping his nose clean, that was his plan.

He was so lost in his thoughts about how he would avoid getting sucked in if anything kicked off, that when the short, wiry man in his fifties sidled up to him and tapped him on the shoulder, Barry jumped as if the man's hand had burned into his flesh.

'All right, Ellis, get a grip, mate.' The man cleared his throat with a nastily phlegmy hack. 'What's the matter, got a guilty conscience, have you?'

Barry said nothing, knowing that the most innocuous of replies – if wrongly taken – could earn you a stripe on the arse from a bit of sharpened tin can stolen from the kitchens. Or even worse if someone really took offence.

The man remained beside him until they reached the recess. Still Barry hadn't said a word.

'Don't be like that,' whispered the man as he tipped his foul-smelling, dark brown urine into the sluice. 'Just trying to be friendly, ain't I?'

It was now Barry's turn at the sink, but the man was still at his shoulder.

'Listen to me, Ellis. I know everyone's keeping it from you, mate, but, in my opinion, a man's entitled to know these things. Specially when it's already being talked about all over the fucking wing.'

Barry made as if to walk away, but the man grabbed him by the arm. 'Listen to me, Ellis. We all know it's bad enough that O'Donnell's gone and married your old lady. I mean, *everyone* thought that was well out of order. Even the blokes who don't like you, and who don't usually give a fuck about nothing.'

Barry stiffened. The man had to be off his head. *Sandy and Brendan married?* They wouldn't do that.

'Blimey, from the look on your face, Ellis, I reckon I've just put me number nine right in it. What can I say? I'm sorry, mate. I was sure you must have known at least that much about what was going on.'

Barry resisted the impulse to shake his head.

'Well, you might as well know the rest. Sorry to be the one to have to tell you, mate, but he's messing her around good and proper. Acting just like that prat of a brother-in-law of his – you know, that Peter MacRiordan. Poking any bit of stray he comes across. And I mean *any* bit of stray – some right old dogs. I wouldn't fancy your old woman's chances of keeping herself all nice and minty fresh if he's doing that with all them old slappers, would you? And that's all apart from the laughing stock the arsehole's making of her. See, the poor girl ain't got a clue what he's up to behind her back. Thinks she's still the blushing fucking bride.'

The man waited for Barry to respond, but he said nothing – so he carried on.

'But, all that apart, mate, fancy you not having a clue about them two getting married. That's bad, that is. That must hurt a man. Can't imagine what that'd feel like if a bloke found out that sort of thing's happened with his bird, while he's stuck in here, not able to do nothing about it cos he's on remand.'

He waited just long enough to make his point. 'And then to hear how the cunt's been treating her . . .'

Barry left his pot standing in the sink. Then, ignoring the complaints and abuse from his fellow inmates about him disturbing their morning routine, Barry stuck himself in front of the PO watching over the recess.

'I wanna see me brief,' he said.

Those were practically the only words – apart from 'No, sir' and 'Yes, sir' – that the officer had heard Barry Ellis utter in all the time he'd been inside.

Chapter 27

Sandy was sitting at her desk, in the escort service's office, upstairs in her and Brendan's home on Old Ford Road. She was supposedly interviewing a long succession of escorts to find out if any of them would be capable of taking over the day-to-day running of the business, when her pregnancy became too advanced for her to continue working. Which was going to be in about a week's time if Brendan had anything to do with it. It had been bad enough finding one of the girls who was suitable to act like a nice little housewife, and stay in Brendan's place that he'd been using as the film studio over in Hackney. But this was even worse. Especially now, after what had happened to Ellie, Brendan was practically wrapping her in cotton wool.

While Sandy was as devastated as everyone else about what had happened to the poor girl – although she still didn't really understand how such a bizarre accident could have happened without the dog even getting slightly scalded – Brendan really was driving her mad being so overprotective.

And now she had been interrupted by a telephone call that was nothing to do with the agency, but that the caller had insisted was urgent and really couldn't wait. She'd kill that Paula for passing on the number.

'Okay,' she said, the exasperation obvious in her voice. 'Now what's so bloody important?'

'So?' asked Brendan as she put the phone down. 'What was it? Another one of the silly tarts can't remember the address? We're gonna have to rethink this. Get someone reliable.'

'It wasn't anything to do with the agency.'

'So how'd they get the number then?'

'They said Paula gave it to them.'

He narrowed his eyes. 'Paula, now there's an idea. P'raps I should get her over from the cab office to stand in for you. She's bright as anything. And it'd be good to know she was here in the house with you in case you need anything.'

'Brendan. Will you stop talking for a minute and listen to me? It was –'

'It wasn't the doctor, was it?'

'For goodness' sake, no. It was Barry's solicitor. He wants to see me.'

'Why'd's he wanna see you? They cleared you of everything ages ago.'

'No, not the solicitor. Barry. It's Barry who wants to see me.'

'Why?'

'I don't know, Brendan. It's been so long, I thought

313

he'd just given up on me. That he'd heard we'd got married somehow, and . . . Aw I don't know.'

Brendan stood up and moved round the desk to stand behind her, gently massaging her shoulders. 'Don't you go upsetting yourself over him, Sandy. You're carrying a precious load there, girl. And you don't have to do anything that that –' He bit back his words, weighing up what he was going to say. 'Listen to me; Barry can't expect you to go running after him. Not any more he can't.'

'I suppose not, but –'

'There's no suppose about it. I'm looking after you now, Sandy. You're *my* wife. And you're having *my* kid. And you do not have to do anything just cos someone says you do. You got that?'

'Yeah, course.' She didn't need all this. She felt knackered enough as it was, without having to fight with Brendan. 'I know all that. But because I'm having the baby maybe I should go and see him.'

'I don't think I'd be very happy about that.'

'I don't feel exactly happy about it meself, but I am sort of relieved he wants to see me at last.'

She reached up to her shoulder, clasped Brendan's hand, and let her head drop back so she could see him. 'And I think it'd be only right, don't you, telling him face to face?'

'No, I don't, as it happens.'

She rubbed her other hand over her stomach. 'Brendan, I don't even know if the poor sod's found

314

out we're married yet. Please, I wanna do this. It'll be like putting an end to the past before the baby comes along.'

'If you're really going, then I'll go with you.'

Sandy shook her head. 'I don't think that'd be a very good idea, do you?'

Brendan shrugged. 'If that's how you feel.'

'Don't be like that, Brendan, please. I'll be fine, and you've got more than enough to do as it is, running backwards and forwards to the hospital and that.'

'Well, you ain't driving. Kev can take you.'

As she waited in the clammy heat of the waiting area of HMP Brixton, with its depressingly institutional decor, Sandy felt physically sick. All around her, fractious children were irritating their already tense mothers, who sat smoking obsessively, tugging at their ill-fitting clothes and patting their over-lacquered hair.

The feeling of desperation was as palpable as the odour of stale sweat coming from the POs in their heavy uniforms.

It'll be over soon, Sandy kept repeating to herself, uncomfortably aware that she'd started taking for granted the charmed life that she was now leading with Brendan. A life so far removed from the last few years she had spent with Barry that she couldn't think how she could have endured staying with him through all those terrible, unhappy, frightening times. Times when she had probably acted and looked not much different from most of these women she was now pitying.

It was like they said: it's lovely when you stop bashing your head against the wall.

She sensed the other women flashing curious glances at her. Most of them seemed to know one another, or at least to be able to fall into easy conversation. But she knew they had her down as an outsider – and they were right.

She felt as though her floaty chiffon dress, her well-cut hair, and her diamond solitaire engagement ring were glowing like neon signs saying *I know I'm better off than you, you poor cows. I'm not a pathetic waste of space, with cheap catalogue clothes and nicotine-stained fingers, with an old man who's gonna spend most of his life in and out of the nick like he's dancing some soul- and life-destroying version of the hokey-cokey.*

She fiddled with her ring, turning the stone to the back so that just the platinum band showed, and kept her eyes on the worn lino between her brand-new shoes, wishing she'd put on an old shirt and a pair of jeans.

At last, the door opened and the most military-looking man among the POs led them through into a room the size of the school dining hall at Sandy's secondary modern in Stepney Green. But in this room there was no childish swinging of school bags at your mates' backs, no shoving and joshing, or high-pitched laughter. If anything it was more like the dining hall at exam time.

There were rows of Formica tables with chairs facing each other on either side, all set parallel to the far wall that was decorated with nothing more than a large, plain clock, already ticking off the seconds to the end of visiting time. The room had no windows, but was brightly lit with harsh fluorescent strips that made even the visitors with their faces tanned from the hot weather outside look pasty and unwell. At the far side of the room, opposite the double doors by which they'd entered, there was a serving counter set in the wall selling tea, sugary and salty snacks and chocolate bars with gaudy wrappers that stood out in the otherwise dreary room like precious jewels.

Sandy looked around her in bewilderment. This was a world she knew nothing about, and one she would never willingly enter again. But she was here now, and she knew what she had to do.

Barry was already at one of the tables. Right at the front. Sandy wove her way towards him, apologising and catching the whispers as she moved forward.

It was an odd sensation, but from the snatches of conversation she picked up it really sounded as if some of the people there – the other prisoners – had known she was coming today, that they were expecting her, and were now sharing the information with their visitors.

She tried to shake it off – this place was making her as paranoid as Barry when he'd done too much cocaine – and did her best to conjure up a happy, but concerned smile ready to greet him.

'Hello, Bal,' she said, leaning across the table to kiss him.

He closed his eyes as her lips touched his cheek, and left them closed as he took a deep breath, taking in her scent, trying to find the words to say to her.

'Hello, San,' he said eventually. 'You're looking good, babe. Beautiful.'

'Thanks,' she said, 'that's really nice. Just what a woman in her thirties needs to hear.'

She felt pleased. This was getting off to a lot better start than some of the scenes she'd been envisioning over the past few days. She'd imagined everything from embarrassing screaming matches to heart-breaking accusations and denials, and even her walking out without saying a word because she just couldn't face him.

'I'm feeling really good.' Her face crumpled the moment the words left her mouth. 'I am so sorry, Barry. I didn't mean that the way it came out. It sounded like I feel good about you being stuck in here or something. I don't mean that. You know I don't.'

'That's all right. This ain't easy for either of us, is it?'

'No. You can say that again.' She scrabbled around in her bag. 'Here. Have a ciggy.' He unwrapped the cellophane and offered her one.

'No thanks. I don't any more.'

'Blimey, you not smoking?' He actually smiled, looking almost relaxed, bringing back memories of the old Barry, the one she'd known and fallen in love with when they were just a pair of daft schoolkids. 'What's happened? Someone told you it interferes with your vodka-and-tonic intake?'

'I'm off that and all.' She handed him her lighter. 'You might as well have this. I won't need it any more, and it might bring back some good memories.'

He took it and weighed it in his hand. 'Bought you that after me and Kevin did our first week at Gabriel's scrapyard. Give it to you when we went to that pub on the river. Thought I was the right bollocks, I did. Money in me pocket, new whistle on me back, and the prettiest girl in the East End on me arm.'

He lit a cigarette. 'Feels like it was a lifetime ago, when Gabe give me that job.'

'Don't seem possible he's been dead nearly twelve years, does it?'

'There's a lot happened since then.'

Sandy couldn't look at him. 'Yeah,' she said quietly. 'Like me marrying Brendan.'

'So I heard.'

Her head snapped up. 'You know?'

He made a noise that sounded like a laugh. 'One of

319

my fellow *guests* here in Hotel Brixton told me. Really enjoyed it and all, he did. Rubbed it right in, like salt in a wound. Loved it, the cunt.'

'I should have told you myself but you wouldn't see me.'

'How hard did you try?'

'Don't be like that.' She looked away again. 'I tried, okay?'

'Don't worry about it. I'd have been glad for you, knowing you was happy. Only problem is, you're not, are you?'

Sandy frowned angrily and jabbed a perfectly manicured finger at him. 'How dare you say that? After all the shit you put me through? But if you must know, I am happy, thank you very much. In fact I've never been happier.'

'You sound like you're trying a bit too hard, San. Gotta convince yourself how great everything is, have you?'

She leaned back in her chair. 'No, I've not actually, Bal. I'm happy because I'm gonna have a baby. Gonna congratulate me, are you?'

'Tell me you just said that in temper.'

She picked up her bag and started to rise to her feet, but he grabbed her hand, stopping her. 'Don't, San, please. I've got something to tell you. And it's too important for you to run off without hearing it.'

'Barry, why can't you just be pleased for me?'

'Pleased for you? How could I be pleased?'

'After what you put me through . . . How dare you? Surely me being happy means something.'

He stuck his elbows on the table and held his head in his hands. 'You haven't got a clue, have you?' he said, staring down at the cigarette burns on the Formica top. 'The reason I got you here was to try and help you, to protect you. I wanted to speak to you because I want to make *something* right after how I've messed everything up.'

He dropped his hands and looked into her face. 'Sandy, that *husband* of yours is fucking you about. The arsehole has got untold birds on the go. Dirty whores. Tarts from the clubs. Brasses. I never messed you about, not in that way, I didn't. I always had too much respect for you.'

Sandy's face betrayed nothing, but her voice wavered as she spoke. 'You're lying, because you're jealous. And I'm sorry about that, Barry, but –'

'No, babe, I ain't lying. I just wish I wasn't in here so that I could do something about it. So I could put a stop to that bastard hurting you. But I am in here, so all I could do was let you know. I couldn't think of another way. Believe me, San, I never ever hurt you on purpose. On my life I didn't. I never have and never would.'

Barry stood up and turned to the prison officer who was standing behind him. 'Get me out of here.'

He was about to leave, but first he turned to her and said: 'And I'll tell you something else, San. I'm gonna fucking have O'Donnell for doing this to you. I swear I am. One way or another.'

He walked out leaving Sandy sitting there.

The PO began unlocking the door to lead him back to his cell. He smiled imperceptibly as Barry spoke, having expected something like this after hearing all the gossip that had been circulating on the wing since Ellis had first asked for the visiting order.

'I wanna see DC Medway. He knows who I am. Tell him I've got some things to tell him. A lot of things.'

'Blimey, Ellis,' said the PO, 'once you start opening that mouth of yours, there's no stopping you, is there?'

By the time the car was crossing London Bridge on the journey back to the East End, Sandy could feel her heart drumming against her chest as if she'd run all the way from Brixton. Over and over she heard the doctor's words – *You have an infection, Mrs O'Donnell. Nothing to worry about.*

'That bastard works for Brendan, so course he's gonna say there's *nothing to fucking worry about.*' She hadn't meant to say the words out loud.

'Sorry?' Kevin frowned into the rear-view mirror, convinced he'd misheard her. 'You all right, Sandy?'

'No, not really. But I'm gonna be.' She shuffled forward in her seat. 'Look, I forgot to say, there's something I've got to do, Kev. Instead of taking me back to Old Ford, could you drop me over at Whitechapel?'

As Sandy climbed the front steps leading up to the entrance of the London Hospital, she understood what Eileen O'Donnell had done to her husband as clearly as if someone had written it up for her in ten-foot-high letters on the hospital walls.

You protect your child no matter what.

Even if it means you have to destroy its father.

Chapter 28

When Brendan came in, Sandy was sitting at the table in their bright, airy kitchen. She had a cold mug of tea in front of her that she was cradling in her hands; she was frowning, staring down into it as if she was searching for something.

'Hello, San. You know, I'm glad I never went with you in the end. I had the chance to talk to Ellie's consultant. And I told him, I said – no matter what it costs, mate, I want her sorted out. He was a bit toffee-nosed, and didn't say that much, but they all reckon he's the top bloke.'

Brendan threw his jacket over the back of the chair next to Sandy's. 'So, how'd you get on then? Doing all right, is he?'

He bent to kiss her head, but Sandy pulled away before his lips could make contact with her hair. She stood up and went over to a cork pinboard next to the wall-mounted phone.

'What the fuck is that supposed to be?' she said, ripping a scrap of paper from the board without bothering to take out the drawing pin. She threw it on the table in front of him.

'What's what? What you talking about?'

'That.' She pointed at the bit of paper as if it disgusted her.

'Would you mind telling me what you're going on about?' He turned and looked about the room, his arms spread wide, as if appealing to a dithering jury. 'Because I don't take kindly to getting a coating. Never have done.' His voice grew very loud and he spat out the words through his teeth. 'And especially not in me own fucking house.'

'I asked you a question,' she said, sitting back down in her chair, refusing to be intimidated.

'How do I know?' He shrugged, turning down the corners of his mouth. Then sat opposite her, picked up the piece of paper and studied it. 'Phone number by the look of it.'

He rolled his eyes and smiled, the fury completely gone from his voice. 'I get it, Barry's had a go at you, 'n' he? Gone and got you all wound up. I said you shouldn't have gone.' He reached out to take her hand, but she wouldn't let him touch her.

'Yes, it's a phone number,' she said. 'And do you know what else, Brendan? I rang it. Her name's Priscilla – *Priscilla* – and apparently she's really missing you.'

His smile disappeared. 'Where did you get it?'

'Your leather jacket.'

He was back on his feet. 'You've been going through my stuff?'

She too stood up. 'You've been fucking whores?'

'Is that what all this is about? Me having a bit on the side with a tart?' His smile returned. 'It's you I want, darling. You know that.'

'Do I?'

'Course you do. Now come here.'

'Don't you even think about touching me. I am four months pregnant, *and I've got an infection*. The hospital says that they can only hope the baby won't be affected.'

She began weeping. 'You rotten, cheating, no-good bastard.'

'What hospital?'

'The one I went to because I didn't trust your stinking doctor, that's what hospital.' Tears were running down her face but she made no move to wipe them away. 'The one who's in your fucking pocket, too scared to do or say anything that might upset you.'

'No, San, you've got it all wrong.'

'I said, don't touch me.'

'Look, why don't we go out for a nice meal, and –'

'Because I don't want to, that's why.'

Brendan picked up his jacket and slung it over his shoulder. 'I've had enough of this. I'm going out for a drink. You'd just better be in a better mood when I get back.'

'Had I? What you gonna do to me if I'm not? Shoot me? Scald me? How about telling the truth for once? What really happened to Ellie?'

'Fuck off, Sandy.'

*

DI Hammond was sitting in the saloon bar of an old-fashioned pub – one that hadn't yet been reinvented as a wine bar – just over the border from the East End in the City of London. He was surrounded by men in suits enjoying early-evening drinks before getting their trains back to the suburbs. The noise level was deafening, but DI Hammond's laughter and the sentiment of his expression – despite his broad Midlands accent – still conveyed themselves very clearly to his London-born-and-bred colleague.

'That drop of poison someone had dripped in Barry Ellis's ear obviously worked a treat, Medway. And you handled the interview with him this afternoon very well. Couldn't have done a better job myself. And now,' he raised his glass, 'it appears we have our very own supergrass. Shame we can't get him to say a word against Luke O'Donnell as yet, but the rest of them are going to go down like bloody ninepins. And – joy oh joy – Medway, I hear on very good authority that there are gentlemen working in the Kesslers' dirty bookshops, who are getting a tad fed up with taking all the risks for none of the big money, and that they might well feel like doing some grassing of their own, if we pull a few raids and put the wind up them.' He sipped on his light-ale shandy, the enthusiasm glowing in his eyes. 'The time has come for me to show these cockney bastards who's in control. No offence intended, Medway, of course.'

'None taken,' said Medway, doing his best to hide his contempt for his superior. If Ellis's story hadn't been such dynamite, and that bloody brief hadn't been there, he might well have told him just to keep schtum and he'd see what he could do about getting him a few privileges. But now they'd all been landed right in it – right up to their bloody necks – and not only with the O'Donnells. Now the stupid Brummie bastard was talking about going after the Kesslers as well. The man didn't have the first idea about what the *cockney bastards* were capable of.

'Do you know, Medway, I'm going to make sure that you get a very generous "reward" for this.'

Medway brightened up a little. Having even a very small share of what the O'Donnells owned would be a little compensation for the mayhem that would break out if Hammond really did go after them. Perhaps the Brummy git wasn't entirely bad after all. 'Another drink, sir?'

'No thanks, Medway,' smiled Hammond, contentedly. 'I'm fine as I am. You know, I just love it when a plan comes together. Even if it is sometimes by accident.'

Nicky Wright unlocked the door of the flat, and walked straight into Luke who was in the hallway, obviously on his way out.

Luke gave him a hug. 'I know we've got plans, Nick, but Brendan just phoned me. He sounds like he's been on the piss for hours, but I can tell he's really worried. I'm not sure what's up, but I reckon it's gotta be about all these rumours that someone's got it in for him.'

'Add me to the list.'

'Don't be like that.' He stroked Nicky gently on the cheek. 'Sorry, but I reckon I'm gonna be a good couple of hours.'

'D'you want me to drive you?'

'No, it's all right, no point both of us having our evening spoilt. You listen to some music, have a drink, and I'll get back soon as I can. Let's see, he wants me to go over to his, and then I reckon I might have to shoot over to Kilburn –'

'Old Ford and then Kilburn, eh?' Nicky smiled at him. 'You get to go to all the best places. Now go on, get moving, and you'll be back all the sooner.'

Luke hugged him again, and touched his lips to the top of Nicky's head. 'Couple of hours tops. Okay?'

It had taken all of Pete Mac's solicitor's considerable skills and persuasiveness to achieve it – and even some references to Pete Mac that Pete had taken exception to, such as him hardly being a criminal mastermind – but he was now benefiting from those efforts, as he had been released on bail. It had also taken a lot of Patricia's money, as she had done as he asked and avoided letting anyone in the family know what was going on. It hadn't even occurred to Pete

Mac that he owed Patricia not only his freedom – however temporary – but also his good health, in that she had saved him from getting his head kicked in by Brendan.

He was now lounging on the sofa in the living room of their house on Jubilee Street, sniggering like a kid at an episode of *The Wombles*, while his daughter Caty glowered at him as if he were a moron.

The sitting-room door opened and Pete Mac and Caty both looked round to see Patricia standing there. She looked really good, with her stylish new haircut and her fashionable, well-fitting clothes, but she definitely didn't look very happy as she walked into the room.

Caty quickly decided that this was nothing to do with her and hopped it up to her bedroom.

Neither her mother nor father said anything as she left, acting as if they hadn't even noticed her.

Patricia stood in front of the sofa where Pete Mac was stretched out like a flabby ginger odalisque.

'Move out of the way, Pat, I can't see the telly.'

'Bugger the telly.'

'What did you say?'

'After everything you've done to me, I still sorted out the solicitor for you, got you bail, and you just walk back in here like you've got every right. Listen to yourself whining and moaning, while my little sister's stuck in that hospital. Her face burnt to hell, and her future ripped away from her.'

'I get it. That's what this is all about. You're upset cos of Ellie.'

'Upset? You don't know the meaning of the word. But you will do, believe me. Cos I've decided I don't want you here. And I don't want to help you any more either.'

'You what?'

'You nearly destroyed me once before, when Catherine got shot –'

'How many more fucking times? *That wasn't my fault*.'

'I want you out of here, Pete. Now. You're stuff's in there.'

She threw a holdall down on to the white curly rug. It was the first time he'd noticed it. This was no good. His brief had pulled the family-man card to get him his bail. If she went and chucked him out now, and they found out about it . . .

'Pat, darling, you can't do this. You've gotta help me.' He struggled to a sitting position then hauled himself to his feet.

'Maybe I'll see how you shape up after the trial, and think again. Maybe.'

'But you've gotta stick by me or they'll throw the book at me. You know what they think of anyone mixed up with the O'Donnells.'

'*Mixed up with the O'Donnells*?' Pat's voice was menacingly calm. 'You're more than mixed up with me, you bastard, I'm your fucking wife.'

He looked affronted. 'No need for that sort of language, Pat. You ain't a sodding docker, girl.'

'I really don't believe you.'

'There ain't nothing to believe. Just start acting like a sodding wife should act.' He paused, as he thought of how his mother-in-law had acted like a wife – she'd murdered her bloody husband. 'What I mean is, if you don't do your duty by me, I could wind up going inside.'

'Well, perhaps you should have thought of that before you got mixed up with all your tarts. Now get out, Pete, before I really lose my temper and call Brendan, and tell him about you getting nicked.'

'He still don't know yet?' This was the first bit of really good news that Pete Mac had heard in days.

'Not yet he don't, but don't tempt me.'

'Look, Pat, why don't we keep it like that? You know, just between ourselves. I mean, he ain't got no need to know now, has he?'

Patricia picked up the holdall and thrust it at him. 'I'll see how you behave before I decide what I'm gonna do. Now get out of my sight.'

She dropped down on to the sofa weeping – for Catherine, for Ellie and for herself – listening to her pig of a husband blundering his way down the hall to the street door.

Chapter 29

'I got here as soon as I could.' Luke followed Brendan along his hallway towards the kitchen, silently praying that all his brother wanted to see him for was to confirm the story that had started doing the rounds – that Barry Ellis was going to turn supergrass. Not that that wasn't bad enough in itself – it could mean the end of everything for all of them.

'So what d'you wanna do first, Brendan? Clear out the money from Kilburn? Or d'you want me to get Kevin to go and –'

'Fuck Kevin.' Brendan twisted round and leaned in so close to Luke that he could feel his breath burning on his face. 'And fuck Kilburn. I go out for a drink, I come back a couple of hours later, and she's gone. Left me a note saying I shouldn't try and find her. So, don't piss about with me, Luke, just tell me where she is.'

Shit. Luke swallowed hard. This was just what he'd dreaded. It was about Sandy. Brendan had guessed – rightly – that she'd turn to him for help. 'She's staying in one of my flats.'

'Give me the phone number.'

'Brendan, why don't we sit down and have a drink?'

'I've had a fucking drink. I've had a whole fucking bottleful of the stuff. Now give me that number.'

'Hadn't we better sort out Kilburn first? You know what they're saying about Barry talking, and there's all that dough –'

'Give me the number, Luke. No one walks out on me. No one.'

Luke stood at the kitchen window staring out at the canal. No wonder Sandy loved it here. It was a scene so peaceful that it didn't make sense that such madness was going on inside the house.

There was a very good chance that Barry – *poor old Barry* – was about to be the cause of their world blowing up around them, while his big brother was making a telephone call to a woman who could have made his life wonderful for him, but who he had treated like shit – just like he treated everyone else.

Sandy answered the phone. Brendan turned his back on Luke and lowered his voice. 'Sandy, it's me. I'm not having this. I'm gonna come round there and sort this out.'

'No, Brendan, I told you in the note, I don't want to see you.'

'Don't be an idiot, Sandy, you know you won't get away with this. I won't let you.'

'No, don't *you* be an idiot, you just listen to

someone for once, Brendan.' She sighed knowing that what she was about to say was completely stupid in one way – she'd be losing everything that Brendan had given her, everything that made her life easy – but in another way, it was all she could do, she had no choice.

'I really mean what I'm gonna say, so just hear me out. At first, I genuinely believed that we had a chance of having a life together. Despite feeling guilty about Barry, and all the things I knew you were involved in. But, and I'm being very honest here – I was prepared to be a hypocrite. I turned a blind eye so I could have that nice life. But I started noticing warning lights flashing, and bells ringing about what I was actually doing. And I started feeling bad about it all. That it just wasn't right. But then I found out about the baby, and it was all all right again. I was happy. Really happy. But then you gave me this infection, and I spoke to Barry, and I understood you, Brendan. Understood you better than you'll ever understand yourself. You infect everything you touch. Everything. Including me. And that's why you are never going to get anywhere near this baby. If it survives, that is, after what you've already done to it.'

Brendan's face had drained of colour, he wanted to do nothing more than find her and give her a good slapping. And he would have done if she hadn't been carrying his child. 'Is this all that women's-lib shit that Ellie's poisoned you with?'

'Only you would drag in that kid while she's lying in hospital. You are such an arsehole, Brendan. Don't you get it? I've just seen you for what you are, that's all. Try and be a man and accept it.'

'But them birds I had, they didn't mean nothing to me.'

'Well, more fool you for throwing away everything for something that meant so little.'

'I told you, I'm not gonna let you get away with this, Sandy. I'll make you see I'm right.'

'Brendan, please, try to listen to what someone else has to say, for once in your life. You don't solve your problems by shouting at people or threatening them, or by pretending they're not there. Your problems follow you around wherever you go. The trick is to turn round and face them. And that's what I'm doing. Facing up to the fact that you're no good. And try, just once you arrogant bastard, to see the world through someone else's eyes – not mine necessarily – anyone's. You're alive, you've got a choice. But poor old Barry, he's as good as dead.'

'What you on about now?'

'Luke told me what everyone's saying about him turning supergrass. So, it's obvious, innit? Soon as he gets out – you'll get to him and kill him. Or he'll go into hiding and be so terrified he'll get back on that shit, and so he might as well be dead. So you'll get him either way. You win as usual. Except with me. Because, whatever else you get away with, you are not gonna get away with polluting my child.'

'Why the hell d'you think you can treat me like this? You knew all about me, knew I didn't live in a world like other people. My world's a place where everything's . . .' He raked his fingers through his hair. 'Aw, I dunno.'

'And whose fault is it that you live in that world? Not this baby's.'

'It's the only world I know.'

'You chose it, Brendan.'

'So did you. And it gives us a good life.'

'A good life? Yeah, I thought so an' all. It was like all them years I was with Barry, I learned to ignore the shit and the violence. Just saw it as the way you lot earned your living.' She let out a humourless puff of laughter. 'But cheating on your wife with whores? That I couldn't handle.'

'Sandy, please.'

'One final thing, Brendan. When I went to the hospital to see Ellie, Eileen was there. She told me what really happened. That the boiling water was meant for me. Because of you, and because I'm Brendan O'Donnell's wife. You're evil, Brendan, do you know that?'

There was the unmistakable sound of the receiver being put down in its cradle, but Brendan went on ranting as if she could still hear him. 'You won't get away with this, you cow. Do you hear me? That's my mother's grandchild you're carrying. My baby.'

He smashed the receiver against the wall, sending shards of plastic across the kitchen floor. 'Give me the address, Luke.'

'You know she'll be gone by the time you get there.'

'I said, give it to me.'

As soon as Brendan left the house, Luke went upstairs to the escort office, where there was a phone that hadn't been smashed to bits, and called his flat.

No reply. Nicky was probably in the shower. Perhaps something good had come out of this bloody mess. If he left now they could get to the restaurant and maybe on to a club. He'd call the maitre d' and get him to hold their table, then he'd shoot home and get showered and changed. He'd leave the phone numbers for the restaurant and the club, so Brendan could call him later if he decided he wanted him to do something about Kilburn and the shops.

As he scribbled a note, he took a deep breath and tried to figure out how this mess was going to finish up. Perhaps Brendan really had gone too far this time.

Luke, ripping his tie from his neck ready to jump under the shower, opened the door to his flat, and immediately froze. He could hear voices coming from the living room.

Fuck, surely it wasn't the law. They'd only started hearing the tales about Barry a few hours ago, and even then they hadn't sounded very likely. But who else could it be? Not pissing burglars, surely? He'd kill them if they spoilt his bloody flat. Or if they'd so much as touched a hair on Nicky's head.

He stayed out on the landing, and pulled the door almost shut in case anyone came out into the hall. Then he leaned as close as he could to the jamb, straining to hear what they were saying.

He could make out Nicky's voice. Shit, he wasn't gonna be chatting to burglars, was he? It must be the law.

Then there was another voice. Luke frowned. It sounded familiar somehow. He listened a bit more. *David Seymour*, that's who it was. That bloke who'd gone to the boxing do with them.

Luke smiled, relief washing over him. Nicky had asked a friend round for company. All this shit with Brendan was turning him into a bloody lunatic.

He was just about to go and join them, when the smile dropped from his lips. Nicky was shouting. Luke shook his head, not wanting to believe what he was hearing.

Then David was shouting over him.

'Just hear me out, Nicky. I know it was a bit underhand, the way I went about it, hanging around the record shop, pretending I was your new best mate and everything. But when I got the tip-off at the paper about you and O'Donnell, how could I resist it? This story's gonna be dynamite. Biggest I've ever handled. Queers, cockney bad boys, murdered sisters and poisoned fathers. Jews. Irish. It's fantastic. Just talk to me, let me get your side of it, and it'll earn you thousands.'

'If you think –'

Nicky didn't finish. Luke burst into the sitting room, slamming the door behind him. 'You arsehole, Seymour.'

'Luke, thank Christ you're back.' Nicky ran to his side. 'I am so sorry. I had no idea.'

'It's all right, calm down, I'll handle this.'

Luke strode across the room to David, who was sitting on the edge of the sofa. 'Get up.'

David tried to object but Luke had him by the collar of his flowery shirt, hauling him to his feet.

'Now empty your pockets, and that bag, or I'll do it for you.'

David took his notebook from his jacket and handed it to Luke, then opened his briefcase and took out a tape recorder.

Luke snatched the machine from his hand and threw it the length of the room, smashing it to pieces against the far wall. Then he spun round to face David again. 'If you know what's good for you, you sit back down, and you keep that fucking trap of yours shut. Got it?'

It was over an hour later when the barman in the Bella Vista handed Brendan the telephone.

'Sandy? That you, darling?'

'No, Brendan, sorry, mate, it's me, Luke. Can you do us a favour and get over here? To the flat? Right now if you can. I think we might have a problem on our hands. D'you remember David Seymour, the bloke who came to the boxing with me and Nicky . . .'

Brendan's mood hadn't improved, and when he arrived at the flat, Luke seriously wondered if he'd done the wrong thing in calling him. He steamed straight into the living room, grabbed David by the hair and dragged him out to the kitchen.

Brendan and David were back in the living room in less than five minutes. David's left eye was already swollen shut and blood was pouring from his nose and his left ear.

Nicky gasped, 'What have you done to him?'

He moved as if to help him, but Brendan was too quick. He lashed out his arm, and struck Nicky across the face with the back of his hand, sending him crashing into the coffee table. 'Don't even think about it, you little prick.'

'Brendan, what the hell are you doing? Please, don't hurt him.'

'Save it, Luke, for someone who deserves it.' He pointed at Nicky who was flat on his back, his face grey apart from the red swelling across his cheek-bone. 'That little fucker is nineteen years old. Fucking underage.'

'He's what?'

'You heard. And what with matey boy here – the bloke we entertained like he was family, treated him like he was something worth talking to – being a fucking journalist . . . Well, he's hit the fucking jackpot. Christ knows what he's already passed on to the papers. But I'm gonna enjoy meself finding out.'

'I swear –' David began, but Brendan just talked across him.

'This must have been what Hammond was going on about. All these rumours that're flying round about us. And we thought it was Barry Ellis we had to worry about. He might have fucked things up for Sandy and me, but I should have known he'd never grass on us.'

Luke was shaking his head as if none of it could be true. 'You told me you were twenty-three.'

'I'm really sorry, Luke.'

'Why did you lie to me?'

'You wouldn't have had anything to do with me.'

'I just don't believe all this is happening.'

Brendan put his hand on his brother's shoulder. 'Don't get yourself wound up, Luke. We've got things to do. I'll find out from that berk what he's said and who he's said it to.' He jerked a thumb at David. 'While you go and find Kevin and clear out Kilburn. Get the dough over to the lock-up.'

He tapped his thumbnail against his teeth. 'And I'll phone Pat to let her know what's happening, just in case the law decides to pay a visit.' He looked at his watch. 'Her and Mum should be back from the hospital by now. Then I'll meet you round hers later.'

'Brendan, if Seymour has been mouthing off, what do you think's gonna happen?'

'Just do it, Luke.'

'But how about Nicky?'

'What harm can come to him while I'm here? Now will you just get going? Go on, I'll see you round Pat's.'

As soon as Luke was safely out of the flat, Brendan picked up the phone.

'Sorry to disturb you in the evening, love, but can I have a quick word with Anthony?'

Brendan could hear Anthony's wife calling him, and the sound of children laughing in the background.

'Hello, mate,' said Brendan, 'watching telly with the family, was you? Send me apologies, but there's a couple of things. First of all, did you do that little job for me? Sorting out the trouble I had over that kettle?'

'Yeah, done and dusted, mate. That ain't gonna scald no one no more.'

'Right. Good. Now, I need you over here. At Luke's place. Soon as you can. I need a bit of help sorting out another little problem that's cropped up.'

Chapter 30

Brendan walked into Patricia's kitchen at just gone midnight. His hair was limp with sweat, and his clothes looked as if he'd worn them for a week.

He nodded to Luke as he sat down across the table from him. 'How was Ellie tonight, Pat?'

'You know.' Patricia fetched another cup and saucer from the cupboard over the draining board. 'I think she was glad that Mum went in again.'

'That's nice. Where's Pete Mac?'

'Him and Pat have had a bit of a falling-out,' said Luke, shooting a warning look at Patricia, who, from the expression on her face, really didn't need one. 'And he's cooling off in a hotel for a couple of nights. It's all right, Pat knows where he is if we need him.'

Brendan let out a long slow sigh. 'No thanks, Pat,' he said, as she set the cup down in front of him. 'Got any whiskey?'

'Course.'

While his sister went to fetch a bottle and some glasses from the sitting room, Luke leaned across the table and whispered urgently: 'What's happening back at the flat?'

'At least that's one thing I've managed to sort out,' said Brendan. 'Pity I can't sort out the rest of this fucking mess.'

'How do you mean?'

'Well, when I was phoning everyone, trying to find out what was going on – basically, what that bastard Seymour might have already blurted out – I had a bit of bad news. It seems these stories about Barry might well be true after all.'

'That he's turned grass? No. You sure?'

'Yeah. Can you believe it? *Poor old Barry*. First he sets me own wife against me, and now he's gonna stitch me up with the law.' Brendan shook his head in bewilderment. 'After how good I was to that man . . . Still, like I say, I've solved one of our problems. Them two won't be talking to no one.'

Patricia came back into the kitchen with the whiskey.

Her two brothers were staring at each other across the table with an intensity that made her stomach churn and her hands shake as she put down the glasses. She'd seen that look on the faces of men in her family too many times before. It was the sort of look that could turn trouble into anger, and then into violence, leaving women to weep and to pick up the pieces.

Luke grabbed his brother's hand. 'Brendan, you didn't hurt him, did you? Please, tell me you didn't.'

'What if I did?'

'I love him.'

'Don't talk shit.' Brendan's face was screwed up in repulsed contempt.

'But it wasn't Nicky's fault.'

'Aw no? So who let Seymour into our lives? Who conned you over how old he was?' Brendan filled his glass to the rim with whiskey. 'And anyway, by the time I'd finished with that other little toerag, he'd seen too much. But don't worry, I'm sure the lying little cunt didn't feel a thing.'

'Hang on, when you said you'd sorted it out . . .'

Brendan swallowed half the whiskey and immediately refilled his glass. 'I got shot of the pair of them.'

'No!' Luke was on his feet. *'You bastard, Brendan. You fucking bastard. You know I loved him.'*

Brendan sneered at his brother. 'That ain't love you feel, mate. That's your prick talking.'

'What would you know about anything? You're just like the old man. Everything you touch goes rotten. Catherine, Sandy, Ellie. And now Nicky.'

He moved towards the door, but Brendan got there before him and stood there, barring his way. 'You won't find 'em, Luke. They're gone for good. And they were lucky as it happens, cos they deserved a lot worse than what they got.'

Luke's chin was down on his chest and his arms were dangling loosely by his sides. 'He'd never have done anything to hurt me. Never. He would have kept quiet. Because no matter what filth you talk, I know he loved me.'

'Don't make me laugh. Why can't you just accept it? He had you over, Luke. Took you for a fucking mug.'

'*You bastard.*'

'Yeah, so you already said. But I don't get you, Luke. I only did it for you.'

'You've never done nothing for nobody. Nobody. It's always for you, no matter how you try to pretend otherwise. And you make me sick, do you know that? Sick to me stomach.' He slowly raised his head until they were facing one another. 'And I never want to set eyes on you again.'

'Please, don't do this, you two.' Patricia was still standing by the table, tears streaming down her cheeks. 'I can't take much more of this.'

Brendan stood away from the door to let him go. 'What, gonna go and stay with Sandy, are you? And don't look at me like that. I know you've gotta know where she is.'

Then he went over to the table and finished his drink, waiting until Luke had gone before he spoke. 'I'm going round Mum's. Dunno how long I'll be.'

He turned to look at her before he left. 'I ain't sure, Pat, but I think things are gonna go a bit wrong, girl.'

Brendan trudged down the steps into the familiar basement kitchen on the Mile End Road. Despite it being the early hours of the morning, he wasn't surprised to find his mother sitting there, knitting, with the dog at her feet. She never seemed to sleep much these days.

'All right, Mum? What you knitting?'

She actually smiled at him, making his heart lift with pleasure, as she held up an almost completed, white lacy baby's jacket. 'I started it at the hospital, while I was sitting with Ellie. I know it's difficult to say at a time like this, but we mustn't forget your good news, son.'

He knelt down on the floor beside her. 'Mum, I've gotta tell you something. Something important. There's something wrong.'

'You turn up here at this time of night. Why should it surprise me that something's wrong?'

'I've done something, Mum. I got rid of two people. And before you look at me like that, I only did it to protect Luke. He would have been sent to prison, Mum, and he could never have stood that.'

Eileen felt as if someone had forced concrete down her throat and into her chest, filling it up so only tiny gasps of air could get into her lungs. 'Is he safe now?'

'He'll be all right. I'll make sure of that.'

'I don't want him going away, Brendan. Please, take care of him.'

'Course I will, and I'd have looked after you an' all if you'd have let me. I'd even have done your time for you, Mum, you mean that much to me. The world.

You've gotta believe me, cos I really mean it.'

'I know you do, son, in your own way. Trouble is, you're too much like your father. You've never been able to love anyone as much as you love yourself.'

'What's wrong with me, can't I ever be good enough for any of you?' Brendan covered his face with his hands. 'Sandy's said she won't let me see the baby.'

'Oh, son . . .'

He dropped his hands and stared down at the floor. 'Yeah, I know. And that's all I want, Mum. To have Sandy and the baby. Hold 'em both in my arms.' He took out his handkerchief, wiped his face, and then stood up. 'I think I need a bit of air. I won't be long. Tell you what, I'll take the dog out for you, while I'm at it. Come on, Bowie, come on, boy.'

'Okay, son.' Eileen picked up her knitting automatically, but she looked at it and put it down again. More wasted time.

Not for the first time, or for the last, Eileen O'Donnell wondered at the madness of it all, the madness that could do such terrible things to a family.

Chapter 31

A soft trickle of sweat ran down his spine, as he moved slightly, adjusting his position to get the full benefit of the rays on his body. He'd wear the new linen suit tonight. Look the right business down in Puerto Banus. A month and a half in the sun had made him brown as a berry and twice as handsome.

When he'd got rid of the other place in Estepona, he really should have thought about buying a villa closer to the coast. There wasn't even a breeze up here in the hills. And, even with his eyes closed tightly shut, the sun still made patterns on his eyelids: blue and yellow shapes dancing around and aggravating him.

Fuck it, he loved it really.

He sucked in his gut. If he wasn't careful he was gonna go the way the old man had gone, flabby round the middle, old-looking. And he definitely didn't want that to happen. Not when there were birds like Anya around – tall, tits out to there, and a natural blonde. Very nice.

He fumbled around under the side table and found the suntan lotion, then rubbed the cream over his legs and face. He could do with Anya being here right now

– just to do his back for him, of course . . .

He grinned as he felt himself harden at the thought of her long, cool fingers running over his skin. Still, he could wait a couple of hours. In the meantime, he'd just have to make do with a nice cold beer.

He reached out for his drink.

Nothing.

He opened his eyes, squinting into the sun. Someone was standing over him. *Holding his fucking beer.*

'Bowie,' he shouted. '*Bowie!*'

'For Christ's sake, calm down, Brendan,' said the looming shadow that was still holding his glass. 'It's me.'

'Luke?' Brendan was up off the lounger, the sun cream mixing with the sweat on his forehead and dripping down into his eyes and making them sting. 'You daft cunt! No wonder the dog didn't fucking bark. Where the hell have you been all this time? Is Mum with you? How's Ellie and Pat? And what about Sandy? You heard from her?' He shook his head, grinning, and clapped his hand over his brother's shoulder.

'Why the fuck didn't you let me know you was coming over, dozy bollocks? I'd have sorted out a party for you.'

'I didn't want you to know.'

'Why not? Is something up?'

'I wouldn't know, Brendan. I've been staying over

at Aunt Mary's, keeping me head down, trying to think all this through. How to make sure the girls and Mum were all right. How to sort out this whole fucking mess. And do you know what, I thought about you every single day, and I realised exactly what I had to do. And that I was the only one who could do it.'

Brendan rubbed the back of his hand across his now streaming eyes, making the stinging and blurring even worse. 'Will you stop talking in fucking riddles, Luke?'

'I'm gonna put an end to it. All of it.'

With that, Luke dropped the beer, raised the sawn-off shotgun he was holding in his other hand, and shot Brendan full in the face, spraying shreds of his brain and fragments of skull all over the baking tiles of the poolside terrace.

Bowie ran off yelping and screaming into the scrub at the back of the villa.

Luke tried calling him back but the dog was too spooked to obey.

He took a breath, and stroked what had once been the top of his brother's arm. 'You destroyed everything I ever loved.'

Then he put the gun in his own mouth and squeezed the trigger.

July 1975

Chapter 32

Sandy sat in the old-fashioned offices of Tighe, Martin and O'Flaherty waiting for Mr Martin to read her the contents of the big brown envelope he had taken so much time to fetch from the clunking great safe set in the wall behind his chair.

She really was losing her patience. She had given up half a day's work – and pay – in the hotel where she worked in Brighton to come up to London, and that wasn't even taking into account the extra money she'd had to shell out for the baby minder to keep an eye on Lisa. And then there was the price of the train fare.

It was all right for the likes of Mr Martin, he had bloody money coming out of his ears, the money he charged people to give them advice. She could only hope it wasn't another attempt by Patricia for the bloody O'Donnells to get their hands on Lisa. She was just about sick of getting letters saying how much it would mean to bloody Eileen since she'd lost 'her boys' and since Pete Mac had been put away. They could beg and plead all they liked, they weren't getting their hands on her, Sandy wasn't going to let her child make the mistakes she'd made.

'Thank you for coming along today, Mrs O'Donnell.'

'It's Wilson. My maiden name. It's what I use now.'

'Oh dear, I see,' said Mr Martin, finally opening the envelope.

'I think it's my business what I choose to call myself, Mr Martin.' Sandy was very close to walking out, but . . . she was here now.

'Certainly, it's your business, Miss Wilson. But I'm afraid that it might present a problem.'

'Problem? How? What for?'

'Your inheritance. You see, Mr Brendan O'Donnell and Mr Luke O'Donnell have both left you considerable amounts of money and property in their wills, the stipulation being – and I might add that it was Mr Brendan O'Donnell who insisted on this – that you and your child should be known as O'Donnell, and that Mrs O'Donnell – senior, that is, Eileen – should know about it, and be able to send letters to your child, and be able to play some part in your child's life. Apart from that, this *very* considerable inheritance is yours to do with as you wish.'

Sandy flopped back in her chair, gripping the arms as though they were all that was keeping her from tipping over on to the floor.

'Can I have a minute? To think?'

Mr Martin nodded. 'Certainly, Miss Wilson.'

What she thought about was the tiny room that she shared with Lisa. The damp, the cold, and the scratching noises above the ceiling that kept her up most of the night. The long hours she worked, and how little she saw of her beautiful baby girl.

'Mr Martin, can I sell the property on?'

'It will be yours to do with as you choose, Miss Wilson.'

Sandy took a deep breath, and then pulled her chair up close to Mr Martin's desk.

'Sorry, Barry,' she said, making the lawyer frown in incomprehension. 'Where do I sign?'